JAZZ BABY

JAZZ BABY

Beem Weeks

Fresh Ink Group
Roanoke

JAZZ BABY

Fresh Ink Group
An Imprint of:
The Fresh Ink Group, LLC
PO Box 525
Roanoke, TX 76262
Email: info@FreshInkGroup.com
www.FreshInkGroup.com

Edition 1.0   2012
Edition 2.0   2016

Book design by Ann E. Stewart

Cover design by Stephen Geez

Cover photo by Shirley Michael

Cover model: Melady Weeks

Cataloging-in-Publication Recommendations: General Fiction; Historical Fiction; Coming of Age (Fiction); Noir Thriller (Fiction); Prohibition (Fiction); Speakeasy (Fiction); Gangster (Fiction); Illegal Drugs (Fiction); Southern (Fiction); Mississippi (Fiction); New Orleans (Fiction); Storyville (Fiction); 1920s (Fiction)

Library of Congress Control Number: 2012931495

ISBN-13: 978-1-936442-10-2

For my mother, Shirley,
for standing by my side
when I needed it most.

For Jason Weeks.
You left us way too soon, brother.

For Donald Weeks.
I miss you, Dad.

Acknowledgements

Special thanks to the following:

Stephen Geez, for showing me how to write it better.

Ann Stewart, for your tireless work.

Darin Weeks, Lisa Walworth, Dennis Glover, Nonnie Jules, and everybody at Fresh Ink Group.

CHAPTER ONE

I can't say for certain how it is a life can so easily come apart at the seams, like a favorite old dress gone to pieces, leaving little more than a pile of worthless rags. It just happens—never a warning, nothing in the air that smells of change.

That's the cruelest part.

There were two of them come to fetch me just before noon—a chubby man and a schoolmarm of a woman, each gone well beyond Mama's and Papa's years. The fella, well, he couldn't be bothered with the whole deal, like maybe he'd done well enough in his own sight just to have been talked into driving out to dumpy old Rayford. He stood sentry beside that shiny black Model T Ford, his beady eyes searching neighboring cotton fields like he just knew somebody of a lower social station lurked unseen, waiting for a chance to swipe that fancy piece of machinery from underneath his very nose.

And the lady, she didn't want to be here any more than her companion. Uncertainty clouded her countenance like one of those plagues Moses dealt with in the Bible, the sort that could easily blot out that Mississippi sunlight, turning afternoon into evening with the shake of a stick.

Didn't matter much to me. I didn't want them there, neither—even if they *could* help me along in my dream. Mama caught me spying through the parlor window. "You just gonna gawk at 'em all day, Emily Ann, or are you gonna meet 'em at the door?"

Papa's lone chuckle softened the moment. "Ain't no reason to be scared, Baby," he said, peeking over his morning paper. "Just invite the nice folks in for cookies and lemonade."

"I ain't ready for this, Papa," I complained, holding fast my position beside that window. "Besides, *we* don't know they're nice."

His shifting weight sent that ancient oak rocker to squeaking. "Too late. A deal's a deal."

"'Cept I ain't the one shook on it. Who told Pastor Pritchett to set this up, anyway?"

The *Rayford Gazette* fell away; Papa's tight gaze snatched hold on mine. "I did. Now get to bein' neighborly before you catch a lickin'!"

Eunice Spatch offered one of those forced smiles meant to conceal something akin to disdain—or disgust—at my station in life. Rheumy grey eyes picked apart my threadbare sundress. "Well now," she started, in a voice humming through her bulbous nose. "You're a bit smaller than I imagined." Her icy gaze stumbled upon those two new bumps pushing against the thin yellow fabric at my chest. "Pastor Pritchett made claim you're a teenager."

A scarlet heat caressed my cheeks. Words caught in my throat, kept my intended invitation inside our home from ever making sound. Uppity rich folks just had a way of stealing my voice.

Mama barged into the moment. "She's a late bloomer, is all. But that don't mean the child can't sing." She jostled in close to the woman, raised that stupid tray of cookies. "I've made refreshments; come inside for a spell."

'Cept old Eunice Spatch, she just waved that tray away, as if Mama's simple offering somehow offended the woman. "Can't stay," she said, stepping clear of the proffered treats. "Only came to give the girl a proper dress. But the one I brought won't fit her."

Mama's pride lay in jagged little pieces scattered across the front porch. I hated her for such a show of weakness, for always trying to fit in with folks who ain't a thing like us.

I don't reckon it really mattered much. Not to me, anyway. It just meant Eunice Spatch—and others like her—would never set eyes on our battered blue sofa with the stuffing coming out the back. She'd walk off without any laugh-out-loud tales of sagging floorboards or the ever-present odor of rancid bacon leavings. And nobody would ever have to know that the Teegarten home lacked indoor plumbing and electricity.

Only colored folks had it worse.

"I'll have to trade the dress for a smaller size," the marmish woman promised. Her long, thin fingers fit snugly beneath my chin, raised my downcast gaze. "Awful pretty child, you are. I've never seen eyes so green—like a china doll's."

The subtle smile playing at the corners of my mouth had nothing at all to do with her stupid compliments—if that's what she intended.

"I ain't wore a new dress in such a long while," I confessed, thinking back two summers, when Papa first brought home the very garment covering my body at that moment.

"Yes, well…" Eunice Spatch latched onto Mama's arm and pulled her in close again. "Bathe the child, please. And wash her hair; it's just *filthy*."

*   *   *

I hugged tight to the rear corner of our house, and kept sight on that fancy Ford's slow fade toward town. They'd be back soon enough. Still, I didn't dare budge from behind the lilac bush till the dust settled on Posner Road and I could be fairly certain those two wouldn't double back just yet.

Mama flung a handful of words through an open window. "Take a cake of soap with you, Baby—if you're going to the pond. And don't dawdle, either!"

I checked my tone, mumbled a clipped, "Whatever," and broke hard for my secret place hidden in a rough tangle of trees smack in the middle of dirty old Mister Kuiper's cotton field.

Sharp-angled blades of sunlight sliced open the heavy green canopy above, bleeding lemon-yellow splashes of warmth and light into the cool shade of my private oasis.

Here, I didn't have folks eyeing me like I'm poor white trash.

That creaky ancient dock squeaked brief protests beneath the weight of my sudden intrusion, but kept its end of our unspoken deal and held me safely above the still water.

Across the pond, a million butterflies rose and fell in unison, courting some grand symphony only they could hear. Or maybe it's jazz that sparks that sort of mood—a mood that lately had me warm and slippery where it counts most on a girl.

I sloughed away that ratty old sundress and took down my underpants. A warm breeze like a first-time lover's hands stroked my bare skin, stirred up a hunger inside of me had nothing at all to do with food. Days like this made me awful glad to be a girl.

Alone, it's easy to find my voice. "Look at me, the real me, the one who lives inside," I sang aloud. "Ain't got much money, no fancy dress, but still I have my pride."

'Cept when are we ever truly alone?

The immediacy of that wolf whistle directly at my back knocked me ass-over-tea kettle, dumping me into the cool drink. I broke the surface out where the water runs deepest, and searched for the culprit.

My voice came high and tight. "You get out of here, Billy Blood!" I hollered.

That stupid Choctaw boy paid me no mind, though. He just slithered on down to the end of the dock and squatted leapfrog beside my discarded clothing. "Don't look like you're in no kinda way to tell *me* what to do, Teegarten."

Anger like sharp barbs formed on my words—anger more at myself for getting caught without a stitch. "What do you want, Billy?"

"Came out for a swim."

"Gonna have to wait. I got here first."

"You ain't the one owns this mud hole." He snatched up my under-pants, caressed that worn white cotton between his long fingers.

Such a bold move—for an Injun.

"Put those down!" I demanded.

"Or what?" he dared.

"Or I'll scream."

Didn't matter a lick to that stupid boy; he carried never so much as an inch of fear toward the white man. "You're awful nice to look at, is all, Emily Ann. Can't blame a fella for having a peek, can you?"

Ain't never let a boy come so close to me this way—not without his name being Jobie Pritchett. But even Jobie would never gawk like this one. "You can have it," I said. "Just let me get dressed first."

"Mighty white of you, Teegarten." Billy gathered up his true height and ditched his grin. "But what exactly are you offering me? I mean, can't be Kuiper's mud hole—since it ain't yours to give."

Scarlet heat burned my cheeks. The idea of a snappy retort just melted inside my head like an ice cube on an August sidewalk. Flirt with me, Billy boy, but don't you dare play me a fool.

"Cat got your tongue, Teegarten?" Those long fingers worked at the buttons on his dingy gray shirt. Billy never bothered with permission; the boy acted on instinct. "You're a touch underdone—what with no grass on your front yard. But that don't mean we can't enjoy each other's company, does it?"

I could cross the pond and rush the clearing. 'Cept how would I get to my clothes?

Did I really even want this to end?

I fixed that Injun with a sideways glance. "Ain't you scared someone might catch you out here?"

Billy's grin came as lopsided as the boy himself. "Ain't nobody comes out here anymore, Emily Ann. Only ones gonna know is me and you— and *I* won't tell."

"Suppose *I* tell?"

"You won't."

"How do you know?"

Billy tossed up a stray shrug and let those dirty black trousers fall from his narrow hips.

"Lord a-mercy," I breathed softly. I'd be a liar running through hell wearing gasoline-soaked underpants to make claim I didn't gawk. But a thing like that—I ain't never seen a boy so raw, so beautiful. The sight called to mind one of those carved sculptures they show in magazines; a museum piece come to life. Thin and wiry, that boy; his smooth red skin had gone dark from days spent in the sun. Shiny black hair spilled to his shoulders. And down there, well, it looked as if a long, fat snake had fixed hold and refused to turn him a-loose.

"We gonna share us a swim, Teegarten?"

I leaned closer to the dock, tried like the dickens to commit his every curve and angle to memory. "We can share…"

'Cept stupid Jobie Pritchett had to go and ruin everything.

That preacher's boy rolled onto the dock like he owned the thing. "Whatcha doing out here, Blood?"

Billy yanked his pants up. "Just came for a dip."

"With a white girl?" Jobie snatched up Billy's shirt and threw it at him. "Best get gone, Blood."

An awkward still moment passed while Billy finished putting his clothes right. "See you around, Teegarten," he said, taking his grin with him.

I waited until me and Jobie were alone before asking the question burning brightest inside my head. "Are you fixin' to tell Papa?"

Jobie jammed his hands inside the pockets of his denim overalls and floated one of his dreamy smiles. "Tell him what?"

Good boy. This would be our little secret.

I swam into the shallows, over where black muck squished between my toes. "How come you're out here?" I asked, hoping he'd look at me the same way Billy did.

'Cept Jobie, a preacher in the making, set his blue-eyed gaze on some spot across the pond. "Just came out to maybe sketch some pictures, is all."

"How come you won't draw *me* anymore?"

"I've drawn you a dozen times, Baby."

"Not like this, you haven't."

The boy's cheeks pinked up a nice deep shade. "Can't do *that*, Emily Ann."

"Why not?" I demanded.

"Wouldn't be right."

"Says who?"

Jobie pushed a stray blond curl from his forehead, made like he'd pondered this very notion a time or two in his quiet moments—like maybe he could be bent to my will.

I moved into his line of sight. "You could do a drawing like one of those French fellas you're always bragging on."

'Cept stupid old Jobie had to go and open his big mouth. "If folks even 'spected I made dirty pictures, they'd never let me be their pastor when my daddy's time is done."

Dirty?

Is *that* how he saw me?

I gained the dock and pushed past the boy. "I ain't dirty, Jobie Pritchett," I said, taking up my clothes.

"I didn't mean it like that, Emily Ann," he pleaded, though he wouldn't so much as look at me until I had my dress on.

"Didn't mean it," I hollered over my shoulder, retreating toward home, "but you still said it."

*   *   *

That shiny black Ford glowered at me from our driveway. They were back already, just waiting to spirit me away.

Papa's the one had the big notion for me to go sing over to Jackson. "Use that voice to get you someplace ain't Rayford," he said.

Ain't nobody but church folks wants to hear spirituals, though.

I climbed the steps and sneaked through the back door, hoping for a reprieve. Mama had supper on the stove. Fried potatoes hissed and popped in that ancient cast-iron skillet, the smell mingling with onions and something else I couldn't quite place. Something familiar and acrid.

Mama spun on me quick as a top. "What took you so long, child?"

I tried my best to act like nothing had happened. "Just been talking to Jobie, is all," I said, leaving any mention of the Injun from my explanation.

"Did he watch you bathe?"

My head went to wagging back and forth. "Jobie wouldn't do that."

"Preacher's boy or not, I don't trust him. Besides, he's too old to be coming round here sniffing after you."

Jobie ran five years ahead of me, which really didn't count for much after a certain age. But you couldn't argue that point with Mama. In her opinion, I'd never reach that certain age. I'd always be a child.

I reckon we shared more than just the same emerald-green eyes and honey-brown hair, Mama and me. We both kept secrets.

She pressed a kiss to my forehead and gave my bottom a quick swat. "Go on and get those people out of my house," she said. "I'll keep your supper warm."

They didn't say anything to me directly, the church lady and her chubby fella. They just thanked Papa and drifted out the front door, expecting me to follow.

I dropped beside Papa on the sofa. "Come with me," I begged.

"Can't, Baby. You know that."

"Why not?" Seemed like I'd been asking that question an awful lot lately.

"I'll drive out there and pick you up. You just sing your heart out."

I let the screen door slam in my wake. Not out of anger, mind you, but just enough of a bang to register my final protest.

The chubby fella helped me into the back seat of Henry Ford's finest. "We'll be there in twenty minutes," he promised, sliding behind the wheel.

Eunice Spatch sat up front with him, though I can't say for sure if they were married or just friendly. Every now and again she'd glance over at him with that sort of hungry twinkle in her eyes that's common in the younger set.

A warm breeze slipped through open windows and set my hair to dancing.

Addison Markley gawked at us from her front porch as we drove past her house. Addie likes girls the way boys like girls—or so most folks in Rayford make claim. I reckon it could be true, though I'd never seen any proof of it.

The man found me in his rearview mirror. "And what are your plans, young lady?"

"Plans?" I asked, certain I'd missed a chunk of discussion I'd been meant to chew on.

"Surly you have a young beau asking for your hand—start a family maybe."

I folded my hands in my lap, found a distant tree in the passing land-scape, and fixed my gaze to it. "Uh-uh. I'm going to New York to sing jazz just as soon as I can."

"Sodom on the Hudson," he grumbled disapprovingly.

The lady tossed in her own jagged opinion. "The *devil's* music."

I pulled in a deep breath and tried for my true voice. "It's nineteen twenty-five, and things are different now. Girls don't have to get married off and start having babies just because we reach a particular age. We got the vote now. We can be whatever we want to be." It got good to me. I met his burning gaze in that mirror and marched on with my truth. "Won't be long till we have a lady in the White House telling us what's what!"

His sudden burst of laughter twisted my newfound confidence into a tight knot deep inside my belly. "And then what?" he bellowed. "A *Negro* president?" He found third gear and shot us down that state road toward Jackson. "You're a dreamer, little girl. A silly little dreamer."

It didn't help having that church lady cackling away as if she'd been listening to some vaudeville funnyman telling jokes.

I slouched low in my seat, intending to disappear altogether, leaving those two to wonder if maybe I'd been nothing more than a ghost.

'Cept life doesn't work that way.

Jackson, Mississippi, sprang up quick as a sucker punch to a blind man's nose, had me gawking wide-eyed at bustling crowds walking here and there along either side of Main Street. Fancy glass-covered storefronts showed off stylish dresses and handsome suits. Flappers gathered at a side-walk café and boldly sucked on cigarettes with their brightly painted lips. Klaxons sounded warnings, fellas hollered insults at one another, and somewhere above the cacophony a colored man breathed smoky notes from a shiny saxophone. I didn't even need to see him to imagine the scene.

But then a high steeple breached that pale blue afternoon sky and yanked me back.

Eunice Spatch sprang from the Ford like the fires of hell got on her. "Hurry up, child!" she demanded, as if she herself had a stake in this whole foolish notion Papa dreamed up. "We can't keep Mister Duncan waiting."

My shoes banged a hasty rhythm against the cement walk leading to the front door. Half a dozen white-haired church ladies milled about the foyer, each giving me a looky-loo. I didn't belong in their fancy church; that seemed to be the prevailing opinion.

'Cept I didn't come for their benefit.

"Can we just get this over?" I asked.

Eunice Spatch latched on to my arm and jerked me into a small room off the foyer. "Don't be an ingrate," she scolded. "It's not often a girl from *your* station is presented with this sort of opportunity."

A white-haired lady came in with a brand new pink summer dress just happened to be my size. She didn't say much. Didn't smile, neither.

Elizabeth Purdy trickled in behind her. I only knew of Elizabeth on account of she came to Rayford Christmas last—to sing carols for all us poor folks can't afford to sing for ourselves. Mama said they only came to make themselves feel as if they did an alms.

Elizabeth ran a year or two ahead of me, though she carried herself like a grown woman. All the boys back home went loopy over her, with that fake smile of hers and stupid golden hair. Couldn't sing a lick, you ask me.

Hands belonging to Eunice Spatch snatched hold on the hem of my dress, and before I could say mother may I, the woman yanked the garment over my head.

Elizabeth's cool blue gaze found the small swell of my breasts. Her shallow grin showed all the telltale markings of some sort of mischief.

'Cept Eunice Spatch is the one went and opened her big mouth first. "The girl's mama made claim she's a late bloomer."

Childish titters filled that cramped space. They were schoolyard bullies, nothing more.

Whispers buzzed through their tight huddle like hungry mosquitoes in search of a crimson meal.

Elizabeth broke a-loose from their clutch, leaned close to my ear like maybe we might could be secret friends. Her soft breath warmed my naked shoulder. "Do you people wash up in swamps out there? You smell like an old dirty frog."

Eunice Spatch said, "*Ribbit!*" and their laughter rang louder.

I know we ain't supposed to hate folks who do us wrong; turn the other cheek, Jesus said. 'Cept these snotty rich people, they make it hard for a girl to practice that Golden Rule.

"Just take me home," I demanded.

Eunice ignored me like I'd not uttered a single word. "Splash her with perfume, and let's send her out."

A soft mist of sweet lilacs fell against my bare skin, brought to mind that bush Mama planted a few summers back.

The white-haired lady helped me into that lovely pink dress. I'd guess it to have cost somebody a tidy little sum—certainly more than Papa might manage. And it fit just like I'm the one its maker had in mind as he passed the garment through his fancy sewing machine.

I'm just as proper as Elizabeth, I told myself, eyeing my image in that long mirror stuck to the wall. Better days, my reflection promised.

In this dress, I could be a whole other girl.

*   *   *

We marched into that cavernous chapel like a small funeral procession in search of a stray corpse needing a decent burial. A handful of curiosity seekers sat scattered among the pews, men and women alike, no doubt expecting a swell laugh.

'Cept I can sing. No brag, just fact.

Stanley Duncan pranced about the pulpit like a newly-minted deity demanding worship from somebody, anybody. He gave a nudge to his gold-rimmed spectacles, slid them up the bridge of his pointy nose, and laid down a beady-eyed gawk that walked up one side of me and down the other.

His words spilled out in one of those high-falutin' Yankee tones. "Well get on up here, child. We haven't got all afternoon."

Whispers and giggles fluttered freely in that hot June air as some unseen force drove me up the aisle like an uncooperative bride-to-be gone to settle this arrangement.

Or maybe I'd been meant for sacrifice.

It's called a scholarship, Mister Duncan explained, an opportunity to study proper vocal technique in his school—which happened to be there in that church—and it wouldn't cost Papa a cent.

My fingers stroked that delicate pink dress. "I already know how to sing," I told him, suddenly certain of myself.

Stanley Duncan peered over his glasses, fixed me tight in his sight, said, "Very well then." His skinny backside found the empty piano bench. "Let's run through the fixed-do."

"Fixed-do?" An achingly lonely bead of sweat skittered down my spine, disappeared against the snug waist of my new dress. "Um, I don't know what that means."

Mister Duncan—bless his soul—didn't have the disposition to put me on display like a head with its chicken cut off. "Perhaps you'll give us a song," he simply said.

I gave him my back, gathered a dozen lazy gazes from the congregation, and took up an old standard. All those folks there—I reckon they expected some scared little girl's idea of a nursery rhyme.

I fed them "Amazing Grace" instead.

I scattered those mournful words like seeds tossed on thorny ground, certain they'd reach the rich soil underneath, the way they always did in the tiny church back home in Rayford. One by one old ladies drew out fancy silk handkerchiefs to dab at stray tears of repentance.

Why would people cry at such a beautiful song? I mean, music is supposed to be a joyous sound, isn't it? Tap your foot. Hum along. Maybe even dance a little. Just please don't cry.

But then that delicious applause wafted through the congregation like the sweet smell of cotton candy, and it had nothing at all to do with folks just being polite; these were my new fans.

'Cept old Stanley Duncan didn't quite have the same read on my moment. "You sound a bit too Negro for a white child," he proclaimed. "But don't you worry about a thing; we can train that heathen tone from your voice."

I spun off a confident retort, certain my newfound adoring public would side with me. "Some folks *appreciate* the way I sound."

Duncan shot me down with nary a thought. "Only those with a predilection for hell would foster such an opinion, young lady."

Ain't a churchgoing soul alive wants to be put in league with the devil. That's how Mister Duncan managed to pluck up what had only just begun to sprout. That mean old man tore it out, roots and all.

Pieces of broken dialogue came a-loose and spun through the air. Items like "devil's music" and "not in *our* church" landed at my feet. Maybe they'd carry me out and toss me to the street.

Would they dare lynch a *white* girl?

Above the growing fray came a familiar voice. "You rascals wouldn't know talent if it bit you on your self-righteous asses!" Tanyon Thibbedeaux stomped down the aisle like a jilted groom come to reclaim his girl from some fella stole her away. "Next one says boo about Baby, I'll rattle their teeth," he promised.

And he'd do it, too.

Big, strong Tanyon.

He snatched hold of my hand and pulled me toward the foyer.

Eunice Spatch trailed back of us like a scared hound hoping for table scraps. "I'll need that dress, young lady," she said.

Tanyon spun on her. "Ain't it Baby's?" he demanded.

Eunice sputtered before dropping a clipped "No!"

I couldn't bear such a loss, to return home the same old nobody. "Just— Can't I—?"

"Three dollars, is what it costs!" the woman argued. "Pay, and it's yours. Otherwise, take it off before you befoul the thing."

Tanyon drew back his hand.

Eunice Spatch's eyes went wide as a pair of pies cooling on a windowsill.

I jumped into the gap, tossed my arms around his waist. "Let's just go."

Dollar bills fell from his offending hand like three loose feathers. Bought and paid for, that's the message he meant to send.

I stumbled along behind him into the midday sun, proclaiming my undying gratitude for his act of generosity. He didn't have to buy me that dress. I mean, ain't nobody ever confused Tanyon Thibbedeaux with a wealthy man. Truth be told, he fared little better than Papa.

"You sing like a colored girl, Baby," he said, opening his car door.

I climbed up inside, scooted to the passenger side. "Ain't gonna do me no good here," I said.

Tanyon slid in behind the wheel. "You don't belong here anyway. A voice like yours belongs over the river."

A million butterflies took motion inside my belly, their gossamer wings stroking my soul. "New Orleans?"

"N'Orleans." Tanyon retrieved a half-empty pack of Lucky Strikes from his shirt pocket, fished one free, took it between his lips. "Lots of opportunities over there. Plenty of money to be had."

That soft Cajun accent lulled me into a lazy state of mind. Tanyon and Papa went way back. They ran the streets of Baton Rouge as boys, got into all sorts of tomfoolery together. I'd be a liar to say I didn't have a certain draw to the man.

I inhaled the lilac scent on my skin. "So how come you're here instead of Papa?"

Tanyon dragged a blue-tipped Lucifer matchstick across the dash of his old Chevrolet, dipped that Lucky into the orange glow, and pulled smoke deep into his lungs. "I'm real sorry to have to tell you this, Baby…"

Every one of those happy butterflies suddenly went still. "Tell me what?" I asked.

Tanyon's gaze searched out some faraway place beyond that church parking lot. "Your daddy," he said softly, giving his Lucky another suck, "your daddy passed on."

Chapter Two

Early morning sunlight spilled through my bedroom window, splashed its warmth across my face, refused to turn me a-loose. I'd been caught in that place between asleep and awake, savoring the fading remnant of a nasty little dream I fought desperately to cling to, when the real world decided to jam its foot into the moment with no intention of letting me forget.

"Get up, child!" Mama hollered from somewhere in the house. "Can't sleep this thing away."

Life has no beginning to the tales it weaves, no real end, neither—only additions and subtractions, is all. Papa became a subtraction the morning he died, erased from my life, never to return. I mean, I'd lost grandparents before. And everybody in Mississippi knew someone who passed on when that influenza tore through our corner of the world in the final year of the Great War. 'Cept Papa wasn't old or sick. And he didn't march off to fight that Kaiser fella. When I'd last set eyes on him, Papa had been the biggest, strongest man I knew.

How does a man like that just quit stepping among the living?

I tossed onto my back and kicked free from the scratchy linen sheets tangled around my legs. I tried like the dickens to recall his last words to me, to remember his face. Didn't seem right to forget so soon.

Fragmented images of naked Billy Blood dripped softly from that lost dream, saturating my still-waking mind with puddles just dirty enough to wet heaven's wrath—should I splash around in them too long.

But Mama's harsh call wedged itself between me and that Injun boy. "I ain't gonna tell you again, Emily Ann!"

My bare feet gave the floor a frustrated thud. "I'm up!" I hollered at the closed door. My voice dropped to a whisper. "Sorry, Papa."

I yanked my nightshirt off and wiggled my body into that new pink dress. I never did suppose that old Eunice Spatch would come back by to fetch me over to Jackson again. And truth to tell, it really didn't bother me. Ain't nobody needs to train anything out of *my* voice. I didn't have much inclination to sing spirituals anyway; it's jazz that puts nickels in a girl's pockets.

Stella eyed me with suspicion from her place atop my dresser.

"Ain't gonna make me feel guilty," I said, stroking her porcelain chin. "It don't count if it's only a dream. Besides, Billy's an *Injun*, not a Negro."

Mama barged in before I could dig up any more dirt on myself. "Who are you talking to?" she demanded.

I nodded toward that china doll Papa bought for my eighth birthday. He chose her on account of she has hair the color of thick brown honey and eyes green as emeralds. My twin, he called her. Cost him two weeks' pay.

A subtle nervous twitch poked at Mama's left cheek. I'd have missed it if I hadn't been looking at her.

"What's the matter?" I asked, though I'd never get a straight answer from her. Mama kept a tight lid on *her* box full of bones.

"I'm gonna send you to stay with Aunt Frannie for a spell." That wretched name just tumbled from her lips like loose pebbles bent on disturbing still waters.

My belly looped a knot even Houdini himself couldn't untie. "I don't wanna stay with *her!*" I cried. "All she ever does is make me go to church seven days a week."

Mama took on that look usually meant a lickin' lurked nearby. "I don't recall giving you a choice, girl!"

"But that ain't fair," I protested. "I mean, you ain't the only one lost Papa."

There went that twitch again, 'Cept this time it left off being subtle. Mama lunged. "Don't you *dare*—!"

I ducked her open-handed slap and tumbled into the parlor.

Tanyon Thibbedeaux peered in through the front screen door. The intensity of his gaze snatched hold of Mama like just maybe he'd had a peek inside her bone box. "Morning, Norma Jean," he said, certain of himself. "How's about you let me in, and let's have us a little talk."

*   *   *

Addison Markley's boyish specter drifted lazily up the front drive. Black trousers and a white shirt clung to her narrow frame; her right hand boldly clutched a jar of corn liquor.

"My daddy sent this for your mama," she said, climbing the porch. "He says a few sips at bedtime will help her sleep some."

I tossed a nod toward the door, told her Mama and Tanyon were inside doing an awful lot of hushed mumbling. "You can wait around if you like."

"Nice dress," she said, eyeing my legs beneath the hem. A dirty little smirk tugged at the corners of her mouth. "I always figured you to be the pink sort."

My cheeks burned hot scarlet.

We weren't what you'd call friends, Addie and me. But neither could we be counted as enemies. She just ran three years ahead of me, is all. I reckon in her sight I'd been nothing more than a snot-nosed baby couldn't tie her own shoes.

'Cept now, well, we had something in common.

"How long's it been since your mama passed?" I dared ask.

Addie leaned her tall body into the porch railing and pondered my question. "Ain't really thought about it much lately," she said, drinking in the curves of my hips. "Four years, I guess."

I took up perch beside her, away from the screen door, away from Mama. "Does it still hurt?"

Her shrug said no, but her dark eyes told a simpler truth. "Life goes on, Emily Ann. Can't bring a soul back—no matter how many tears you cry."

I pushed forward. "Can you still remember her voice?"

Addie ignored my question, offered up one of her own. "How'd he die?"

"Doctor Royster claims his heart quit him," I explained, giving her what little I'd been privy to. "'Cept Papa, he'd only just turned thirty-five. That's way too young, you ask me."

The sharp edges of Mama's voice cut through the screen door. "Come inside, Emily Ann. Tanyon has something to say."

Addie grabbed my arm, pulled me close. Her lips brushed my ear as she whispered sweet secrets directly into my head. "We ain't gotta be strangers, Emily Ann. You ever just wanna talk, maybe do something…"

Addie likes girls the way boys like girls, I reminded myself.

'Cept all's that did is stir up a mess of curiosity in the pit of my belly.

"I'd like that," I told her, holding her gaze longer than intended.

Mama snatched the liquor jar from my hand and marched me into the kitchen. "Choice is yours," she told me, "but you ain't going over the river. Biloxi's one thing, but New Orleans ain't the place for a child."

Her words darted through my mind like minnows in shallow water. Biloxi? New Orleans? My choice? What on God's green earth did the woman mean?

Tanyon patted the chair next to him at the supper table, asked me to have a seat and hear him out. "A place in Biloxi," he explained. "A speakeasy, really, but they're in with the local law. Only a tryout. Jazz, Baby, that's all they play."

His face blurred like a funhouse mirror. My head went to wagging back and forth. "I can't," I heard myself say. 'Cept why would I say no to the thing I'd long dreamed about?

Tanyon's fingers slid beneath my chin, raised my gaze to meet his. "You can at least try, Baby. Ain't no harm in giving it a whirl."

I shoved his hand away and tried like heck not to cry. "Ain't nobody wants to hear a kid sing jazz—especially in a speakeasy! They'll all *laugh* at me, I try something like that."

And of course Mama had to jump into the fray. "She's not ready, Tanyon—just like I told you. Maybe a few years from now—"

Tanyon clipped her short. "She has the voice, Norma Jean! It makes no sense to go on wasting her talent singing spirituals to folks ain't capable of appreciating the girl."

"They appreciate her just fine," Mama protested, offended over any notion that implied otherwise.

Mama had dreams of her own once. She danced ballet. And to hear Papa tell of it, she belonged on stages scattered in faraway places like Paris and Rome, London and New York. Even that Hearst fella put her in his newspapers a time or two, made claim of her graceful beauty. She made it as far as Atlanta before I came along and snatched it all away.

I shifted in my seat, wiped at my tears, and latched on to Mama's hand. "I'm gonna give it a try," I said. "Papa would have wanted me to. He'd have even driven me there himself." And that's the gospel truth; I had no bigger fan than Papa.

Tanyon went for Addie's jar, gave the lid a twist. "Gotta do it for *you*, Emily Ann. Ain't gonna work if you're doing it for anybody else."

"They gonna pay me?" I asked.

"It's only a tryout."

"A tryout for what?"

"For Friday nights. That's when you'll see some money."

*   *   *

Tanyon's Chevrolet rattled along that rough stretch of road leading south to Biloxi. His mouth went to running like a whippoorwill's ass, intent on selling me what I'd already bought. I reckon the corn liquor deserved blame for that.

Suppose they hate me? That's the question kept gnawing at my mind, chewing its way into my brain, devouring the part that supplies confidence to a girl foolish enough to believe she can sing jazz. Ain't nobody gonna boo you in church.

Tanyon fished up a Lucky Strike, dragged a Lucifer across the dash. "How'd you get familiar with jazz songs, Baby? I mean, you ain't got no radio to home, ain't never been to a speak."

Sharecropper shacks pocked the flat scenery like a tin-roofed plague. Cotton fields raced toward the graying horizon.

"Aunt Frannie has a radio," I confessed. "I listen whenever I have to stay with her."

Tanyon gave his Lucky a long suck. "Uh-uh. Ain't no way that woman allows the devil's music in *her* home."

The salty air of the Gulf mingled with the breeze, took me back to trips I made with Papa. "She goes to Bible study every morning. Gone over two hours most days."

Our destination pounced on us just outside of Biloxi. Nothing fancy, really, just an old general store turned speakeasy. A dozen cars lay scattered about the dirt lot, practically hidden in the growing darkness.

"I'm scared," I admitted, hoping for an escape route where no questions would be asked.

Tanyon wheeled the Chevy behind the building, settled us in a greasy yellow light pooling at the speak's back door. "Take a sip," he said, slipping a shiny silver flask into my hand.

Sweet jazz leaked into the night when the engine died away. Laughter danced between the notes.

I drew that proffered hooch to my lips, pulled its liquid heat against my tongue, and breathed off those vapors—just the way Papa taught me New Year's last.

A cough or two dropped into my lap. I managed a weak "Lord a-mercy" before daring a second run at that flask.

Tanyon tossed smoke rings into the air and let go a soft chuckle. "Gonna have to keep my eyes on you."

Voices broke through the speak's back door, warm and loose by tone, though I couldn't piece together any one single conversation.

And that band! Lord a-mercy! They poured a sticky-sweet melody into the mix, and I could just tell by the joyful ruckus folks were cutting a rug inside that small space.

I scooted closer to Tanyon. "I wanna dance tonight."

He capped that flask and returned it to his back pocket. "You only get one song, Baby, so you better knock 'em dead."

We tumbled out of the car like a girl and her beau doing the town right. Tanyon's arm fell across my shoulders and hugged me tight to his side.

"Stick close to me," Tanyon admonished. "This place can get rough."

We broke the threshold and crossed into the sort of scene I'd conjured up during a hundred sleepless nights:

Flappers cut all the latest moves out on that makeshift dance floor.

Fellas in brand new suits lined up at the bar, eager to spend some of that ill-gotten gain sending smoke signals from their pockets.

Four colored boys dished out a delicious run of notes atop a low-slung stage jammed into a far corner.

Tanyon nudged me into the swirling crowd. "Don't get scared now, Baby," he hollered over the din. "Tonight can be very good for us."

"Can I have another drink?" I begged, choking on a dry notion prodding me to get gone and be quick in doing it. These people would never take me seriously.

'Cept Tanyon had ideas he'd no doubt spent a lot of free moments constructing. "Ain't no different than singing for them church folks," he claimed, dragging me into a short hallway just off the back door. "You just sing that jazz, and they gonna love you like one of their own."

The office door had a name on it: *Ari DuMaurier*—and a title to give weight to that name: *Owner.*

Tanyon's voice came stiff and hushed. "Be polite, say please and thank you, and let's hope for the best." His knuckles rapped a coded knock against the door.

Behind us, shadowy figures shifted in the dim setting; some stopped to gawk at me, but most paid me no mind.

The door gave up a wide yawn. A short bald man leaned into the gap. His gray-eyed gaze took hold on me good and tight. "Dis da girl?" he asked, each word dripping with that familiar Cajun twang.

Tanyon's head went to bobbing like his neck got broke somewhere between home and here. "Baby Teegarten," he said. "From Rayford."

"*Baby?* I should say so." The little man backed away from the door and waved us inside. "I got five dollars says she still has her mama's tittie milk on her breath."

My cheeks went hot with that angry scarlet burn. I held my tongue, though, left it up to Tanyon to defend me.

"She can sing like a colored girl, Ari," Tanyon promised. "Just give her that one song, that's all I ask."

DuMaurier leaned against his cluttered desk and let the devil's grin wrap itself around his thin lips. "I'm g'wan give her dat one song." Those eyes of his shifted from me to Tanyon and back again. "You best be all da man says you is. Dem folks out in dat room, dey been long time in drinkin'. Dey liable to strip da meat from da bone, you don't give 'em a show."

Tables had no place in the cramped main room. Folks who weren't already on the dance floor huddled at the edges, sharing jars of corn liquor and wild tales of previous indulgences. Cigar and cigarette smoke swirled in the stale air, collecting like gray clouds at the low ceiling.

Tanyon gripped my hand in his and pulled me along the perimeter, bypassing groups of drunken fellas eyeing me with nasty intent. A few hurled wolf whistles. One man pinched my bottom.

Tanyon refused dissuasion. "Pay 'em no mind, Baby," he hollered, determined to present me to the band. "This is good training."

Training for what? I wondered, trying my best to avoid eye contact with those strange faces darting here and there at the fringes of my sight.

Two steps up and we gained the stage.

The saxophone player did all the talking, though I couldn't recall a single word, even if my life depended on knowing the secret he'd just divulged.

"Do you know that song?" he asked, looking right at me.

Instinct had my head nodding back and forth—without actually catching the title.

Tanyon backed away, leaving me alone in front of the microphone. Two dozen faces on that floor eagerly anticipated my first move. Some hoped I would fail—couldn't hide *that* sort of lust.

My belly twisted tight, swore all kinds of promises aimed at evicting my supper.

Sweat rushed down my back.

Blood in the water.

Someone hollered, "Get off the stage!"

A flapper up front yelled, "Go home, little girl!"

My legs took to trembling. I mumbled, "I can't do this," and broke for freedom.

'Cept that saxophone man, he had his own ideas as to how this might turn out. His strong fingers wrapped around my upper arm, tugged me right back to center stage. "Give 'em your back and sing to *me*," he ordered, parking my body at the microphone. "And don't you *never* run off like that, without you don't even try."

Insults fell like rocks from an angry mob seeking revenge against some injustice I'd supposedly laid on their town.

Sax man repeated, "Look to *me*." He straightened my shoulders, raised my chin. "Them folks back of you ain't really here. It's just you and me."

My gaze locked on to that wiry colored man.

I swallowed hard at a tangle of words stuck in my throat.

Smoky notes wafted from the bell of his instrument—a song most familiar. When my cue rang out—that high-minded wail—I leaned into the microphone and lamented on that no-good man done me wrong.

*   *   *

We must have passed a dozen cars during our quiet ride back home, each heading in the opposite direction, trundling toward Biloxi rather than Rayford. Can't say I blame them, neither. Ain't no speaks, no jazz, no fun in that little scrap of space.

I studied Tanyon's profile in the green glow coming off the dash, searched for any hint of the ideas he clearly had stacked up inside his head.

"Did it surprise you?" I dared ask, hoping for any sort of reaction from the man.

He sucked on his Lucky and pondered my words for a drawn-out moment. "Did what surprise me?"

"The way those folks treated me."

"And just how do you suppose they treated you?"

I couldn't keep that grin all to myself. "Pretty damn good, you ask me. I mean, they ain't never cheered for me like that at *church!*"

That silver flask flashed against the dash lights. We passed it easily between us a few times, reveling in my conquest, our shared victory.

I scooted closer to him, leaned against his body. "Do you reckon Mister DuMaurier will hire me?"

"DuMaurier has no use for you, Baby," Tanyon announced. "He'd catch hell from the law for putting a young girl on his stage."

I pulled away, found him in that dim glow, and tried like the dickens to read him. "Then why'd we even bother?"

"I told you it was a tryout."

"Tryout for *what?* I mean, if I can't—"

The Chevy jerked to the side of the road, jammed me tight against Tanyon.

"Now you listen here!" he demanded, mashing the brake to the floor. "We didn't run to Biloxi to audition for a small-timer like DuMaurier."

"Well then who—?"

"Frank Rydekker, that's who! And let me tell you another thing, girl. He liked what he heard." His grin got caught up in the dim light. "He's the one we needed to impress."

I tried to snatch hold on his words and make sense of what he meant. "I thought Mister DuMaurier owned that speak."

"Would you forget about DuMaurier? And forget about that lousy speak, too." Tanyon found first gear and rolled us back onto the road. "Rydekker owns one of the bigger clubs in N'Orleans, Emily Ann." His grin melted into a smile reminded me an awful lot of Papa. "He's willing to try you in his Friday night slot."

A club? In New Orleans? My eyes went wide as two silver dollars in a midget's hand. My dream crouched in the shadows, close enough to taunt me, and still I couldn't reach out and take hold of it.

"Are you forgetting something?" I asked, stewing in the salty broth of disappointment. "Mama ain't gonna let me cross the river."

Tanyon managed a last pull from his Lucky before flicking the spent butt into the night. "Leave your mama to me," he finally said, awash in his own hubris. "You just keep your mouth shut till I can put together what's what."

*   *   *

I recognized that white Cadillac lurking in the shadows along the side of our house, the one with a familiar black star painted on its doors.

Tanyon made no real effort to conceal his natural-born contempt for lawmen. "What do *they* want?" he spat, sliding his Chevy into the driveway.

I reckoned it had to do with Papa, though that jar Addie carried over sat front and center of my thoughts. Sheriff Dantley didn't fool around when it came to bootleg hooch in his county.

Tanyon leaned in close enough for his breath to warm my cheek. "You ain't high, are ya?"

A stray giggle fluttered free from my lips. "Just a touch."

"You were awful good tonight," he said.

"Only did one song."

"One's all it took." He fished a-loose a Lucky and patted his breast pocket for a Lucifer. "Rydekker's offering twenty dollars a night—which ain't half bad for a beginner."

"Twenty whole dollars?" My words burst brighter than the sudden orange glow of his struck match. "Just to sing jazz?"

Tanyon tossed a wad of smoke into the now-darkened space between us. The man had ideas of his own. "We can make ten times that in a week—if we tickle the right ears."

I didn't have time to ponder his grand scheme, compare it to my own dreams, see if they matched up. Sheriff Dantley's wide shape filled the front door, crept onto the porch. This was no social call.

"I best go in," I said, giving the car door a good fling.

My legs took to shaking like a drunk on the wagon the closer I came toward confrontation.

I climbed the front steps.

The lawman removed his hat. "Evening, Emily Ann," he said, like we'd just bumped into each other at the general store.

I only gave him a nod, just in case my words slid into one another and I'd have to explain my whereabouts for the night.

"Okay, well…" His nervous state became apparent in the pale light spilling through the parlor window. "Do you still have that auntie of your'n stays in town?"

Crickets chirred behind me.

An owl gave a hoot.

My gaze shot past him, searched for Mama inside the house. "Why do you ask?"

Dantley's bulk dropped into a slouch. "I know you had it bad lately, Emily Ann—"

"Where's Mama?"

"I don't mean to make it worse."

Tears stung my eyes. "Is she gone?"

"Huh?"

"Did she pass?" I demanded.

The lawman's head wagged back and forth. "She ain't *dead*, Emily Ann; she's, well, she's in jail."

That hooch. That's what happened. He came by to see if we were all right since Papa's passing, and he saw the jar Addie carried over.

I breathed an eager sigh. "It's just one jar," I said, gaining some confidence. "Ain't like she brewed it herself. It helps her sleep since Papa."

His head gave in to a tilt made him look like an old coonhound hearing a penny-whistle for the first time. "What on God's green are you rambling on about, girl?"

"The jar," I explained. "The reason Mama's in your jail."

Exasperation colored his jowls an offended red. "I ain't took your mama to jail for a jar of *hooch!* Kinda man you take me for, dragging a widow in for something like that?"

"Then why?" I dipped into that pale light, gave him the opportunity to look me in the eyes. "Why do you have her locked up?"

His meaty hands worked over that black felt hat. "I took your mama in on account of, well…"

He dug into his pocket and fished out a silver watch dangling at the end of a fancy chain.

Midnight.

I expected an answer. "Well *what?*"

"Your mam's the one killed your daddy."

Chapter Three

Aunt Frannie's ancient Victorian reached high into the morning sky like a lazy fat lady having a good stretch after an early nap. It never did sit right, an old spinster keeping all that extra space for herself, while entire families are forced to make do squeezed inside those puny shotgun shacks ain't big enough for a single grown man. Besides, it could just as easily have been Mama's house—had she thought things through a little better before getting with child.

It didn't amount to much.

My belly went tight with a pain the likes I'd never known before. And truth to tell, it had next to nothing at all to do with Aunt Frannie; we got on just fine, me and her. I reckon it had more to do with Mama and that whole mess she poured into my life. I mean, who kills another soul and then blabs it up to the law? Didn't make no kind of sense. I guess I'd rather not know she had dirty hands. At least then I could still love her.

That jazzy rhythm I flung against the front door carried every intention of crawling under the old spinster's skin. If there's one thing in this world Aunt Frannie detests more than that old serpent himself, it's his music.

A handful of angry words took flight between my syncopated rap, tossed into the air from somewhere out back of the house.

"You filthy beast!" Aunt Frannie hollered. "Don't let it escape, Billy."

Laughter—girlish giggles, they were—tickled the tension from the moment. 'Cept when did Aunt Frannie ever laugh out loud? I'd been one to believe she'd discovered some hidden Bible passage condemning such outbursts of joy.

It's something I needed to witness for myself. Not that I'm the nosy sort, mind you; it's just that I'd never seen anything outside of a half smile from that woman.

I left my suitcase and made for the side of the house, hoping to discover the source of the ruckus that managed to coax a little sugar from an old pillar of salt.

"Get in front of it, Neesie!" Aunt Frannie ordered. "If it gets past, we'll *never* catch it."

I took to my knees and crawled between a pair of azalea bushes I helped plant last time I stayed over.

A sharp ache stabbed my stomach like maybe I'd eaten half a dozen green apples. Even down there, where my legs came together, registered something I could never in good conscience describe to another living soul.

"It's heading for *you*, Billy!"

A rush of footfalls tussled at the dirt; the hubbub spun recklessly toward my hiding place, attacking from left and right.

'Cept all I had a mind to wonder is, Who the heck is this Billy?

My head cleared the tops of those shrubs.

A storm of dust swirled directly in front of me.

That Choctaw boy's eyes pumped mine with all sorts of promised mischief.

"Billy Blood!" I gained my feet, gave away my secret place. "What are you—?"

Thwack!

Ass-over-tea kettle, I went, tumbling through the bushes like a discarded ragdoll, landing at the feet of a colored girl looked at me like I just now fell from the sky.

A swarm of black dots gathered at the edges of my sight, put me in a narrow mind to sock that girl a good one.

"Did you do that?" I demanded, pulling up on shaky legs.

She denied it, though, and set her head to wagging this way and that. "The billy done it," she claimed.

"*Liar!*" I spat. "Billy was standing right beside me."

That's when Aunt Frannie swooped down from wherever she'd been perched, went about restoring order. "She means the billy *goat* got you, Emily Ann." And then I saw it with my own two eyes: Aunt Frannie's laughter. "And it looks like he got you pretty good."

My hands moved gingerly over my wounded backside. Mama always said that's where I kept my pride. "Why'd you get a stupid old goat anyway?" I asked, spying the mocking beast munching on a rose bush.

"I didn't," said Aunt Frannie, turning her gaze to that Choctaw boy. "There's an extra two dollars in your pay, if you can return it to its proper master."

Billy tossed up a nod before vanishing among the various shrubs taking root throughout the yard.

I didn't mean for my words to sound so rude; they just spilled from my mouth all rough-edged and raw. "How come you let that Injun in your yard?"

Aunt Frannie shared Mama's face—though an older version. "Billy is my gardener, Baby." Her fingers stroked my cheek, the way Mama's never did. "Sorry, for your daddy. I guess I always figured it might one day come to this."

Whatever did she mean? I wondered, too much a coward to raise the question to sound.

And that colored girl didn't help matters any; she got on my bad side with nary a thought to the consequences. "This one gots her flowers," the girl said, tugging at my dress.

Aunt Frannie's nose wrinkled up, the same way it will when someone mentions jazz or flappers or corn liquor. "Jeez Louise, Emily Ann! Haven't you learned your cycle?"

She gave no chance for a response, pulling me inside the house by my arm. She dragged me through the kitchen, into the parlor, and up that fancy staircase to the second floor.

To the water closet.

My second favorite place on earth.

"Didn't your mother teach you about this?" Aunt Frannie asked, lifting my dress over my head. "You're in full bloom, child."

The crimson stain ruined my underpants, and painted its mark on the back of my dress. I understood its meaning and rejected it without a thought.

"I ain't ready for this," I complained, climbing into that wonderful claw-foot tub, with its promise to treat me right. Only Mr. Kuiper's pond offered better.

A liquid rope of warmth spilled eagerly from that copper spigot, splashed gently against my bare skin. But the water had gone pink with my shame, and for the first time in my life, I didn't want to be seen without a stitch.

And Aunt Frannie, well, she offered up nothing likely to be confused with sympathy. "Welcome to the curse, young lady." Her grin called to mind a giddy schoolyard bully spying his next victim. "Consider all your carefree days dead and gone."

*   *   *

That long mirror spoke softly, convinced me to have a gawk at what

I'd grown into. I loosed the towel and let it fall to the bathroom floor. Truth be told, I didn't see much of a difference from the last time I stood before that very same looking glass, taking great narcissistic delight in my own nudity. I reckon my hips took on a more noticeable curve since the previous summer. And maybe my breasts had gone past being little more than useless pink nubs. But that ain't saying much; that girl in the mirror still had a long road ahead of her.

The rags are what I hated most—well, that, and the cramps. I'd waited with great expectations for womanhood to arrive, and now that her slender arms finally embraced me, I wanted nothing more than to sock her in the nose, make *her* bleed.

The colored girl barged in without so much as a knock or a warning. Her fingers gripped that ratty old sundress I thought I'd never wear again. "G'wan take some soakin' to clean that other 'un." She made no effort to avert her eyes, sizing up my bare body like I had on all the latest fashions.

"Have you had yours yet?" I asked, taking the proffered dress.

"My flower?" Her head went to twisting left and right atop her shoulders. "Uh-uh. But Miss Frannie say mines is just up the hill a piece."

I guessed her to be my age, maybe a year back of me. An awful small girl—smaller than even me. Dark eyes. Full lips. She kept her hair in two loose braids. She said nothing as I dressed, just watched as if we were old friends gone way back.

"Aunt Frannie says you're her laundry girl," I said, checking my reflection. "You got kin around here?" I only asked on account of I'd never seen the girl before. Ain't many colored folks in Rayford.

"Mines is over in 'Bama," she explained. "Well, they was. My mams done passed, and I ain't knowed my paps. Gots a beau, though, called Simp." A lovely scarlet flush colored her chocolate complexion. The girl kept secrets.

"How come he didn't come with you?" I asked.

A nervous smile played upon her lips. "Can't be black in Mississippi. 'Sides, we g'wan get married when I go back."

A million questions bubbled in the ether, each demanding to be heard: Did she ever kiss the boy? Has she seen him bare? Did they ever lay together?

'Cept Aunt Frannie intruded with a question of her own. "Are you ready to go to Jackson, Emily Ann?"

*   *   *

I came into this life the very same night *Titanic* went under—an omen, Mama called it. 'Cept nobody really knew if it portended to a good life or bad. And it didn't help that I made my debut butt-first, causing Mama all sorts of grief. Lord knows the woman never let me forget such sacrifices.

Maybe that's why she turned against Papa.

Doctor Royster's the one unraveled the knotted mess. He caught whiff of that acrid odor belonged sprayed on a cotton field, to keep the boll weevils away.

That same odor I'd sniffed mingled with Papa's last meal.

I didn't tell anybody *that* part.

Not even Aunt Frannie.

"Do you suppose they'll give her the chair?" I asked, not certain I needed to know the answer.

Aunt Frannie's knuckles went white in her grip of the steering wheel. "They don't usually send women to that godless contraption."

"Maybe she didn't do it." The warm breeze set my hair to dancing some gentle waltz.

"Your mama confessed, Emily Ann. Repented, too." Her clear green eyes moved from the road ahead to me and back again. "It didn't need to come to this. All she had to do was turn you over to me when you were a baby, and she could have continued her dancing."

We'd gone down this path before. "I came from *her*," I said firmly. "Can't change facts."

For all her blustery show of authority, Aunt Frannie possessed in her the warm heart of a natural mother. She just couldn't have her own babies, is all. I reckon that's why she'd long ago taken such a deep shine to me. Maybe I'd been the closest she'd come to a daughter of her own.

Maybe she just really did love me.

Godwyn's Department Store loitered at the corner of Cotton Street and Norwood, occupying a full city block, promising the good folks of Mississippi the very same items available to the well-to-do up in New York. I'd only been inside the place one other time. With Papa. For a birthday present for Mama. The lady at the perfume counter looked on us like we were the mess some poor fool stepped in and carried in there on the bottom of his shoe.

"I don't like it here," I mumbled, sucking back the bitter taste of that past rejection.

But Aunt Frannie, well, she saw life at different angles. "They offer a lovely selection of dresses," she said, tucking her forest-green Pierce-Arrow against the curb. Her smile came with reassurances not normally given to a girl from my station of life. "Besides, you're a woman now. Shouldn't you dress the part?"

I flung the passenger door wide and gained the sidewalk, eager to see where this new transformation might lead. 'Cept inside the store nothing had changed. Every narrow eye in that place fell on me, the poor little dirt-girl in a tattered yellow sundress. I didn't belong.

Couldn't tell such a thing to Aunt Frannie, though. She burst through the crowd like she owned the place, attached her gaze to the slender woman in charge of the ladies' department, and snapped off orders with the expectation of finding each one fulfilled by the end of our visit, assuring everybody with functioning ears there'd be hell to pay should even the least of her commandments fall short of completion.

A slow parade of fashions not common to Rayford came at me like a lazy daydream: cocktail dresses and flower prints straight from Paris, strapless numbers popular with most flappers. Aunt Frannie's the one had the final say in choice, though. She kept me conservative, allowing for little deviation from my normal attire of sundresses.

"Thought I was a woman now," I said, not really complaining.

Her arm fell across my shoulders, hugging me close. "And so you are, Emily Ann." She grabbed at a proffered white blouse and navy skirt. "Go try these on."

That's the outfit I wore out of Godwyn's, leaving behind the tattered remains of that faded yellow sundress. A new girl.

A woman.

*   *   *

"Who in blazes is that?" Aunt Frannie's gaze stuck to that dull black Chevrolet like a bug in pine sap. "And what does he mean by parking in front of *my* house?" She'd die before admitting to such a sin, but Aunt Frannie had a way of looking down on folks who fell short of her own lofty heights.

"It's Tanyon," I said, racing for the front door.

Aunt Frannie chopped off a handful of words that included some sort of rebuke claiming the man had no business with a girl of my age.

I gave clarification to the situation. "He's Papa's best friend."

That tall, lanky fella trod the front porch like he'd been to that house a hundred nights before. "Evening, ladies," he said, eyes bouncing between me and Aunt Frannie. "Sorry to intrude so late."

Aunt Frannie's the one invited him inside the parlor, suddenly playing hostess to some special visitor. "Can I get you something cold to drink?"

Tanyon waved her off. "I just came to check on Baby, see how she's holding up." His gaze drifted through that fancy room, took inventory of the inherited wealth. "Reckon she's doing just fine."

We shared a black velvet loveseat, Tanyon and I, and made small talk concerning Mama's fate, what the local paper had to say about it, and just what might have motivated such an act. Everybody had questions but nobody knew the answers.

"You're looking prim and proper," he said, meaning my new outfit.

My cheeks flushed warm scarlet, like maybe he had a mind to flirt with me right there in front of Aunt Frannie. "We went to Godwyn's," I said lamely, my hands folded in my lap.

Aunt Frannie thumbed through a magazine, feigned interest in some story or other, all the while sneaking furtive glances at me and Tanyon from her perch on the sofa. And what would she say if I climbed on his lap like I used to back home?

"I suppose I ought to be going," Tanyon said, gaining his feet.

Aunt Frannie rose like a hornet got her on the backside. "And do feel free to visit Emily Ann. Only try to make it a more favorable hour."

I caught the look from Tanyon, the one that said, Walk me to my car. Didn't take that Einstein fella to figure what the man meant to talk about.

We strolled down the front walk in the fading glow of a spent day, both acutely aware of Aunt Frannie's hawk-eyed stare watching from behind the screen door.

"It's all set up," he said softly. "For this coming Friday night."

"Ain't no way she'll let me go to New Orleans." My voice came low but steady.

"Can't back out now, Emily Ann."

"What am I supposed to do, run away?"

When we reached his car, Tanyon retrieved a pack of Luckys from his breast pocket and shook one a-loose. "You have friends, right?" He took the cigarette between his lips and dragged a Lucifer across the roof of the Chevy. "Just tell your Aunt you're staying over to some girl's house. Simple as that."

Truth be told, I didn't know any girls friendly enough to drop in on and stay all night. Couldn't tell that to Tanyon, though; he didn't stick around for any sort of excuse. He had his mind all made up.

"I'll pick you up Friday afternoon," he said, sliding in behind the wheel. "And wear that outfit you have on. It makes you look grown up."

*   *   *

I found her in my room, that colored girl, sitting on my bed, cradling Stella like the china doll belonged to her and nobody else. And truth be told, it didn't bother me the way it once would have. It's her song that grabbed hold on me, put me under a spell meant to loosen up a girl, get her in a certain mood—if a *fella* sang that same song.

I trickled inside my bedroom like a slow leak, caught the girl in profile, and studied the way that sweet melody dripped from her perfect lips like nectar from a flower. I swear I could almost smell the jasmine behind her soft words.

I waited until the last note fell before making my presence known. "Where'd you learn that song?" I asked, drifting closer to the bed.

She said nothing at first, just stared at me through a haze of fear mingled with suspicion.

"Well, then," I said, dropping down beside her. "You have a nice voice. Bet you could sing jazz."

That got her going. Neesie shifted in her seat, laid Stella against her lap, still unwilling to turn the doll a-loose. "Ain't g'wan sing no jazz. Jus' wanna gets my *own* baby to sing to."

'Cept I knew things this girl surely didn't understand. "They got folks willing to pay good money, you come sing in a speak."

But Neesie wouldn't hear of any such nonsense. The girl meant only to get by in life, drawing no attention to her own lot. "Don't wants no speaks; jus' wants my own chile."

Those skinny dark arms pulled a stark contrast against the dull gray linen of her work dress.

My body leaned into hers. "You're still a child yourself," I said.

A delicate smile played at the corners of her soft mouth. "So is you."

"Un-uh," I assured her. "I got my flowers."

"And you gots this baby doll, too."

"No I don't." I broke free from her warmth, from the scent of the girl, and gained my feet. "Stella belongs to you now."

Neesie's dark eyes went wide with something akin to joy. "Don't tease," she ordered.

"Ain't teasing," I promised, smoothing an imaginary wrinkle from my skirt. "A girl my age, well, I got no time to be playing with dolls. Besides…" I tossed a quick glance toward the open door, hoping Aunt Frannie wouldn't hear. "I'm fixin' on being a star before too long."

"Doin' what?"

"Singing jazz."

That head of hers went to wagging atop her shoulders. "Ain't nobody g'wan put you on a stage. And 'sides that, Miss Frannie g'wan have *her* say."

"Too late," I told her, moving for the door. "It's already done."

CHAPTER FOUR

Billy Blood moved like shirtless mortal sin through Aunt Frannie's back-yard garden, working hard at that nub of a stump he intended on having gone long before suppertime. Above his head the sky had gone black with the bruise of thick angry clouds that promised cool respite from that sticky heat clinging to my skin like an old set of long johns.

I watched from the kitchen window, taking care not to be seen. Lord only knows all the foolish ideas he'd string together after catching me spying.

'Cept I had a few ideas of my own needed expressing.

"What time does he take lunch?" I dropped onto a chair at the breakfast table and fixed on the colored girl.

Suspicion, like those storm clouds, gathered in Neesie's dark eyes. "What you want with *him?* Ain't good for nothin' but trouble."

True enough. Everybody in Rayford knew that much about Billy.

But I still needed him.

"You mind yours and I'll mind mine," I said, spreading the morning paper across the table.

Neesie dipped into the laundry room, fell away from my sight long enough to let me have a better gawk at that Choctaw boy.

He'll do it, I convinced myself, creeping through the back door. Offer the boy a dollar and he'll jump at my plan.

I crossed the yard without any real sense of what I might actually say to convince him to see things my way. I mean, suppose he expected something that costs more than a dollar? Something intimate, personal.

The thwack of the ax echoed off the back of the house. Billy raised it again and slammed it hard against that stubborn stump like he and it had gone round and round in some long-standing feud not likely to see a conclusion anytime soon.

I stayed back a good piece, avoiding the splintering wood raining down on the area closest to Billy. "Where's that goat?" I asked, scanning the azaleas for movement.

Billy stopped mid-chop and fixed me with a look meant to run me off. "Ain't got time to chatter, Teegarten."

"Wanna earn a dollar?"

That got his attention.

He tossed the ax aside and fished a handkerchief from his hip pocket. "Doing what?" he asked, wiping at his forehead.

I moved in closer, just to show I meant this to be our secret. "Go tell Addison Markley I need a word with her."

Billy wanted more than a dollar for what I was asking. I could tell by the way his eyes dropped to my legs—bare beneath a new lemon-yellow sundress—and did a slow sashay up the length of my body, settling on the small swell of my breasts.

"Tell her yourself," he said, snatching hold on his ax again. "I have work to do."

"It's too far to walk," I complained. "Besides, it won't take you but a few minutes to drive over."

Billy spun on me like maybe he'd got confused over which way the stump went. "And suppose her daddy's there. You think I wanna catch a bullet over his stupid daughter ain't got sense to know she's a girl?"

"He won't be there." I lied, but New Orleans counted on my meeting with Addie. "He'll be out at his still."

"Can you guarantee that?"

I couldn't, even though my nodding head claimed I could.

Sweat shined his upper lip like it meant to water a dark mustache—if only the Injun had the wherewithal to actually grow one.

"Fine," he said, returning to his feud with that old stump. "Gonna cost more than a measly dollar, though."

I figured as much—him being Billy Blood and all.

"How much?" I asked, though I reckon I already had a good count of the cost.

Thwack! went the ax.

"You ain't *that* dumb, Teegarten," said Billy.

Okay then. This is how it had to be. "How far you aiming to go?"

The Devil's grin caught hold on Billy's lips.

It made perfect sense, this taking place in a garden.

Billy leaned the ax against his adversary. "Some kissing, I guess. Maybe a little touching."

Those dark clouds overhead expelled a low rumble. A cool breeze tossed my hair into a delicate dance. A lone drop of rain kissed my bare shoulder.

"Can you handle that, Teegarten?" He drifted in close to me, so subtle in his intentions. Those long thin fingers stroked my cheek, caressed my lips. "I mean, if you ain't ready for… stuff…"

"Monday morning," I blurted, pulling away from his touch, his salty odor. "But you have to go tell Addie," I hollered over my shoulder, scampering for the house. "I need to see her right now."

Neesie drank up that whole scene from the kitchen window, didn't even try to hide the fact she'd been spying. "A head full of nasty ideas, that boy," she said to nobody in particular.

I stumbled into my seat at the table, made like I had an interest in what the newspaper had to say. Couldn't hide my shakes, though. My hands trembled like an old drunk gone new on the wagon.

Billy's sudden touch stirred up all sorts of tingles and warm spots on my body, made the pits of my arms wet with sweat. Ain't no boy ever conjured *that* from me before.

Not even Jobie Pritchett.

I cleared my throat, prayed my voice wouldn't be lost, or stretched too thin. "He ever try anything with you?" I dared ask.

Neesie hoisted a basket of clean laundry atop the table and gifted me with her best smile. "He do to you what he done to me, he g'wan have *two* girls chasin' *him*."

*   *   *

Faded denim overalls hung a-loose on Addie's wiry frame; patches concealed holes in the knees. She'd only just got her hair cut again, short, like a boy's. 'Cept Addie didn't look like no boy in her face. Might could've been in the fashion magazines, if she had a mind for such things.

She jammed her hands into her pockets while taking a short turn around Aunt Frannie's parlor, giving only cursory glances at the paintings on the walls. "Who's the old man?" she asked, nodding toward the oil over the fireplace.

"My granddad," I told her, hanging back near the front door. "He's dead and gone now."

"Your mama's daddy?"

My head went to nodding like it rested on a rusty spring.

Her dark eyes tied me in a knot. "Then how come he let y'all live in that shithole out on Posner Road?"

I knew the story well enough, kept it to myself since I first overheard talk of it a few years back. Ain't the sort of gossip a girl wants to hear about herself.

I told her anyway.

"My mama got with child before she married Papa," I explained.

Addie's black boots banged a slow rhythm against the parlor floor until she stood close enough to touch me. "So you're a *bastard*," she said. "I can respect that."

She didn't smell like a boy, that's for sure. The sweet scent lingering in the air around her conjured girlish images.

Addie's the one took a seat first. "What's your plan?" she asked.

I dropped down beside her, and after a short spell of hemming and hawing, I managed to stammer my intentions.

Her face betrayed little of her thoughts. "New Orleans, huh? Well, it ain't nothing like Rayford, Emily Ann. But I reckon that's the place to go if you mean to sing jazz."

"I just need you to be my alibi, is all," I added again, in case she missed it the first go round.

"What's in it for me?"

"Give you a dollar."

"A dollar? Not everybody lusts for money, Emily Ann." Addie leaned in closer, like she meant to share a secret. 'Cept she pressed her lips to mine—a soft peck at first, lasting only a second or two, before committing herself completely, taking it deeper than I'd ever imagined a kiss might go. The tip of her tongue nudged mine, made all sorts of promises I'd spend the following days desperately attempting to decipher.

Part of me thought to stop this moment of weakness, to pull away from her and run upstairs to the safety of my room. 'Cept I didn't. How could I, when the other part seized control, the part that found in this kiss a most amazing experience?

Addie's the one finally broke the spell, forced the genie back into its bottle—for the time being. "I'll cover for you, Emily Ann," she promised, gaining her feet. "We'll work out some sort of payment."

I stayed fixed to the sofa long after she drove off, replayed our indiscretion from as many different angles as possible.

It didn't make me *that* way, did it?

I mean, it's only a kiss, right?

Neesie traipsed through the parlor, laundry basket on her hip like a too-heavy baby she ain't quite ready to teach to walk. "You g'wan want that skirt washed for your trip?" she asked.

I pulled up onto my feet and cornered the girl near the staircase. "You been spying on me?" I demanded.

"Ain't g'wan tell nobody."

I'd be a liar to say I didn't enjoy that fearful countenance she took up whenever confronted. Aunt Frannie knew how to draw the best ones from the girl.

I closed the slight gap between us, left nothing but the air we shared, pressed my nose against hers. "You say one word and I'll make you sorry."

Neesie's voice came low, ragged. "I promise," she whispered.

I could trust her, I knew as much. 'Cept it didn't feel right, her having to keep a secret without getting something to put into her own pocket.

I backed off, gave her room enough to draw a breath. "Want a dollar?"

And doggone if her head didn't commence to wagging back and forth. "Don't needs no dollar."

Anger burned a hot spot in the pit of my belly. "Well then what do *you* want?"

That smile of hers caught me off guard, doused my heat.

"Maybe you might could learn me to read and write some."

Anger turned to hurt. "You can't read?"

There went her head again, wagging like a coonhound's tail.

Suddenly my belly came up hollow, empty. Even Billy Blood learned to read. "Fine," I said. "You keep my secret, and I'll teach you." I pushed past her and gained the stairs. "How is it that a dollar won't buy anything anymore?"

*   *   *

Tanyon's fist gripped that shiny black ball atop the gearshift, took us down a notch once that bridge came into view—the one leading to my biggest dreams. Rusted iron girders reached high overhead like they meant to snatch at clouds or low-flying crows. Beneath us, angry black water swirled and spat, demanding respect from any fool brave enough to wander along its muddy banks. I'd seen it from a distance a time or two, just never knew occasion to cross over.

The Chevrolet's wheels made quite a ruckus against those loose narrow planks that stood between us and that river. Awful scary for a first-time crosser.

I hollered over the din, "Papa says they got catfish in there—big enough to swallow a grown man!"

Tanyon didn't care nothing about no fish. "This Addie girl—you can trust her, right? I mean, she ain't dimwitted, gonna show up at your Aunt Frannie's place looking for you, right?"

Addie knew better than that. Besides, the girl had intentions involving me. No sense in burning *that* bridge, right?

Tanyon found second gear and brought us to an easy trot. "What's *she* getting out of this deal?"

My gaze fixed on the paddle wheel of a boat passing beneath the bridge. "Don't know yet." I considered the possibilities, tried to sketch out the sort of tomfoolery a pair of split-tails might stumble into. "Ain't gonna be money, though."

Didn't take looking at the man to know his grin had gone crooked on his face.

His voice came all casual. "Addie's that tomboy, right?"

My cheeks went hot with scarlet flush. Inside my head, I attempted to manufacture an excuse, some defensive retort meant to close the book on any such rumors before they'd have a chance to lay down roots.

'Cept Tanyon, well, he had his own ideas. "Just keep her happy, is all. Ain't nobody needs to know your business." He plucked a fresh Lucky from a half-empty pack and took it between his lips. "Besides," he said, dragging a Lucifer across the dash, "you're gonna see all sorts of stuff like that in *this* city."

I snatched the Lucky from his hand and had a long pull. "You got me practically *marrying* the girl," I argued, savoring the taste of tobacco against my tongue.

That's when New Orleans said hello, there, on the other side of the bridge.

The Big Easy.

That's the moniker I'd most often heard in regards to that city. The French Quarter. Bourbon Street. Storyville, with all its forbidden delights. She gathered me into her bosom like an old familiar friend, whispering promises I just knew she'd keep.

'Cept it wouldn't count a tinker's damn if Tanyon fit me for a leash.

"You gonna treat me like a baby?" I asked, expecting the worst.

But Tanyon, well, he didn't cotton much to rules anyway. "I ain't your daddy," is all he said.

*   *   *

"It ain't really called Storyville anymore," Tanyon explained, angling his car along narrow cobblestone streets running this way and that. "Not since nineteen seventeen. They still got all the vice, though. Anything you want can be had for a price."

Scattered piles of horse droppings flaunted their continuing presence in the iron faces of a growing collection of mechanical beasts eager to capture all the heavy work.

Smoky fumes choked the air, mingled with that earthy odor wafting up from the river, creating its own unique scent.

Boat whistles of differing octaves competed for attention down on the river. Paddlewheels slapped at the murky water. Fellas hollered orders meant to be followed.

My head spun like a top. "Is it always this noisy?"

"Uh-uh," said Tanyon. "It gets louder after dark."

Buildings straight out of another time lined all those tight streets.

Wrought iron, like some perennial vine, clung to the landscape, enveloped tiny scraps of land, kept folks from falling off balconies, thwarted burglars from entering through open windows. Couldn't swing a dead cat without smacking against some wrought-iron creation.

The source of all that racket belonged to the loading docks.

Tanyon took pride in this. "Second biggest in the country," he said, grinning like he's the one made it all happen. "Only New York moves more cargo."

A crooked Victorian lingered lazily on the corner of Iberville and Marais Streets, like a decrepit old lady ain't got sense enough to know her time is long past, she ain't nice to look at anymore. And this being Storyville, well, it didn't take no college learning to determine what all took place underneath *her* bonnet.

"This is a cathouse," I asked, "ain't it?"

Tanyon's grin turned awful greasy. "Figured we might make a few bucks on the side, maybe stir up some interest in you."

I leaned into the passenger door, fixed him in a hard gaze, and demanded to know his intentions.

"I'm only teasing, Baby," he said, flinging his door open. "My sister lives here."

I got bold. "Is she a whore?"

"She's a house mother."

I flung my own door wide, tossed my feet to the sidewalk. "So she's a madam, huh? Well I don't reckon that's as bad as being a whore."

"Some girls have no choice; they don't wanna go hungry."

Tanyon didn't knock, he just barged right on in, had hold on my arm, dragged me along like the folks inside were expecting us.

I guess I never really gave much consideration to what a cathouse might actually look like behind closed doors. If pressed, I reckon I'd have conjured some image streaked through with half-naked girls lying about on ratty old sofas, not really caring which of the toothless drooling widowers coming through the front door had money enough to make it all worthwhile.

'Cept that's not the truth of it.

Half a dozen young fellas congregated around a long oak bar, sipping mugs of beer, waiting for their turn upstairs.

A colored boy not much older than me played a grand jazz swell on a shiny white piano.

Pretty girls made up like vaudeville beauties trod the staircase, dipping into the scene every few minutes to carry away one of those handsome boys at the bar.

A big-boned woman lumbered across the parlor, took my chin in her hand, and brought my gaze up to hers. "Would you just *look* at those eyes!" she all but hollered. "Green as polished emeralds!"

One of the bar boys broke a-loose from his perch and landed a step or two to my right. "She a new girl, Rosie?"

My heart went to banging inside my chest like a tiger raging against the cage that stole its freedom. He had me pegged a *whore?* And just what gave him such a notion as *that?*

Rose Thibbedeaux is the one set him straight. She spun on the boy quicker than a bullfrog turning a dragonfly into lunch, threatened all sorts of grievous pain should he not take her hint and get gone.

She relieved Tanyon of my arm and tugged me toward the rear of the house. "Let's retire to the kitchen," she said, "before they *all* come sniffing after her."

Tanyon set on yapping about this and that, constructing a wishing well full of big ideas should we get even a chance to show out to the kings of the city's nightlife.

Rose propped her bulk against a counter. "Who's club is she working tonight?"

Tanyon pulled up a chair at the table and went for a Lucky. "Frank

Rydekker's place," he said, breathing out a silvery cloud.

For brother and sister, they certainly lacked any serious resemblance. Maybe around the eyes they shared a kinship. That, and their noses.

Rose let go a slow sigh. "I suppose she's gotta pay her dues. Rydekker's a slippery one, though. Can't say *I'd* trust him with her." Her gaze took a slow mosey up one side of me and down the other. Ideas like butterflies fluttered around her head. "She could make a pile of money working for me."

That familiar scarlet heat warmed my cheeks. Truth be told, such a suggestion didn't sound nearly as offensive coming from Rose.

"Can't do it," said Tanyon. "Ain't saying there's anything wrong with that particular profession—"

Rose cut him off. "Girl's got a mind of her own, don't she? Let *her* answer."

My belly went tight with knots strong enough to hold back even the wildest of horses. And I swear I meant to toss an emphatic *no* into the moment, set the woman straight about just what sort of girl I was, 'cept I couldn't for the life of Peter find my voice.

I sloughed off a lame shrug instead.

Rose's grin matched Tanyon's. "What's she wearing on stage tonight?" she asked.

Tanyon crushed his Lucky in an ashtray. "Same as she's wearing right now."

Rose's head went to wagging. "Got to dress her up, singing for Rydekker's crowd."

I tossed in my own two cents, made mention that I'd only just bought the blouse and skirt.

Didn't matter to Rose. She held the city's pulse. "Might be fine for church, but Frank Rydekker ain't preaching nothing but good times and no regrets." She snatched at my hand and pulled me back through the parlor and up that wide staircase.

It didn't at all add up to the image I'd conjured only minutes earlier. Closed doors lined the narrow hallway, keeping in all but the occasional moan or hint of a giggle. Muffled voices carried on silent conversations as if belonging to lovers seated in a fancy restaurant. Bed springs picked out a rough rhythm behind one of those doors.

"You stand about the same size as Abigail," Rose proclaimed, barging unannounced into a room at the end of the hall. "She's got some real fine delicates in here."

The sparse clutter of a lived-in life lay scattered like debris throughout the tight space. A whore's life. 'Cept this girl, this Abigail, her room differed little from the very space where I lay *my* head most nights.

"How old is she?" I asked, dropping onto the foot of her unmade bed.

Rose took to rooting through the closet like a merry old sow turning up a compost heap. She never did answer my question.

A photograph on the wall over the headboard showed off a girl lying buck naked on a sofa, eyes closed tight, only pretending to be asleep.

She called to mind one of those French postcards boys are forever going on about—though not a one of them ever actually seems to *own* one.

Rose caught me gawking. "That's Evelyn Nesbit," she said, gathering close to me, a scrap of black silk in her hand. "A Gibson girl, once upon a time."

I'd heard of her before, maybe even saw a photo or two. Nothing like this, though. "They take that picture *here?*" I asked, feeling curiosity's tug.

"She's never even been down this way—so far as I know." Rose Thibbedeaux sized up the image as if she'd only just now realized the girl wore not a stitch. "She certainly was beautiful, I'll give her that. She wasn't too bright, though. She coulda made a fortune—under the right tutelage."

Rose, being that tutelage.

"Ain't she the one some fella killed another fella because of?" I wondered aloud.

"That was the scandal," said Tanyon's sister.

My gaze slid away from the girl on the wall, stumbled happily over a jumble of cosmetics leering at me from atop a squatting dresser.

Rose Thibbedeaux leaned closer, her chubby fingers already halfway through the buttons on my blouse. "Got no cause to smear paint on a face like yours," she said, almost in a whisper.

The house mother had a way about her, a certain something that set a girl at ease just as casually as a vaudeville mesmerist. It took a long moment to fully appreciate the fact that she'd stripped me bare as that Nesbit woman in the photo.

Her voice came soft, motherly. "Awful nice to look at, you are."

I stood before her like a prized hen, one rumored to know a thing about laying eggs of gold. "Think so?" I asked, fishing for another compliment.

"Even nicer than Norma Jean."

The name itself grew legs, kicked me hard in the belly, drove all the breathable air from my body.

I demanded, "What do you know of my mama?"

Her hand stroked my side, my bare hip. "Didn't say I *knew* her, darlin'." That smile of hers had a means to convert even the strictest of unbelievers over to her side. "She wasn't quite a household name, your mama, but she was certainly knocking on the front door."

The words jumped from my lips before I had chance to draw them back, examine the idea behind them. "Did my mama work here?"

'Cept that one they call Abigail spoiled the moment. "Jeez Louise!" she exclaimed, gawking at my naked body from the door. "You pushing *babies* now, Rosie?"

My fists drew up like angry stones, ready to sort this girl out should she not mind her manners. "I ain't no *baby*," I assured her, gaining a step in her direction.

Rose latched on to my arm, yanked me back. "She meant no harm, Emily Ann." She passed that scrap of black silk to my hand, told me to put it on.

"'Cept I ain't no baby," I told the girl again—just in case. Some folks tend to be hard of hearing.

Abigail's blue-eyed gaze coasted over my exposure. "Ain't too awful grown up, neither." Her laughter dumped hot coals into the pit of my belly. "Caught somewhere in the middle, I'd say."

I took up that black dress, wiggled my body into its snug fit. Spaghetti straps dug into my shoulders. The hemline fell well above my knees. I may as well have gone naked as to parade around in something so skimpy.

Abigail's grin came lopsided, like the two sides of her face couldn't agree on any one particular expression. "No wonder all them boys downstairs are so damn restless."

Rose gave my hem a tug; her fingers smoothed a wrinkle near my hip. "Are you still with your virtue, Emily Ann?"

My cheeks burned warm scarlet. Was I still a virgin, she meant to know.

My head tipped a quick nod.

Rose put up her best sell. "Just one time," she promised. "That's all I'm asking. I won't allow no harm to come to you. I swear."

Abigail piped her own tune. "Some of them fellas with deep pockets would go to *war* bidding over the likes of you."

I moved up on the girl. "What do you mean, 'the likes of me'?" I asked.

There went that lopsided grin again. "A man has enough money," explained Abigail, "he'll give most of it away just to be first inside your cunny."

"That's the nature of man," added Rose. "You'd pull down more for that one first time than you'd make in six months working for a thief like Rydekker."

Money's nice. It's a big part of my dream. I'd be a liar to claim otherwise.

'Cept it ain't the *only* part.

"I ain't ready for *that*," I admitted, gathering my skirt and blouse from the floor. "I gotta try singing first." My legs nudged me toward the door before my will could be bent.

Tanyon met me in the hallway. I reckon he'd been there the whole time, listening, maybe even watching.

"It's your choice, Emily Ann," he said, taking my hand in his. "But you made the right decision. Your daddy would be proud."

"Yeah," I muttered, following him downstairs.

But even as that single-word affirmation escaped my lips, I couldn't help but feel disappointed, like somehow I'd just been cheated out of the only sure thing I might likely ever come across.

*   *   *

722 Dauphine Street promised little in the way of excitement—from outward appearances. What once had been a Digby's Department Store now went by the somewhat famous Crescent Club.

Revelers of every color, size, and persuasion lined the sidewalk out front, passing around flasks of bootleg hooch, eager for the doors to swing open so nighttime could finally begin.

Nobody paid us any mind as Tanyon and I split the crowd on our way down a side alley leading to the rear entrance.

Tanyon laid a coded knock against the heavy red door.

A fella's chubby face filled the small peephole.

"I have Miss Teegarten with me," said Tanyon to the man.

That door swung wide; entrance was granted.

Dozens of round tables lay scattered willy-nilly throughout the cavernous main room. A wide stage rose five feet above the floor. Four colored boys worked up a number I could sing in my sleep.

I said, "I'm ready," drinking in a dream fixin' to come true.

That chubby fella let go a laugh. "How's about we open for business *before* you get started, huh?"

Waitresses lit candles and set ashtrays on each of those tables.

Tanyon snatched the one closest to the stage, and ordered a pint of bourbon from a dark-haired girl dressed out like a flapper.

"Tell me something," I began to say.

'Cept Tanyon, he had an answer all lined up. "Your mama was not a whore—if that's what you're meaning to know."

Fine enough by me.

Even if I really didn't believe him.

Frank Rydekker himself brought Tanyon's pint to our table. "So this is the little songbird," said the short, stocky man, pulling me into a splash of orange glowing off a candle. "Can you sing any of these songs?"

My eyes tumbled down the list he presented. "I can sing 'em all," I gladly admitted.

Rydekker nodded toward a big fella up near the bar and hollered, "Let 'em in, Bill!"

"Don't be scared, Baby," Tanyon said, handing me a go at that pint.

I raised the hooch to my lips, had a good pull. "Don't call me Baby any-more."

*   *   *

Cool blue dripped onto the stage from lights burning high above.

My body stood in its gathering puddle.

A boy on drums got us going with a slow shuffle that took up with the bass like a couple of long-time lovers knowing each other's next move before it's even been considered. Sullum Cass kissed his shiny saxophone with the breath of something painful and delicious, tossing delicate notes into the smoky air. When the boy on piano sprinkled all the right keys into the mixture, I eased my body against that skinny silver microphone stand, closed my eyes to the fractured night, and told all about that man done me wrong.

Everybody on that parquet dance floor caught on real quick. It's me they stared at.

Me!

Emily Ann Teegarten.

And wasn't a single one gave a tinker's damn about my age or my station in life. Faces opened in welcoming smiles as wicked rhythms spun us all toward a whole new place—a place tucked up high as heaven.

Bodies shimmied and twirled at my feet.

One song blurred into another with nary enough time to breathe.

If I'd dropped dead then and there on that Big Easy stage, I'd have no real complaints. I reckon I'd tell the first angel I set eyes on I'd lived a full life.

I lived out my dream.

Chapter Five

Raising a child had never occupied a foremost spot on whatever agenda guided Mama's life. I reckon in her eyes motherhood appeared as one of those strange abstract paintings that mostly confuse folks as to the artist's intentions. All those whispers of "She'll grow into it" faded like worthless cobwebs by my tenth year, when the woman still showed no interest in helping me along. And I ain't even mad at her, neither. Some women just ain't meant for mothering.

I only wish she hadn't taken Papa away.

I gained the front steps of the county courthouse and went immediately for Sheriff Dantley's cramped office on the first floor.

Folks swirled around me like chicken feathers in a squall, gawking, asking hushed questions like, "Ain't she the one whose mama…?"

Lottie Kane sized me up from behind her cluttered desk, made like I had no business being in that space. She'd been sweet on Papa—back before Mama went ahead and stole him away.

"Sheriff's busy," she said before I even opened my mouth.

I reckon in me, she saw the very reason she'd lost the man some say she still pined over. An unexpected child can change a whole lot of plans.

"Ain't here for the sheriff," I said, crowding close to her desk. "I need to talk to my mother."

Lottie's head went to wagging back and forth. "Impossible."

Mama's age, I'd guessed her to be. Real pretty—in a plain sort of way. The kind of girl who worked as a sheriff's secretary by day, and waited tables in a speak at night. Awful sneaky. The type of woman you can't really trust, can't really know.

'Cept she didn't scare *me*.

I leaned over her desk, got up-close and personal, my face an inch or less from Lottie's. "I ain't asking for *your* permission."

That smug grin like an ugly vulture took perch on her thin red lips. "Rules is rules, Emily Ann." She tossed her dark curls like a flirt who'd found herself a new fella. 'Cept flirting didn't enter into this moment. "Besides," she said, leaning back in her chair, "you'd need the sheriff himself to bring you down there—this being a capital case and all."

Capital case?

I pulled up a vague recollection of what that term might intend, and shoved it back down into its dark hole just as quickly. Something like that, well, I didn't need to dwell on it.

"I got a right," I demanded.

That's when Sheriff Dantley came in behind me, set about picking Lottie Kane to pieces, like plucking the wings off a nasty old fly. "First of all, this girl's been through enough without you giving her more!" he hollered. "And, ain't nobody made it a capital case just yet!"

"Just yet" is the part that bit into my neck, fed sweetly on my soul. It seemed somewhere in the universe my fate as an orphan had already been determined.

We took the back stairs to the basement, down to where they keep drunks and bootleggers and anybody else who dared run afoul of Mississippi law. Not the sort of place I ever imagined I'd find any kin of *mine*. Least of all Mama.

But she's the one did the deed.

"Don't pay no mind to Lottie," the lawman said, angling us along a narrow row of cages. "Ain't no secrets being kept from you."

My shoes tapped out a mournful rhythm against that hard concrete floor.

Old Methuselah himself tossed in his own melody when he flung a high-ended wolf whistle through the bars at my right. "Lift your dress, darlin'; give a fella somethin' to hope for."

The lawman put him straight, gave it to him good. "I'll stick you back in that closet, you don't mind yourself, you withered old skin sack."

I found her sitting on a cot in the very last cage, staring at her hands folded in her lap. She sported a mask of someone broken beyond repair; those familiar green eyes were sunk deep into her head as if the very marrow had been sucked from her bones by misery itself.

Sheriff Dantley faded into the shadows, gave me my time alone with Mama.

I'd conjured a million things to say to the woman, not a one of them nice. 'Cept all my words grew wings like moths and fluttered a-loose of my head, disappearing to wherever it is lost thoughts go.

Mama met me at the door, reached between the bars and stroked my cheek in ways she'd not done before. Her fingertips traced my lips, my chin.

Her words came wrapped up in cotton, all soft and muffled. "I guess you hate me now, huh?"

I managed a weak shake of my head. Though she deserved nothing less, I just couldn't find it in me to hate my own mama.

My body went limp against her cage. I dug down deep and found the one question needing answering. "Why did you take him from me?"

"It's hardly been a month since I last saw you," she said, "and already you've grown up so much."

"I have a right to know!" I demanded.

'Cept Mama paid me no mind. "Aunt Frannie says you got your first monthly." She drifted back to her cot like a pale wisp of smoke. "Gotta watch those boys now. One's liable to come along and steal away all *your* dreams."

"Papa didn't *steal anything* from you. *You gave* it away."

She worked up one of those smiles the simpleminded get for no particular reason. "Is that so?" she said. Something bitter dripped from her tone.

Silence thick as sorghum threatened to push all the breathable air from that stuffy space.

Nerves had me clearing my throat, testing to see could I still talk. "He belonged to me as much as he belonged to you," I told her. "I got his blood."

Mama picked some imaginary piece of lint from her gray jail dress, caught me in a dark gaze, and got me good in the heart. "You don't know *whose* blood you're living on, missy! You weren't there the night I conceived."

That lonely drop of sweat sashaying down my spine danced with my attention just long enough for me to glimpse Mama unguarded, to sense how pitiful the woman had become, how selfish she'd always been.

"You saying I ain't his?" I dared ask.

Nothing but silence, is all she returned.

I pressed my face between those bars, determined to snatch answers from her very soul, even if it meant climbing in there with her. "You owe me that much, Mama!" I argued.

"Life is a lot easier when you steer clear of big questions, Emily Ann."

My hands stretched toward her, but her body lay just out of reach. "Come over here!" I ordered, no longer the child in this relationship. "Come and get yours!"

'Cept Mama wanted none of that. She tossed onto her side and gave me her back. "Go on now," she said softly. "Let me take my rest."

It's hard to make heads or tails of all that transpired between us that hot afternoon. The only thing I could be absolutely certain of is the change that took place.

"It doesn't even matter anymore, *Norma Jean*," I said, spitting her name from my mouth like two sharp tacks. "He'll always be Papa. You won't take *that* from me." I backed away from the cage, from that lump lying on her cot. "You hear me?"

*　　*　　*

Papa's the one always tucked me in at night, and read to me amazing stories from books he'd collected from his youth, vivid tales called *Moby Dick* and *Oliver Twist*. He told me all about Alice and her journey down a rabbit's hole. And he'd only recently promised a copy of *The Great Gatsby*, a new work of my own generation and time, something to pass on to the next ones to come up after I'd done my bit to raise a fair share of Cain. At least I like to believe that's what he meant, sort of his way of giving blessing to the life I aimed to chase.

The life Mama failed to achieve.

Billy Blood stirred up a ruckus behind the row of overgrown hedges skirting the yard on Faulkland Street where the Bostwick house once stood. For being an Injun, the boy sure couldn't stalk a prey to save his life.

"Ain't like I don't know you're there, Billy," I said, keeping my pace steady along the crumbling sidewalk.

He followed beside me like a red-skinned shadow, crouched low to the patchy grass behind the hedgerow. Billy had a plan. "How about you come back here with me?"

Ain't gonna lie; the boy had a tight grip on my curiosity.

"Why should I?" I asked, slowing my pace. I reckon we both knew I'd be back there with him with only the slightest of sweet talk.

"On account of you *owe* me, Teegarten."

I tossed around furtive glances here and there before slipping unseen through a breach in the hedge.

The boy's gaze pawed at my dress, had me already bare inside his head. That pink tongue of his traced his lips, got them ready for whatever he had a mind to do.

"My bobbasheely!" he proclaimed, walking a slow circle around my tense body.

"What's that mean?" I demanded.

"It means 'friend' in Choctaw."

"Since when are we friends?" I meant it as a joke, a thing to loosen the tension.

'Cept Billy saw it as opportunity.

"Since one of us started singing in a speak across the river," he said.

Stopped in my tracks, I did.

It's strange, the way a found secret carries power over the one hoping to keep it concealed. And just how far would a person go to keep a thing hidden?

I sloughed off that hint of doom. "Who cares if you know?" I said, holding my ground as best I could.

Billy's grin had gone snakelike. "Aunt Frannie just might."

One word from him, and all I hoped to accomplish would dry up quick as a summer sprinkle beneath a hot August sun.

I cast my line, searched for another sort of bite. "If Tanyon finds out about this, he's liable to come after you."

"That, he might." Billy's body pressed against mine; his hands rested at my belly like it was the most natural place for them to be. "Big deal. I might get a black eye, maybe a busted nose. But you, Teegarten, you'd be tainted. Ain't no chance you'd be able to sneak off again."

I'm the one started negotiations. "How far you aiming to go?—and that don't mean you're humping me, neither!"

His touch came soft, delicate, almost girlish; those long fingers stroked my neck; his lips brushed my ear. "There's plenty we can do, Emily Ann," he whispered.

My blood ran hot. That place between my legs went warm and slippery. I couldn't find enough of my voice to raise complaint—or give consent.

This moment belonged to Billy.

His mouth found mine; those callused hands fell on my breasts, squeezing and pinching like he intended to get 'em to full size by sheer force of will.

'Cept it couldn't happen like this. Not out in the open. We'd both find ourselves dangling from a tall tree should some knuckleheaded Klan boy stumble upon us.

"We need someplace private," I said, pulling away.

Billy served bravado by the cupful. "Ain't nobody gonna see us."

I sidestepped his continued intentions and cleared space between us. "I ain't doing this out in the open."

Frustration murked his dark eyes. A sigh of resignation escaped his lips. "My maw won't be home till past five," he said, biting down on sour anger. "Be at my house in ten minutes."

"Fine," I said, agreeing out of more than simple necessity.

Billy's scent of earth and sweat remained with me long after the boy ran off to prepare his lair. His smell filled my head with ideas about the sort of things I'd consider doing, and just where I'd draw the line. But lines, well, they're meant to be crossed, right?

I tumbled out from behind that hedgerow and made like I had somewhere else I needed to be pretty darn quick. My mind walked off a time or two, rushing in on scenarios I hoped might happen and others I prayed would not. I reckon that's why I didn't catch hold on the fact someone thought me worthy to follow.

The gray-primered rattletrap crawled along just over my shoulder, teasing me with its uncertainty. Suppose they'd seen me with Billy. What then?

Ah-ooo-gah! went that klaxon, sending my bones a-skittering every which way beneath my skin.

Addison Markley howled with glee. "Jeez Louise, Emily Ann," she hollered. "You about jumped clean out of your dress!"

I wanted to be angry with her, to give the girl what-for. 'Cept I couldn't quite grab hold on that particular emotion just then. Seeing her behind the wheel of her daddy's truck had me forgetting about everything—including that stupid Choctaw boy.

Sorry, Billy. Nothing personal.

A soft smile kissed Addie's lips. "Hop in," she said, nodding toward the empty side of her truck.

My mind stumbled this way and that, left me unsure, and yet strangely certain all at once.

"Come on," she coaxed. "Let's take a ride."

*   *   *

Because a girl is more familiar, that's how I came to choose Addison over Billy Blood that afternoon. I reckon you could sprinkle in a good deal of curiosity, as well. I mean, it ain't like I hadn't thought of her almost constantly since she kissed me.

My gaze fixed tight to the girl as she angled the truck along that quiet stretch of road that ran toward Jackson. Ideas of the nasty sort bounced like tiny rubber balls inside my head. I even worked up a line or two that I'd surely utter—if given a chance.

Addie's hands were awful big—for belonging to a girl. They locked onto the wheel like she meant to tear the thing a-loose—if only she had reason enough to do it.

'Cept Addie held a secret. "I mean, I wasn't spying or anything," she explained like a child caught making faces at teacher's back. "You were singing at old man Kuiper's pond once." There went that grin of hers again. "Bare-assed and hollering jazz songs!"

"Lord a-mercy!" I complained—though I didn't have it in me to really be mad over her revelation. "First Jobie and Billy spied," I sassed, "and now *you!* Ain't nothing but a bunch of peeping Toms around here any-more."

Addie's laughter carried us straight into the dirt lot out front of the grain elevator. She stifled the engine's growl and flung her door wide. "You're delicious, Emily Ann," she said, leaping from her seat.

I swallowed her compliment whole and paid her back in kind. "You ain't so bad yourself."

It's the best I could manage on the fly.

Addie leaned in through her open door. "You have what fancy folks call *charisma*."

"What's that mean?"

"Means you could wrap *any*body around that pinkie finger of yours and have your way."

"Charisma, huh." The word felt smooth against my tongue, slightly cool; I swear I could almost taste its sweetness.

Without another word, Addie vanished quicker than last night's dreams, faded into the slow movement of tractors and men in denim over-alls doing whatever it is they do at a grain elevator.

I scooted closer to her side of the seat and waited for the girl to reap-pear just as suddenly as she'd gone off. The air carried her scent on its gentle breeze, gave up just enough to start me missing her in no time at all.

A simple scenario filled the space behind my eyes. It'd begin with a kiss, just like last time, 'cept longer. And her hands, they'd take to my breasts, only gentler than Billy's touch. From there, well, I didn't really draw a blank. I mean, I could easily conjure *some* sort of image. I just didn't have any real personal experiences to add color between the lines.

'Cept Dale Kruiger, Junior, drifted purposefully into my stream of sight, putting a clamp on my thoughts of being alone with Addie. His wide shoulders hoisted a couple of fifty-pound sacks of corn. That boy sported muscles where most folks wouldn't even consider.

"Afternoon, Baby," he said, tossing those grain sacks into the bed of the truck.

I eased in behind the wheel and met him at the drivers-side window. "Ain't going by that name anymore," I told him, making no attempt to keep from staring at him. Couldn't be helped; I'd had a crush since as long as I could recall.

"Good thing," said Dale, snatching a dingy red handkerchief from his back pocket. He mopped the sweat from his forehead without once taking his eyes off my bare legs. "Growin' like a weed, girl."

Dale ran more than a few years ahead of me.

But who cared about age anymore?

His gaze found mine, held it tight but tender. "Sorry to hear about your daddy," he said softly. "Horrible thing to happen."

He leaned in through the window, his face no more than an inch from mine. "You spoken for these days?" His breath smelled of peppermint. "You and that Markley girl foolin' around?"

My cheeks burned scarlet at the shock of such a question. I stammered over my own tongue, trying to spit out an answer, something meant to set the boy straight.

'Cept my words all dried up.

"All's I'm sayin', Emily Ann, is I got no problem with such matters." His big head tossed his gaze this way and that, like he had plenty to say but not enough time to say it. "I might even be keen to just watch, that's okay with you."

That's when Addie sidled up to the truck, a cold bottle of Co-cola in each hand, and a smirk on her face. "I wouldn't let you watch me *pee*, Dale," she said, wedging her lean body between her truck and the boy.

"Well then how about a visual I can take home with me?" he said, squeezing past Addie's protection again. "Maybe you might could give her a kiss, Emily Ann."

I tried to hold his gaze, but couldn't. Instead, I found an oil spot on the floor and focused on it until the stain changed shape many times over.

Addie's laughter drained the tension from the moment. "He's only funnin', Emily Ann." She passed a Co-cola through the window and told Dale to back off.

I took the bottle to my lips, had a long pull, and tried to make sense of the situation. Such talk doesn't *bother* Addie? Does the girl even know what folks say about her behind her back?

Dale slipped a finger beneath my chin and drew my gaze to meet his. "I'm only goofin', Emily Ann. I don't mean nothin' by it."

"I know," I squeaked, like some vulnerable little mouse.

Addie reclaimed her place behind the wheel and put us back on the road toward home. A lazy smile played at the corners of her mouth. "Ain't a big deal, Emily Ann," she said, finding third gear. "Can't go on worrying what other people think about you."

True enough. But still, a reputation like *that?*

How did the girl live with such a thing?

"What do you think the good folks of Rayford will say when they hear you singing that devil's music on the radio?"

"*Radio?*" I let slip a loose fit of giggles.

"They're gonna claim you as their own, is what they'll do."

I allowed myself a quick dip into the dream of being heard on a wireless, my voice coming tinny through its speaker, telling of some man done me wrong. Maybe Aunt Frannie would hear me, and then there'd be no need to sneak around anymore.

Addie worked the truck down to a slow crawl before tossing us onto a dirt path wending through a thick patch of woods just outside of Rayford. We were quiet, but for a low growl coming from the engine.

Slivers of afternoon sunlight sliced through the green canopy overhead, left its lemon-yellow glow here and there, like familiar friends gathered at the edges of a secret place where something big promised to break a-loose without a moment's notice.

We met a clearing half a mile in, came to a stop beside a crooked shack looked like it might fall over with only a little coaxing. Thick white smoke billowed signals of the secret sort from somewhere back of the shed.

"Won't be but a minute," Addie said, quenching the engine's throaty rumble. She gathered up those sacks of corn—one at a time—from the truck's bed and carried them inside the shed.

Didn't take that Einstein fella to figure out the source of all that smoke.

"That's your daddy's still, ain't it?" I asked, hoping like heck I hadn't just crossed one of those lines bootleggers are forever scratching in the dirt.

Addie climbed in behind the wheel and offered a quick nod. "Ain't gonna tell anyone, right? 'Cause you know what a queer sort whiskey runners can be."

"Won't tell anybody," I promised.

"Fair enough." Addie's the one scooted over, got me pinned in real tight between her and the door. "You know you owe me," she said, "—on account of I covered for you."

My turn to drop a quick nod.

Those big hands of hers stroked my cheek; her long fingers traced my lips like a blind girl searching for the familiar.

I tried my voice but couldn't find a single word. A soft breath is all I could manage.

Addie's whispered words fluttered around us like butterflies drunk on nectar. "How far have you gone before?"

My head spun like a top that's lost its center. "Not very."

"Come on, Emily Ann. I know that preacher's boy is sweet on you. You ever let him stick his hands in your underpants?"

"Not Jobie!" I exclaimed. "He ain't like that."

"Jobie Pritchett wants nothing more than to have a taste of that thing makes you a girl."

"But Jobie won't even—" Her kiss silenced me, sucked the loose words right off my tongue, replaced them with a simple truth: She and Jobie talked.

Addie pulled back, but refused to lift her gaze. "I won't horn in on you, Emily Ann. It wouldn't be fair to Bible Boy." She slid back behind the wheel and gave the engine its necessary tickle and kick. "Besides," she hollered over the din. "I'm sorta spoken for these days."

My countenance dropped faster than a bad habit in a room full of Baptists. "She anybody I know?"

Could Addie sense my disappointment?

"You know him all right."

My eyes went wide as a pair of shiny silver dollars. "*Him?*"

That grin of hers had me contemplating the Garden of Eden, pondering Eve and the serpent, wondering just which one Addison Markley might be.

"Dale Kruiger, Junior." She said his name as if they'd always been an item. "And don't you go telling anybody, either," she ordered, guiding the shifter into gear. "I have a reputation to uphold."

CHAPTER SIX

We crossed the bridge just before sunset, right as evening tossed its gauzy gray hue over the city, dulling even the silvery shine coming off a low-slung moon hanging just above Dauphine Street. Anxious people with nowhere in particular to go wandered about the place, uncertain as to where or how they intended to lose those few dollars sending smoke signals from their pockets.

Tanyon sucked on a Lucky and laid his knock against that red door back of the club. He chewed on some idea or other I wasn't yet privy to, gnawing away as if there were seeds or pulp needed separating from the truth of the matter.

I squeezed up close to him, tucked my hand in his. "What are you thinking so powerful hard about?" I asked.

He let go some vague grunt meant to answer nothing at all, and drifted in through the open door.

Girls darted here and there like minnows in the shallows of a pond, making ready for the night's crowd.

Up on that stage the colored boys got hold on a dark piece called to mind all sorts of misery, a haunting melody bent on bringing up the devil himself.

"What *is* that song?" I wondered aloud, tailing Tanyon toward his table.

"Something they made up," he claimed, dropping onto a stool.

"Made up, huh?" I climbed the stool beside him and eyed those boys. "I got songs of my own we might could try. I mean, they're just words but—"

"Stick to what people come to hear."

"And who says *mine* ain't it?"

That's when Tanyon's façade cracked wide enough to offer a glimpse at whatever idea he'd been working over. "We could do a heap better than *this* place, Emily Ann," he explained, his voice raw with anger. "They got clubs paying *twice* what Rydekker gives up."

A full bottle of bourbon appeared on our table like a fairly intriguing parlor trick. Tanyon shuffled that complaint of his to the bottom of the deck and poured out two shots. A gift horse, he claimed, forgetting any mention of discontent.

He'd bring it up again, though, in due time. That's just what greedy folks do.

I brought a shot to my lips and sipped at its heat. The fire burned my throat, turned my blood hot. "Maybe *New York* will have us," I said, trying on Addie's idea.

Tanyon's hand found my bare knee; those long fingers tugged at the hem of that skimpy black dress. "You look grown up in this."

And I *felt* grown up, too.

I snatched up a Lucky and dipped its tip in the candle's orange glow. "I saw Mama the other day," I confessed. "She sure don't act sorry for what she did."

"Forget about her, Emily Ann." Tanyon tossed back his shot and re-loaded for a second go. "She ain't never coming home."

I pulled on my Lucky, breathed off a soft cloud. "Reckon they'll give her the chair?"

In that brief moment of silence, in a narrow scrap of space lying empty between my last word and Tanyon's next, I swear Mama's cry came to my ears.

"They don't put women in the chair," Tanyon said softly. "Not even the ones deserve it most."

*   *   *

He caught me before I made the stage, that chubby fella in a cheap wrinkled suit the color of smoked glass. A loose line of French words dripped from his thick lips—that dirty *Louisiana* brand of French.

"I don't understand," I hollered, pushing past the man.

'Cept this fella wouldn't be denied.

He snatched hold of my arm and shut down my escape. "I said, If I was to die making love to you, Miss Teegarten, I would gladly go tonight."

I wrenched free of his grip and set space between me and him. How'd he know my last name? I wondered, lost in his lazy gray gaze. Nobody in that city knew my last name—'cept for Tanyon. That's just simple common sense to keep Aunt Frannie from catching on.

"Do I know you?" I asked, studying his moon face—Tanyon's age, I reckoned, maybe a year or two older.

He squeezed into that gulf, drew close enough to smell the whiskey on his breath. "You just about my favorite singer, is all," he said in that twangy Cajun voice common to the area. "I come all the way from Baton Rouge to see you."

A girl can't help but appreciate something like that. Ain't every day a fella puts that sort of stroke against my ear.

Sullum's saxophone flung a jumble of notes into the smoky air, enticing me with its moaning call.

"You best get a move on," said my admirer, before fading into shifting shadows stalking corners where the candles weren't meant to reach.

I gained the stage with a fresh bounce, took up with that flirting microphone, leaned my body into its skinny silver stand like me and it had something going on, and told all about my new lover got eyes only for me.

Young people shimmied across that parquet floor; bodies brushed against one another, riding the band's constant rhythm like they held no say in the matter whatsoever.

And maybe they didn't.

Maybe we were just the devil's pipers sent to corrupt.

'Cept I didn't think of that until too late.

"Oh, he gonna love me," I sang into that microphone. "Gonna love me like no tomorrow, gonna take me out past the sunset…"

I breathed out a dirty moan, the way the colored girls do when they sing that same song, and put a subtle thrust in my hips, like I had a mind for carnal intentions with that skinny silver lover.

At first I figured it to be a fight, the way folks scampered off the dance floor. It happens like that, when fellas get liquored up and two have an urge for the same girl.

'Cept this wasn't a fight.

This was a raid.

"Go out the back door!" Sullum hollered, scrambling for the hallway behind the stage.

I couldn't go just yet. Not without Tanyon.

"Come on, girl!" DeShay, our piano player, angled me toward an easy escape. "They's revenuers," he shouted, pulling me into an inky shadow. 'Cept the boy couldn't have had more than a few years on me. Certainly not enough to put himself in charge of *my* rescue.

"I ain't leaving without Tanyon!" I argued, breaking a-loose from the narrow boy.

"Gonna find jail, you don't get hid." He bolted past me, got swallowed up by that inky black, left me to myself.

The club emptied quicker than a water cistern got a hole in its bottom. Folks squeezed through the front entrance, hoping to wander away unnoticed by the swarm of agents.

Tanyon went at Frank Rydekker, backed the man in a corner and set about giving him what for—by the looks of it. His head went to bobbing back and forth like it had a strong possibility of coming a-loose.

I cut a move toward the two men, hoping like heck to douse Tanyon's anger, make sure I'd still have a stage to return to once the smoke settled.

'Cept I never made it that far.

My admirer fell on me like a dry drunk on a jar of corn liquor, caught me mid-stride, pinched my wrists tight in those cold metal handcuffs.

"Come on, doll face," he said, jerking me through the mob out front. "Let's you and me go on out past that sunset."

*   *   *

A crowd gathered along either side of Dauphine Street, gawkers mostly, come to see a real genuine raid, even though some had been inside when Uncle Sam came a-calling, like those snooty waitresses who now milled through the scene sporting incensed masks of shock at the very notion a speakeasy might so boldly operate right out in the open.

And not a one sought to get me out of *my* bind.

My gaze pushed and pulled at all those phony faces looking on me like I'm the one called in the law. Tanyon's absence turned my belly to water. Did he even know I got caught up?

"Watch yourself, doll face," said that agent fella, putting me into the back seat of his dirty black Ford. He took up behind the wheel, found me in his mirror, and fetched up the very same grin he hit me with before I went on stage. "Does your Aunt Francine know you're here?"

I shifted nervously against the cold leather seat and tried to read the man. "How do you know Aunt Frannie?"

He turned the key, pressed the starter button, and brought life to the angry engine. "A fella in my position knows all sorts of things."

"Like what?" I demanded. "What do you know of *me?*"

First gear took hold and rolled us along those narrow streets of the Quarter, carrying us toward the edges of the city, out to where no lawman's gonna keep an office…only secrets.

My belly growled loud as that engine.

I leaned forward and gave my voice a try. "Where are we going?"

His laugh came cold and black. "We goin' to the Atchafalaya, girl. You and me got some business needs tendin'."

A quick jog to the right put us on a rough stretch of dirt crawling lazily through an ancient stand of oaks looked like they'd been there since long before the French came snooping around the place.

Even that low-slung moon had a time trying to scatter all those nosy shadows crowding in on the Ford.

The trees coughed us out into a clearing set beside standing water.

That revenue agent shushed his engine.

He turned in his seat, found me in the dark. "Sing for me, doll face."

I recall how Papa used to tease me sometimes, make me sing for my supper. 'Cept this, well, *this*—How's a girl supposed to find her voice when she has to sing for her *life?*

"What should I sing?" I asked, tucking fear between each word.

"Surprise me."

It came out without much thought. I just closed my eyes and opened my mouth and "Amazing Grace" filled the sticky still air inside that car. If it could move old ladies in church to tears, it might could find the lawman's soft spot.

His head dropped low like he'd suddenly found sleep for the first time in days. "That was beautiful," he finally said, fixing me in his gaze again. "They sang that song at my mama's funeral."

Hope fluttered in my chest like lightning bugs in a jar. Maybe I found that soft spot. Maybe I stroked it just right.

"Tell me something, doll face," he said, fishing a Chesterfield from a near-empty pack. The orange flash of a spun lighter scattered those shadows for only a moment. "How came your mama to kill your daddy?"

'Cept the man had no mind for an answer.

His door yawned wide, let in the smell of earth and pond water, filled my head with fragmented images of Mister Kuiper's swimming hole.

"You tell *anybody*," he said, sliding in beside me, "and I'll snatch the life out of you." His fingers worked the handcuffs from my wrists. "Won't nobody find you out *here*—least not till the gators have had at you."

My voice managed just enough power to tame this man for only a moment, but it could never make him good.

It could never make me safe.

Silence thick as cold sorghum spilled over the night, blotted out all but the shallow rasp of nervous breaths shocking my lungs.

Does he have a wife waiting for him back in Baton Rouge? I wondered, even as he yanked me onto his lap. *What about children? Is that why he drove us away from the city, so nobody would know? So his world might remain protected?*

And what of my world?

A rush of fear mingled with my blood.

He pulled up the back of my dress, took my underpants down to my ankles.

"Wait!" I pleaded, choking on the sharp edges of my own vulnerability.

"For what?" he growled, pressing his body into mine.

I bit hard on a scream, kept it from becoming sound.

The lawman's hands pinched down on my bare hips, held me tight to his lap while he pushed and pulled at me, dug deep into my core, threatened to burrow straight through.

Even bleeding me did nothing to slow the man.

A high, steady penny-whistle hum filled my ears, lured me away from all those old wives' tales coming against my mind—if only for a moment.

And that's all it lasted.

"God*damn!*" He gasped, releasing his grip on my hips. He shoved me off his lap and zipped his trousers. "Get out."

I took up my underpants and stumbled from his trap.

Would he kill me now, toss my bones into the swamp?

The lawman tumbled after, met me in that clearing. A piece of moonlight touched on something shiny in his hand.

A knife?

"Time for us to part company," he said, closing up that narrow space keeping us apart.

"I ain't gonna tell," I promised, stepping back into ankle-deep muck.

"I know you won't." He put a Chesterfield to his lips, and that something shiny showed itself a fancy silver lighter. "I been by your Auntie's place; I can come get you anytime I feel."

Sweat trickled down my back, beaded up along my spine.

Mosquitoes big as sparrows touched at my shoulders, searched for a meal.

"You stick to the road," he said, drawing on his cigarette, "and you'll be back in N'Orleans short of an hour."

I tossed him a quick nod and stepped up from that nasty old black muck. My shoes were ruined, sure, but at least I still had the breath of life in my lungs.

"You got something real sweet between them legs of yours," he said, easing in behind the wheel. "Be an awful tragedy, you up and fiddle away your true talent by foolin' in two-bit gin mills."

Did he mean I ought to take up whoring?

Maybe he meant I should fool with someone might could move me along to better places—like New York.

Truth be told, even the Big Apple didn't matter a tinker's damn after the goings on of the night.

"I'm all finished with New Orleans!" I hollered at the retreating red glow of his taillights. And even as tears stung my eyes, and my voice gave way to a whisper, I just knew it had to end right there. "And I'm all done singing, too."

*   *   *

Frank Rydekker leaned against the bar inside his empty club like a broken old cowboy in a Hollywood picture show nobody wants to watch. His trembling hand swiped at his dingy gray hair, swept a mess of bangs away from a flat forehead had more shine to it than a brand new Ford.

Hatred, clean and pure, burned in my gut.

The kind of hatred makes a girl wanna cry before she hits someone.

'Cept I'd not lose one solitary tear in sight of *that* man.

"Where's Tanyon?" I demanded, stamping through the place.

Rydekker brought a shot glass to his lips and tossed back its fire. "Gone looking for *you*, I 'spect."

I tripped up well short of anything might be confused with sidling up to him, held on to a scrap of parquet flooring a good space from where he propped himself.

"Is he coming back here?" I asked, despising that greasy timidity slicking up my voice.

The old coot tending drinks dribbled another shot of bourbon, grinned like this talk had to do with him, went back to counting the till.

Rydekker offered some spiel on why there'd be no more raids to contend with, and how I ought not fret over being put center of a scene dealing in handcuffs.

"Only happens to the pretty ones," he said matter-of-factly.

"Then I don't wanna be a pretty one."

"A thing like that ain't your call." He raised a shot, studied its amber hue like it might could tell the future. "He won't bother you again, Emily Ann. You have my word."

Shame had a go at me, yanked my gaze to some spill on that dirty floor.

My words came tinny, hollow, like they were waiting for some sort of filling to give them weight. "I wanna go back over the river."

Frank broke a-loose of his stool, barged up tight to me. "And what waits for you in Mississippi?" he demanded, breathing whiskey and cigarette smoke against my face.

I meant to back away, to clear a little space between us, give myself a moment to think.

'Cept Frank Rydekker had ideas of his own making.

"Ain't got *nothing* over there," he assured me, making like he understood my situation better than I did. "And knock off this naïve routine. Ain't nobody buying it, the nasty moves you cut on my stage. Your future is right *here*, girlie. Get used to it."

This isn't what Papa meant by finding my own way.

Can't carry a tune and the weight of someone else's world, too.

"Take her over to Bienville Street," he hollered at shadows lurking near the darkened stage.

That narrow colored boy broke into our moment, nudged me toward the rear of the club, made like I needed rescuing again.

This time I followed him into the alley out back.

"What's on Bienville Street?" I asked, standing outside that red door.

DeShay spun on me quick as a cat. "Don't you go gettin' Mista Frank riled!" he said in an angry but controlled tone. "You gon' scratch it up for the rest of us."

"I ain't singing anymore," I proclaimed.

"You is. And they ain't a thang can get done 'bout it."

"Tanyon—"

"Tanyon don't know *nothin'* over this side the river." He maneuvered my limp body into a corner, kept us away from nosy nobodies got nothing better to do than turn up muck and mess. "Mista Frank say he want you in his club, you gon' be in his club."

I shook free of his grip. "And if I don't?"

The boy's head went to wagging back and forth. "They's men been kilt over less."

He flung open the rear door of a rusted clump of metal pieces once might have been a Chevrolet, and motioned me inside. "And keep hid," he whispered, "less we get strung."

"You ain't answered my question," I complained, looking up from his ragged back seat. "What's on Bienville Street?"

DeShay prompted the door closed with an eager slap. He peered through its glassless window, teased up a grin called to mind some Old Testament lesson on why trusting a stranger ain't never a good idea, and cleared his throat like he meant to give answer to my question.

He gave me nothing more.

His engine sneezed once, twice, before catching hold.

The smell of burped gasoline stung my nose.

First gear submitted with a painful grind.

The boy dipped us into a stream of quick-moving hustlers on their way to the next big to-do, flung us willy-nilly out front of the pack, before putting us down beside a flat, oblong shack looked out of place among tall cathouses crowding that particular stretch of street.

Rabid piano notes leaked from the next house over.

A loose confederation of girlish giggles challenged from across the way.

"Where's Tanyon?" I asked, nervous at the potential.

DeShay's hand found the small of my back, angled me up the front steps of that peculiar shack. He didn't knock, didn't wait for an invitation, just barged right on inside the place.

A colored fella gone soft with age smiled from a black velvet love seat. "This the girl?" he asked, rising to greet us.

"She waitin' on Tanyon," said DeShay. "And that don't mean she gon' want her picture made, neither."

Just off the parlor, four men tossed bets over some card game or other. Coloreds, mostly, 'cept one Injun. Their beady-eyed stares cut straight through the smoky haze and fixed tight to my scarce black dress.

A Victrola spun off a familiar jazz piece.

"You the one sings, huh?" the old fella asked, offering his love seat.

"Uh-uh!" DeShay wedged his gangly frame between me and the man. "She gon' go upstairs."

"Say who?"

"Say Mista *Frank!*"

Even in absence, Rydekker held sway. Wasn't a man in the room willing to argue against that name.

"The old fool," DeShay explained, leading us up a narrow flight of stairs, "he my granddaddy. Gon' get strung, messing like he do."

A single space occupied the upper level—a loft, DeShay called it.

"This where I stay," he said, grinning like the cat that stole the cream.

A wicker chair kept a corner up front. A lone mattress reclined center of the room. Aside from that, DeShay owned little else.

"How come I'm here?" I didn't sprinkle my words with malice or anything resembling anger; I just didn't appreciate not having a say in the matter.

DeShay dropped onto the mattress, kicked his shoes off. "Tan gon' fetch you from here."

"When?"

"Come mornin'."

"And where am I supposed to sleep?"

His loose laughter got me to grinning.

I drifted and dropped beside him. "Got anything to drink?"

"Corn liquor," he answered, making no bones about eyeing my bare legs. "Ever taste hop?"

I shook my head, offered no protest over where he chose to rest his eyes.

DeShay retrieved a cigar box from beneath his mattress, made claim this "hop" would put hooch out of business before too long.

"Awful bold," I said, fingering the long wooden pipe. "Bet all those rum-runners won't be too happy, you go proclaiming stuff like that."

The heavy scent filled my head.

DeShay dragged a Lucifer across the floor, touched its flickering orange tongue to the pipe's bowl, offered me the first go-round.

I took the stem between my lips, drew easy at first, rolling that sweet smoke against my tongue before pulling longer, taking it deep into my lungs.

"Lord a-mercy," I breathed softly.

"He a photographer," said DeShay between pulls. "My granddad, I mean. He shoot all the jazzers play N'Orleans."

My second go at that pipe put me on my back, my eyes sorting through the ghostly images hiding among water stains painted across the ceiling.

Words no longer mattered.

Neither did thoughts.

DeShay's hand stroked my shoulder. Lines of smoke swirled from his nostrils like dizzy snakes.

I could lie naked beside him and not know shame.

"Where'd you get this stuff?" I asked, taking the pipe again.

DeShay fell alongside of me, his hip pressed tight to mine. "Fat man lives round the corner. Runs a hop house."

The warmth of his soul breached my skin, teased my blood.

Words soft as cotton came to my tongue. "Take me there."

"Can't."

"Why not?"

"Man don't like no split-tails comin' round; says you all is bad luck. 'Sides, Pig got a thing for *boys*, you ask me. Boys and *bugs*. Got a room *full* of spiders—spiders and *snakes*. Keeps 'em in jars, he does."

My body lazed in the air above that mattress, like just maybe I weighed nothing at all. A burst of butterflies took flight inside my chest; gossamer wings traced ideas against my soul, marked me as one of *those* sort of girls.

"You can kiss me if you like," I said—though my voice sounded borrowed.

The colored boy's lips brushed mine, left a hint of caution there. "Are you sure?"

We fell into it like we'd been working that angle since way back, took it long and deep, the way familiar lovers would.

I needed this boy, needed to get that revenuer's touch and smell off me, off my skin, out of my clothes, my hair, my head…

My request came tangled in my breath. "Touch me."

'Cept it never got past that one kiss. And we had no say in the matter, neither.

Tanyon Thibbedeaux barged into our moment like he belonged.

"Best not smoke that stuff, Emily Ann," he announced. "It's liable to ruin your voice."

He said nothing at all about finding me there, lying with a colored boy. I ain't too certain he didn't catch our kiss, neither.

"Ain't gon' hurt her voice," said DeShay. He gained his feet, tucked the cigar box beneath his mattress, and made for the door. "Gon' give her a nice smoky soul, is all."

Tanyon took perch beside me, fished a Lucky from his pocket, and lit up. "Did he hurt you?" he asked, once the boy had gone.

I sat up, snatched his cigarette, and had a long pull. "DeShay ain't gonna hurt me."

"Ain't talking about DeShay." He combed his fingers through his hair, made like his head had a pain deep inside. Like maybe he'd failed somewhere along the way.

Failed *me*.

"I'm fine," I told him. "Nothing I can't handle."

"Did he…?"

I lied, shook my head. "Just touched, is all."

"Good," he said, "because a girl don't need something like *that*. Especially since everything else going on."

I reckon it's the way his body tensed, the way he wouldn't look me in the eyes, that set me off to the idea he had a notion to dump something bad in my lap.

"What 'everything else'?" I demanded.

He hemmed and hawed, shuffled his feet like a petulant schoolboy doesn't want to fess up to a wrong deed done. "It's just that, well, I ran into Sheriff Dantley before we came over."

I pulled myself upright, paced a space over by the window, searched inside my mind to find room enough for what I figured he meant to tell me.

I fixed him a hard gaze supposed to blacken both his eyes, wear him down, bend him to my will. It always worked with Papa.

Tanyon's head lay at a right angle, made him look lopsided, like something inside came a-loose, put him crooked. He sifted words like sand, tried to mingle what's right with a perfect tone, lessen the blow he never meant to administer.

"She's gone," is all he said. "Your mama."

Plain and simple.

No sense in holding back.

Chapter Seven

Sheriff Dantley made claim Mama strung herself up a short piece after she and I had our final go-round. Olin Cawfield's the one found her during his evening walk-through. She'd gone blue by that time, stiff, the way the dead will when they ain't coming back.

Aunt Frannie raised a rebel's ruckus over the matter, got a notion in her head that fault might somehow lie at the feet of Olin or the sheriff or the state of Mississippi.

'Cept the only tang of blame I got a whiff of wafted up from what remained of Mama's way of living.

She took a life and died a coward.

And they actually had nerve enough to lay her down with Papa, in the very next plot, as if she held rights to that piece of earth by virtue of him. She possessed no such claim, though, so far as I could discern.

Course, that had been Aunt Frannie's doing, she being the one holding the purse—just like Judas.

Put *me* in charge, and that killer of Papa would have gone the way of wicked old Jezebel—eaten by dogs!

Aunt Frannie reclined on the sofa, pressed her fingertips against her shut eyes like they might roll out of place, should she lose diligence.

We were all the kin we had left in this world, me and her.

Seemed an awful thin thread, you ask me.

Aunt Frannie stirred, tipped her head in my direction, though she never did open her eyes. "You ever give thought to that Pritchett boy?"

"Jobie?" I squirmed in that big chair beside the ancient fireplace. My hand smoothed away some fictitious wrinkle on my navy skirt. "Why would I think about *him?*"

I could see the string dangling from her thoughts like a kite got caught in a tree.

"You'll need a man to take care of you," she said, settling into the matter.

My naked toes peeked from beneath my hem, pleaded for a quick retreat. I didn't need Jobie Pritchett or anybody else to look after me, and I told her as much.

"Suppose something happens to *me?*" she said, framing each word as if doom waited right outside our front door.

That colored girl shuffled through the parlor, a basket of folded laundry on her hip. The soft brown of her calves enticed my gaze, lured me from the moment.

"I wanna get my hair cut," I said, unprompted, once Neesie climbed the stairs and vanished like last night's dreams.

"What ever for?"

I could feel it down there, that warm, slippery touch where my legs come together.

Aunt Frannie's body came bolt upright. "You are *not* intending on chopping it down like that Markley girl you're so fond of, are you?"

I couldn't find a single *no* in all those words she flung at me.

This choice belonged to me.

"I might," I answered.

"I'd rather see you wear a flapper's style," Aunt Frannie huffed.

Giddy giggles tickled the back of my throat. "What's wrong with Addie's style?"

"She's one of *those!*"

"A tomboy?"

"Oh, she's no ordinary tomboy." She tossed her feet to the floor, found me in her stare, held me tight. "You want people around here to talk?"

I ain't exactly sure how I happened upon such gumption, but I took to my feet, met her at the sofa, and called questions against her line of thought. "You ever *seen* Addie kissing on another girl?"

Her nose went all wrinkled, like maybe she caught whiff of something been long-time dead. "I don't need to *see*—"

"Hypocrite!" I spat.

Aunt Frannie rose up tall as Mama. Her mind plucked at the air between us, searched for words that soothe. "Don't you get fresh, young lady!" is all she managed.

"Judging a book by its cover, ain't you?"

Confusion smoked her eyes. "But everybody knows—"

"But nobody has *seen!*"

Truth to tell, I got nothing good from yanking away that sheet so neatly concealing her skeletons—not with that growing bone collection starting to clutter my *own* closet.

"Addie has a beau," I admitted, drifting a-loose of this scene. "A boy, works over to the grain elevator." I touched my bare feet to those cool wooden stairs going up to where that colored girl finished her chores. "Ain't supposed to gossip."

Aunt Frannie's head teetered atop her shoulders, unsure of which way to turn. "There are none righteous," she finally confessed. "No, not one."

*   *   *

Aunt Frannie's words hummed inside my head like a nest of angry hornets some fool poked with a stick. I sank into that cool bath water, made attempt to wash away the hubbub of her truth, 'cept a noise like that runs way too deep.

My conscience bit down on my bones.

I didn't *hate* my mother—how could I hate the one gave me life? It's anger that picked at my marrow, had me running gimpy through something no girl oughta have to face. It's bad enough she took Papa away, but did she really have to go and set me among the orphans?

My eyelids fluttered shut; my head sought refuge beneath the water. I drew up Jobie Pritchett. His face came easy; that silly grin of a boy unsure of his own destiny; smooth-cheeked and curious; those long, thin fingers; the way they hold a sketching pencil…

My knees opened butterfly-wide, rested against either side of the bathtub. Would he still have me now, even after that revenue agent took away what I could never get back?

My own touch gave me a start.

Vulnerability crept into this brief moment, scattered memories like falling leaves behind my closed eyes, laid wholesale change to that night in the agent's back seat. Suppose Jobie came along, interrupted the scene, made claim to that part of me?

Would he kill for me?

A timid knock pried me a-loose of my thoughts.

Neesie's tiny voice pierced that thin slab of oak meant to keep the world at bay. "You in there, Emily Ann?"

I came upright like a snake got in my bath, eyed that door with an equal mixture of anger and some simmering thing I couldn't quite admit to myself just yet.

"What do you want?" I hollered, taking hold on the anger part.

"I gotta wash up," she answered.

I pulled myself on the edge of that deep claw foot tub even as differing ideas tugged me right and left. "Can you wait a little while?"

Neesie's tone cut an urgent swath through the air. "Ain't g'wan take long!"

"Fuck!" I grumbled, tasting that bitter word for the first time. Its immediate heat burned my tongue, worked my mouth to savor its rough, jagged edges.

I swiped at the wet hair stuck to my forehead and laid level that thumping in my chest. "You alone?" I asked, rising from my wet rest.

Neesie skipped a beat on her answer, as if searching for hidden intruders waiting to pounce from shadows clinging to corners in the hallway. She slid an "Uh-huh" beneath the door.

I flung my feet to the floor; the soft wrinkled white of my soles slipped against the cool green tile, threatened to spill me a time or two.

"Ain't mean no wrong," said Neesie, still trying to talk her way inside.

I snatched up a towel, took it to my front, and yanked the door wide. "Don't be all night, neither," I barked, not meaning a word of it. The girl could stay with me till morning and I'd not utter a single complaint.

A nervous smile played along the edges of her lips. Those eyes, so dark and searching, dared darting glances here and there of all I left uncovered.

A mess of words meant to call apology to this intrusion stammered a-loose of her tongue.

My stiff posture melted into something not quite relaxed. "Ain't no big deal," I said, pushing the door to.

She left off talking at first, just went about humming some tune sounded vaguely familiar, while coming out of that gray linen dress, keeping only her underpants on.

I took up beside the tub, made a show of drying myself, and stole more than a passing glimpse of that narrow girl, her ribs pushing at taut skin, showing through like some musical instrument just yearning to get played.

I suppose you could call it gawking.

I'd admit to that.

Neesie perched at the sink and found me in the mirror. "So," she finally said, soaping a washrag. "You really g'wan cut off'n your hair?"

I leaned against the tub, abandoned all pretense of modesty with the drop of my towel, and drank freely the colored girl's near-naked exhibition.

"My choice," I said, my gaze drifting lazily along the shallow valley of her spine.

"G'wan cut it tomboy?"

My head tipped a nod—as if change had already been determined.

"G'wan *dress* tomboy?"

A flinch issued from my shoulders. I guess I hadn't really distilled it down that far, this notion of change. I mean, there ain't a song or prayer strong enough to put me in that skimpy scrap of black silk ever again. But I didn't have to run in trousers, neither.

"Reckon I'll keep with plain old sundresses," I decided.

Neesie swallowed courage by the glassful, rolled up slow to where I leaned on the tub. "You want, *I* could cut it down." Her bony fingers pushed back my hair, moved it clear of my face. "Ain't g'wan look no boy, though, pretty as you is."

Ivory soap mingled with the girl's natural scent, lent credence to the very idea of purity.

I sifted a pile of useless words through the fabric of my mind, came away with a stupid "Yeah, well…"

Tainted, is the word I let slip through my hands.

"Do I seem different to you?" I asked, holding down a fear that stank of that agent.

Neesie's teasing touch, a careless stray fingertip, brushed against my neck, spun me dizzy, poured me giddy into this moment I'd given more thought to than I'd ever dare confess.

"If they's scaring you," she said, her voice near a whisper, "then you oughtn'ta cross over."

I dared my own touch, traced her ribs along her sides. "Ain't that easy," I admitted. "I *have* to go."

Neesie persisted. "Nuh-uh, you don't! Can't nobody *make* you."

My fingertips breached her waistband. The blood ran warm beneath her skin, put me to thinking on yearnings had nothing at all to do with New Orleans or singing.

My voice came soft, nervous. "Has she gone to bed yet?"

Aunt Frannie answered for herself.

Her voice rang up from the parlor like a pealing church bell announcing the second coming. "Company, Emily Ann!"

Neesie's panicked hands rushed her chest to conceal those delicate buds trying awful hard to become breasts—as if the one come calling just might barge in and register complaint over size and shape.

"Probably just Tanyon," I said, wiggling my body into a gray flannel nightshirt.

"Tell him you quit," Neesie demanded. "Say you ain't g'wan cross over no more."

His laughter gave him up long before I hit the parlor floor in my bare feet.

I found him lounging on the sofa, sipping iced tea, acting like he owned the place. His words came smugger than any preacher's boy had a right to. "Evening, Emily Ann."

"What are *you* doing here, Jobie Pritchett?" My feet slapped at the hard-wood floor.

"Mind your manners," said Aunt Frannie, claiming the spot beside him, grinning like this had been long in the planning.

Jobie lost interest in that glass of tea, met me tall and sure middle of the room. "What say me and you have us a powwow, make peace on a future can make us *both* happy?"

I spun on Aunt Frannie, found a ghost in her place. Sympathy clouded her eyes.

"Can't hurt to listen to the boy," she said. Used to be she'd ride a witches' fit to find me among mixed company in only my bedclothes.

Used to be it mattered.

"You got your truck with you, boy?" I asked, jamming my feet into my shoes.

Aunt Frannie issued no threat, offered nothing by way of resistance to my wanderings.

She simply let me go.

*   *   *

It's funny, the way some folks look different from the side compared to straight on. Jobie's profile took away from the boyish charm I'd come to appreciate over the course of time, put him in a realm closer to being a man.

Closer to being his father.

"Where we going?" I asked, staring at the boy in the green glow of the dash.

A warm breeze tousled his hair. "Wherever you want."

"Cypher Point," I said

"Why Cypher Point?"

"Why do you think?"

"Ain't gotta go *there* if you wanna kiss, Emily Ann."

I scooted closer to the boy. "How about Trader's Landing?"

The tang of black water came to us a fair piece before we ever set eyes on that manic river. Jobie dug deep into first gear, slung us like the stone that ended old Goliath, dropped us in a clearing long ago used to gather slaves coming fresh off the boats. Some say it's blood of sold men still stained that red clay beneath our wheels.

"Do you suppose they'd ever try slavery again?" I wondered aloud.

That preacher's boy located me in the dappled moonlight dripping willy-nilly into our private moment, offered no notion toward talk of salvation, the Gospels, or Sunday hymnals.

Jobie Pritchett had a mind of his *own* doings.

"What are you—?" I started.

His lips fixed on mine, snatched the very words from off my tongue, left me dumb as a lamb before the shearer.

I'd called up a situation like this at least a dozen times in just the previous week, though it hardly ever came attached to the likes of Jobie.

"I ain't dead to passions, Emily Ann," he said, full of piss and vinegar. "It's just gotta be done right."

My body melted against his, and in the squared hollow space of an unused minute I'd have gone along with any idea that boy had gumption to bring up.

'Cept *our* minute filled up well ahead of his proposal.

"Marry me, Emily Ann." His words hurt to hear. "Let *me* be the one looks after you."

I pushed away from his touch, shook a-loose his request from my ears.

"And do what?" I demanded. "Stay here in Rayford, waiting for your daddy to step aside so you can be next in line to tell all those sinners to repent?"

"It's my *calling!*"

"But it's your *daddy's* voice doing that calling." My gaze stumbled through sticky shadows taunting us directly outside the truck. Could have been anybody out there: men carrying a full share of bad intent, lovers in need of a quiet moment, ghosts of men once free but now owned. "You ask me, it's drawing and painting that's calling you."

His soft sigh gave the boy a smooth edge I'd failed to notice in times past—the sort of edge causes a girl to go loopy.

"And you have an idea?" he asked.

Didn't need to bid *me* twice.

I wedged myself into the opening his simple question unzipped in that inky black night, determined to have my say in all matters concerning me. If the boy's intentions rang true, he'd at least *ponder* my schemes and possibilities.

"New York," I said.

Jobie's blue-eyed gaze went wide and bright, fell into competition with that low-hanging moon.

I moved closer to him again, took his hand in mine, let it rest there on my lap like that was the most natural place for the boy's hand to take ease.

"The Lord gave you talent, Jobie Pritchett—same as he gave Michelangelo," I explained. "*That's* what you're meant for."

His heavy hand relaxed, pressed against that part of me I'd freely give to him if he'd only let me have my dream.

"How would we live?" His voice came soft as that blond mess atop his head. "Can't be more than a few bucks between us."

"I have thirty dollars saved up," I confessed. "Plenty enough to get us there."

"This old truck won't last a trip up north. And what do we do when we get there?"

He meant jobs and a place to stay. At least he had it in him to give an ear to the very idea.

"They have jazz clubs I can sing in," I explained, bending him to my will. "You wouldn't believe what singers earn up there!"

'Cept Jobie's head got that certain wag to it—the one says he ain't anywhere near being convinced enough just yet.

"Can't have you in no jazz club, Emily Ann."

"Why not?"

"Ain't proper."

I evicted that hand from my lap "Ain't proper? Says *who?*"

The boy furnished no immediate response; he just stammered on about something had a lot to do with nothing, kept up this idea of the two of us remaining chained to a master called Rayford.

Jobie spun a-loose from his babblings and set down the beginnings of his own idea—if it really did indeed originate from inside himself. "I could buy your old house from Mister Kuiper and fix it up for us to put down in."

I don't know that I'd call it fear, that sharp taste at the back of my throat; but that boy's words swooped down on me like angry swallows coveting a barn, turned my belly to water.

"I ain't staying in Mississippi," I blurted.

Jobie's hands found the wheel. "And I won't pack off to no New York. I can't do that to my folks."

Silence as heavy as baled cotton fell in between us, pushed us to opposite ends of that truck.

Jobie Pritchett would allow himself a dream of his own to fool with from time to time, but that's as far as he'd take to it. He'd never give it life, though, never let it grow.

"Best take me home," I said, looking down on that muddy river, knowing I'd have to cross it all over again.

Jobie jabbed at the starter button, spooked his ornery engine.

"I'm sorry, Emily Ann," he lamented, grinding on a gear. "Really, I am."

I believed the boy.

I truly did.

CHAPTER EIGHT

I tucked into a dim corner just inside that scrap of space back of what used to be a furniture shop, ordered a cold Co-cola from an Injun girl, and made like I belonged in that speak on Basin Street.

An odd collection of folks found place on a makeshift dance floor; their bodies shimmied to a sublime melody flung through the air from the opposite corner.

DeShay's melody.

That skinny colored boy sat hunched over a battered upright piano no doubt recalled better days during the previous century. Those long, tapered fingers pecked away at the black and white keys, scattered notes like chicken feed atop a syncopated rhythm slapped between bass and drum.

Couldn't put boundaries to a piece like that; it offered little footing for a girl to stand by and toss words into its raw mixture. Some songs just ain't meant to get sung.

Tanyon folded himself against the chair next to mine and pinned me with his gaze. "You didn't have to cut it so—" He bit down on his words and flagged that Injun girl. "Reckon it don't matter. It's your *voice* gonna make us rich, not a hairstyle."

I wouldn't call it *boy*-short—though that colored girl sure did take it lower than I'd expected. At least I could still run my fingers through it.

Tanyon shook a Lucky from a full pack, dragged a Lucifer across our rickety table, and took to gawking at my new look. "Why'd ya do it?"

I snatched his cigarette and tossed him a shrug in return. "Don't always need a reason," I said, sucking smoke into my mouth.

"A girl changes her looks, there's *got* to be a reason."

DeShay shifted his tempo, jogged along a path I'd never considered.

"How come he's playing *here?*" I asked, working at that Lucky.

Tanyon shuffled smoke rings in the air above us, hung a lopsided grin on his face. "That's your new band up there."

That Injun girl cut into the moment with Tanyon's shot of hooch in hand. Her dark-eyed gaze gave me a tug. "You the one gonna sing to-night?" she asked.

My spine jerked me upright; I narrowed in on the one supposed to look after me. "What about the Crescent Club?" I demanded.

Tanyon gave up a sigh, tried to play it like *I'm* the one couldn't handle the truth. "Let *me* do the bookings, Emily Ann."

I grabbed his shot glass and swallowed its heat. "Did I get fired?"

"We quit!"

"*We?*"

"Me and you and DeShay."

Seems Frank Rydekker didn't cotton to the idea of paying his acts any more than the scraps he'd already been tossing at our feet.

I jammed the Lucky into an ashtray and had a long pull on my Co-cola. "Maybe what he pays is fine enough for some of us," I argued.

Tanyon leaned in closer, like maybe he had something dirty to whisper in my ear. His sweaty scent mingled with the speak's stale cigarette air, old beer, beans and rice.

"Listen to me, Emily Ann." Hot whiskey breath laid up snug against my neck, stirred the heat creeping slowly through my blood. "Even if Rydekker put us on five nights in a week, he'd *still* only pay us same as one. Believe me, I've already asked."

"And this place?" My arm fluttered a-loose as if swatting at flies. "They gonna give me more?"

The only answer Tanyon knew for sure concerned that Injun girl's offer of another shot.

Couldn't squeeze more than a few dozen folks in that cramped space—certainly nothing like the Crescent Club. 'Cept it *did* promise a familiar charm in its bones—like a dirty old man ain't afraid to pinch a girl's bottom, to hell with whoever's watching.

I stole that second shot, took it down faster than silk underpants in a cathouse. "Am I singing tonight?"

"Manager wants one song—and none of that wiggling stuff, either."

"And after?"

Tanyon's laugh came soft, almost girlish. "You want, you can stay over to Bienville Street." His pause darn-near swallowed up the ruckus spinning all around us. "I'll come for you in the morning."

I floated up to that dinky stage like a ballerina's big debut.

DeShay tossed a wink my way, said, "Shall we?" and flung a handful of notes over the dance floor.

A familiar song.

I leaned into the microphone, closed my eyes against those who would gawk, and hollered on and on about jumpin' jive and stayin' alive in those Big Easy nights.

*   *   *

Tanyon lied—or at least put the truth through a taffy pull. He didn't quit us over to the Crescent Club; we just stopped showing up. And that's sporting with danger, you ask me. Fellas like Frank Rydekker, well, those rum-runners ain't keen on getting stiffed where money leaves her scent.

"Suppose they come for us," I hollered from DeShay's back seat. "Frank knows where you live, right?"

The colored boy snugged us up to the curb behind his house and laid a hush to the engine. "Mista Frank *own* this shack," he said, eyeing me in the mirror. "He got Granddad runnin' card games and movin' hooch out the place."

I got myself upright, smoothed a wrinkle from my sundress. "Do you think he'll come by?"

"They ain't a thing can get done 'bout it. He come when he come. 'Sides, it's Tan he gon' poke a stick at."

Our doors flung wide, and out we tumbled into that narrow alley slithering back of those houses along Bienville. Shadows flaunted their freedom only steps from where we left the car. High trees brooded over the night, kept back the moon's shine.

"Who's them words you spit tonight?" DeShay asked, halting just short of the back porch. "I mean, I been doin' that piece since 'fore I can walk, and they ain't *never* been no jumpin' jivin' goin' to it."

I found him through a squint, tried to read his mood. "They're my own words," I admitted. "I got a bunch of 'em needs music."

That smile of his put the moment right. "We gon' do jus' fine," he promised, gaining those creaky steps. "How come you ain't wiggle around tonight?"

An up-tempo ditty spun a-loose of that Victrola from somewhere inside the house, called to mind a good sort of nasty.

"Just don't need folks gawking, is all," I said, studying his features in a greasy yellow glow spilling through the screen door. "It's supposed to be my *voice*, not, you know—"

"That how come you cut your hair?"

A quick shrug usurped my intended nod, left us dangling together in a warm pause had the makings of something neither of us could deny. That kiss we last time shared come to mind.

I leaned into a rickety railing, folded my hands behind my back. "You got any of that stuff we smoked before?" I asked, hoping my new look didn't put him off.

DeShay's head went to wagging side to side, riding time with that song on the phonograph. "Might could get us some, you don't mind waitin' here."

'Cept that wasn't fixin' to happen. Those drunken bits of talk trickling through the screen put me on a mood to protest the very idea. "Ain't leaving *me* alone with fellas talk like *that!*"

"Told you, Pig don't cotton to no split-tails. He gon' run us off he even 'spect you pink 'tween the legs."

"I'll dress like you," I argued. "You gotta have *something* can fool him."

"Yeah, well…" He sized me up like some prized lamb at the county fair, ordered me to turn this way and that. "I might got somethin' could fit." His nose went to sniffing at me. "Still gon' smell like girl—and that ain't no store-bought perfume, either."

We stumbled inside, waded through liquid stares tugging at my clothing. The Injun fella's the one caught hold on me, pulled me onto his lap, prodding those other fellas to sling complaints claiming my presence stepped all over their high-stakes dealings.

"Dang, baby doll," my captor hollered. "How come you to know I got a sweet tooth for tomboys?"

I squirmed against his grip, 'cept his hold only went tighter.

A white man, old as Methuselah, grabbed up a silver dollar from a pile on the table, made his offering. "I give you this, huh?" he said, grinning like the devil himself put him up to it. "You jes' lift that dress and give us an eyeful of that thing makes you a girl."

That Injun relaxed his grip, made like I had options to consider— though he never really did add to the measure.

DeShay had his own ideas. "Leave her be," he ordered, trying awful hard to still the rattle behind his words. "Mista Frank don't want nobody foolin' with her."

His granddad broke into the scene like a thief holding the key to the store. "Mista Frank say she ain't protected since she don't show to his club tonight." He took up my hand, yanked me off the Injun. "But we ain't forcing no girl in *my* place. She wanna make a dollar, *she* be the one tell us."

Every eye fixed me hard—including DeShay—to see would I give in for a piece of silver. Seems that's all anybody in that town wants from a girl.

I stepped back a pace or two, putting space between me and them. I'd outrun them all, they give me reason.

"I ain't doing that," I finally said.

A colored fella not much older than DeShay slapped the table, broke the tension. "Can we get on with the game now?" He snatched up a jar of corn liquor, had a good pull. "Only a *fool* gonna pay a whole buck jus' for a *peek!* And she a scrawny thing at that. No sir. A girl gots to have some meat to her, she means to get at *my* money."

It's their laughter put me to flight up that narrow staircase, well ahead of DeShay. Anger worked a mix-up with shame, yanked me this way and that, put me in a mind to find a stick big enough to learn those fellas some manners.

If Papa were there, he'd show them what's what.

DeShay slipped inside his room, closed us in. "Ain't no sense you cryin' after them," he said, meaning to soothe my wounds.

I flung myself on that ratty old mattress, had a go at wiping my eyes. "I *hate* those dirty old cusses!" I spat.

"They's only havin' fun, Emily Ann. They don't mean no harm."

"They weren't laughing when they thought I might lift my dress!"

The boy settled beside me, offered up a lit Lucky, and sprinkled soft words on my shoulder. "That's jus' N'Orleans. That's how folks is."

"I don't *do* stuff like that."

His fingers swiped my cigarette, took it to his lips. "Fair 'nuff," he said between pulls. "'Cept you can't be good always. Sometime you want a thing, they's ways to trade. That's all Granddad meant."

"I don't need anything *that* bad," I assured him.

"Ain't no shame if you do." His wink and grin put us back where we meant to be. "Now, then, let's see we can scratch you up a *proper* disguise."

*   *   *

That long mirror looked me head to toe, made like something simple as denim overalls and a dingy gray shirt could easily trick even folks back across the river—at least from a distance.

'Cept how about up-close?

"Suppose he gets a look at my face," I said, tugging at that oversized T-shirt hanging a-loose of my shoulders. "Think he'd lay a slap to me?"

DeShay drifted through his room like a living image conjured from smoke or fog, something not quite there. He caught hold on my reflection, had a time of hiding that silly grin of his. "Ol' Pig blind in one eye, dusty in the other." He spun me round, yanked me closer, topped my head with a blue baseball cap. "'Sides, ain't no 'lectricity in his place. Can't hardly see past the shadows."

Would *DeShay* part with a silver dollar so willingly?

And suppose he favored something gone past a look?

His salty tang teased my nose, mingled with that smell of tobacco clinging to his clothes, the sting of liquor on his breath.

If he wanted more, well, it wouldn't be anybody's business but ours—you ask *me!*

"What if he talks to me?" I said, tumbling into the dark pool of his gaze. "He'd know by my voice."

Such a gentle touch, the way he stroked my cheek, traced my lips with his fingertips. "He gon' believe you can't talk a lick," he said softly. "Gon' tell 'em you's a mute boy called Charlie."

My own words came wrapped in a whisper, spilled a confession I hadn't meant on disclosing just yet. "I saw you peeking—when I was changing, I mean."

His countenance fell hard against my intentions. "I tried not to look," he swore, tossing his gaze somewhere beyond me. "I know you ain't like it when fellas get all bug-eyed…"

My breath caught at the back of my throat. Another confession settled on my tongue, rested there a fair piece of time before actually taking to sound. "Maybe sometimes I don't mind an honest gawk."

I'd call it mischief, that sparkle in his eyes. "What you mean, '*honest gawk*'?" he asked, twisting his grin into a smirk.

I backed off a step or two, put space between us—not that I feared him. Fear had little to do with that butterfly soirée inside my belly.

"Those other fellas," I explained, "they just wanna look at what's under my dress. 'Cept you don't look. You *see*. See *me!*" The gap between us closed up again, though I'd be hard-pressed to say which one of us moved. "Besides, why let them look when they ain't even listened?"

DeShay's fingers dipped into his hip pocket, fished a-loose a shiny piece of silver. "This 'cause I peeked," he said, pressing the dollar against my palm.

A token of trust.

*　　*　　*

We did a slow trickle into that dark alley, took to those shadows promising freedom under their cover, and made toward Robertson Street.

DeShay strode a few steps ahead, certain to catch the brunt of whatever lay in wait. "Think you can walk like a boy?" he asked, tossing the words over his shoulder like spilled salt.

I jammed my hands into the pockets of those overalls and let my gait go a-loose. Jobie Pritchett's walk worked its way into my stride, carried me lazily out of the alleyway and onto the street. A million thoughts rushed my mind, though I couldn't snatch hold on any single one.

A car trundled past, but paid us no mind.

"Keep your head down," DeShay ordered. "And slump your shoulders."

Vague figures played a ghostly game of catch-me-if-you-can within the safety of the very same shadows concealing me and the colored boy.

Girlish giggles danced somewhere behind a gang of shrubs.

DeShay grabbed my arm, yanked me lockstep with his charging march. "Cathouse on every damn corner," he complained, "and them fools gotta do it in the bushes."

"Won't be like this in New York," I promised, though I knew nothing of that city outside of magazine tales. "They got jazz clubs and fancy hotels. We can get famous in a place like that."

DeShay's march caught a hitch, slowed us back a pace. "Not for me, thank you," he said.

"Sure you can. Tanyon will see to it."

'Cept the colored boy had ideas of his own…ideas having nothing at all to do with jazz clubs, New York, or living anywhere else besides New Orleans.

"Jus' give me a house I can run gamblin' out of, sell some hooch, maybe get me a girl wanna work the fellas."

I gave his arm a tug meant to stall him on a barren corner. "But you have a talent," I said, searching the scene to protect our privacy.

He just pulled away. "'Cause God give you a talent don't mean we gotta get famous." He picked up walking again, left me to catch up on my own. "*You* want that, *you* go get it. Jus' leave *me* be."

We came off at Canal Street, along a narrow stretch littered with shacks and hovels should have been yanked down when the French still ran the city.

Shadowy folks wandered across dusty lots like ghosts in search of the living.

DeShay's whisper found my ear. "Remember," he said, angling me toward a crooked house, "you can't talk a lick. And if he *do* get you alone, don't go upstairs—not unless you ain't scared of no spiders and snakes."

My feet gained that rotted wooden porch. "Why's he keep 'em in jars?"

The colored boy fit beside me. "Voodoo, I 'spect."

A coded knock issued from his knuckles.

My legs set up for a run. "Do you believe in that sort of thing?" I asked. "Voodoo, I mean."

That red door pulled a tight yawn.

A porcine face filled the thin crack. "What you want, boy?"

DeShay's confidence fell flat. He offered up a sawbuck in place of an answer.

A fat hand snatched that bill quick as sin, worked the heavy green paper between porkish fingers—as if testing its legitimacy.

His angry glare lost its edge. "Who's he?" he barked, eyeing me.

"This Charlie," DeShay explained. "He don't talk."

The door went wide as a scream, exposed the Pig's full girth. "Can't talk, 'eh?" Those greedy brown eyes bit into me, refused to turn me a-loose. "Reckon that ain't a bad thing. I mean, the boy can't run off and tell my business, can he?"

My chin fell against my chest, hid my face beneath the bill of that baseball cap. Maybe he couldn't tell. Maybe we'd pull the trick.

DeShay entered first, yanked me in behind him.

Pig closed us inside, kept his size between us and the door. "Well now," he said, taking up a lone candle. "You want what's smoked, or you want what goes in your arm?"

DeShay became my shadow, deflected most of that orange splash coming off that candle. "Smoke," he muttered. "Jus' hop."

"Gonna smoke it here?" Pig said it to me, like just maybe I'd give up and answer and blow the jig.

"Uh-uh." The colored boy's head went to wagging. "Got things need doin' to home."

"Bet you do," Pig said, tossing a smirk at me. His bulk put the creaky floorboards in a complaining mood as he crossed the darkened parlor in search of what we came to claim.

The smell of bacon leavings and rancid butter clung to every bit of breathable air, called to mind home and Papa.

Papa wouldn't know me anymore—not like this.

Pig took up a clenched fist, passed it over to DeShay like he intended a transaction, 'cept he yanked it back before a deal could get done. "How come Charlie here can't talk?" he demanded, issuing a quiet promise to squash plans already been made.

Shadows rendered DeShay faceless, but couldn't a thing be done with that nervous pinch in his voice. "His mama say he born that way, say voodoo done it to him."

Fat man lined up a grin didn't need any light to get noticed. "But he *can* hear and understand, right? I mean, he ain't soft in his head, is he?"

"Nope, he ain't." The colored boy opened space between us, left me vulnerable.

Pig closed the gap, brought that candle along. "Awful pretty—for a boy."

Panic swiped the air from my lungs, set me atop a pair of shaky twigs used to be my legs.

DeShay played into the game, scooped up some vague hint Pig tossed at him, slipped past that faded door, and left me alone to decipher the moment.

Pig's tone came low, and cool, each word tucked beneath a soft wheeze. "You got a habit needs tending?"

My frantic gaze stumbled through that bare parlor, searching for escape.

"Ain't a reason for fear," he said, slow-dancing me into a corner. He put that candle on the floor. "We just gonna figure out what's what, is all."

I reckon I could have screamed, maybe gave his shin a good kick that might have got me through the door, 'cept damned old curiosity got hold of the cat.

A violent twist set me face-first to the wall.

A desperate gasp clipped the silence—though I can't really say if it belonged to me or him.

Heavy hands tugged roughly at those denim overalls, jerking me this way and that, popping the snaps along one side.

Thick lips brushed my ears. "I got a theory," he whispered. "Wanna know what that is?"

I sucked ragged swells of air into my lungs, certain his intentions would be awful forward.

He didn't disappoint.

Pig pulled his words long and slow. "I'll bet dollars to dirt you ain't no boy." Sour breath warmed my neck. A meaty hand breached those overalls, found entry between the open snaps, took a moment's rest at my belly. "When I get to where I'm going," he whispered, "what do you reckon I'm gonna find?"

My breath caught.

Daring fingers slipped inside my underpants, penetrated my disguise, took notice of what's what.

Where my body meant to cringe, it craved.

Pig's words frolicked among low grunts. "Double or nothing says you ain't mute, neither."

"Okay," I confessed, leaning into his bulk. "I can talk just fine."

He spun me a-loose, grabbed up that nub of a candle, and took to gawking at me in its orange splash. "Yes, ma'am!" he crowed, breathing in my scent on his fingers. "You're all girl. Ain't a soul can say otherwise."

A familiar scarlet heat burned my cheeks. "Can I go now?"

"Just one thing," he said, blocking my escape. "I ain't up for no trickery. Understand?"

I tried placing blame where it rightly belonged, invoking the colored boy's name—*he's* the one left me to work things out.

'Cept Pig wouldn't hear of it. He waved off my words like they were so many mosquitoes. "Ain't gotta mess with no monkey, you need a hit. We can work us a deal, just me and you, Charlie."

"It's Emily," I said.

A grin creased his moon face. "Emily ain't part of the deal, only Charlie is."

My gaze hit the floor like a dropped quarter.

Didn't take that Einstein fella to get a read on Pig's angle.

He found my hand, pressed a glassine packet to my sweaty palm, and tossed a nod toward that boy on the other side of the door. "And when you come back," he said, sure of his proclamation, "you can leave that coon to home."

*   *   *

DeShay snatched that packet away from my hand like he's the one had the most claim to it, and examined it against the dull shine of a hissing gaslight somewhere along Bienville Street. "That's a whole lot more than

Pig ever give *me*," he said, unable—or unwilling—to hide his joy. "We might could smoke up the night, have a little somethin' for tomorrow."

"'Cept you left me alone with him," I blurted, only now aware of my own anger. "Suppose he tried something."

"But he didn't, did he?"

"Got close enough to know I ain't no Charlie!"

The boy's laughter only stirred my wrath.

I plucked the packet from his grasp and tucked it in my pocket. "Laugh now!" I demanded.

DeShay leaned against the lamppost, retrieved a pack of Luckys from his shirt, and fished out a cigarette. "I stayed on the porch," he explained, pulling smoke into his lungs, "had my ear to the door. He try anythin', he gon' know pain."

I swiped his Lucky, rolled smoke over my tongue. "He has you by two-hundred pounds. All Pig has to do is sit on you."

"Yeah, well…" The pistol in his hand sparkled in the gaslight's glow. "Ain't no one fixin' to sit on *me*—'less she female."

My gaze sipped on that cold piece. "That thing real?" I asked.

The boy's head wobbled a short nod.

"Ever use it on anybody?" It seemed possible, maybe even likely, given DeShay's station in life.

"Not even on a bad day," he confessed, offering it to me like some sort of prize.

"I best not," I said, backing off a step.

"Go on. Ain't gon' bite."

I took it in both hands and caressed its oiled steel. Something akin to authority crept into my blood, got me warm and slippery down there where my legs come together. I could shoot someone, I told myself, if it come down to me or them.

Somebody like that revenue fella.

I hefted its weight, took aim some distance down Bienville Street, caught sight on a dark car wading through shifting shadows.

"Reckon that's the law?" I asked, imagining a standoff there on the streets of New Orleans.

DeShay seized the gun, smuggled it inside his waistband, and laid a quick pace toward home. "Ain't gon' find out," he hollered over his shoulder.

My shoes picked up a pace of their own, banged a frantic rhythm against the cement sidewalk.

That car gained speed.

The colored boy harbored no intentions of sticking around for a genuine chance to finally use that pistol. "You run up Robertson, circle round, catch me to home," he yelled, vanishing quick as a rabbit down a hole.

I raced out onto the street, meaning to break right, get lost in the shadows. 'Cept that dark machine cut into my angle; its growling engine nipped at my retreating heels.

A klaxon wailed an urgent promise of wicked entanglement.

My pace picked up, caught a hitch, flung me faster than my legs could possibly manage. I hit that road with a thud, scrunched my eyes shut against certain impact, and offered my prayer of hope.

"*Please!*" I cried.

Tires on either side of me yelped like a dog got his tail slammed in a door; the stink of burning rubber filled my nose.

That grumbling engine breathed hot at the back of my neck.

"Dammit, girl!" exclaimed a familiar voice. Hands found my wrists, yanked me from under that black Chevrolet. "You trying to get yourself killed?" Tanyon Thibbedeaux gathered me into his arms and hid me away in his back seat.

Safe again.

CHAPTER NINE

They call it the Atchafalaya, that old waterlogged piece of earth Tanyon saw fit to abandon me to. It's supposed to be a river, he claimed, like the one I sneaked across to find my voice. 'Cept all *I* took sight of meant swamp, you ask me.

A house like a square boat floated on black water littered with bits of starlight fallen down from on high. Mosquitoes hummed and crickets chirred; bullfrogs courted companionship somewhere at the center of it all.

"How come I gotta stay out *here?*" I asked, squinting into the dark. "Why can't I stay over to Bienville?"

"Bienville ain't safe anymore," Tanyon answered, snuffing that low-moaning engine. He fixed me in a gaze claiming suspicion. "Why's he got you conjured up like a boy?" He yanked me across the seat for a better look. "Is DeShay laying funny like that, needing you to be something you ain't?"

I paid him no mind, took hold on his first line. "Why ain't Bienville safe?"

"Rydekker—" he began, though he never did complete his thought. Tanyon crept closer still, like just maybe he had a mind to kiss me full on my mouth. "How bad do you want New York, Baby?"

Urges teased my blood warm, nudged me toward a mood I'd spent more time in lately than not. "It's my *dream*," I whispered, all tangled up in his stare.

"Suppose we could leave next week, Emily Ann. Would you go?"

"But Aunt Frannie—"

"Aunt Frannie ain't gotta know. It's just you and me in on this, girl." A quick tug put me sitting pretty on his lap. "Besides." His lips brushed my ear, stirred warm recollections of the Pig. "I got more right to you than she's got."

Silence mingled with that thick sticky air, blotted out all but our breathing. My dream rested there in that narrow space between us, waiting on an answer I honestly didn't have hold on just yet.

I pieced my words together with a paste of common sense. "Suppose she calls the law?"

"They won't know where to look."

"What about money? I mean, how would we live?"

Tanyon hung a crooked grin right where I could see it. "Money ain't a problem, Baby; we got plenty enough to get us started."

I attempted another angle. "Suppose—"

His kiss swiped the words right off my lips, left me with little more than a jump and a twitch, a sense of melting into him.

The driver's door gave up a squeaky yawn and spit me onto my feet.

Louisiana muck sucked at my shoes.

"Ain't no swamps in New York, is there?" I asked, only half-kidding.

"Don't step in the water," said Tanyon, riling his engine. "There's gators in there." He nodded toward that floating house. "Go on now. They're waiting for you."

I stayed fixed to that scrap of muddy ground like a petulant child, determined to bring those fading red lights back to me by force of will alone.

'Cept a blonde girl on that houseboat worked up a whole other outcome to my standoff. "You don't hurry up," she hollered, "you're gonna sleep outside. Some of us would like to get on back to bed."

My feet gained the rickety gangplank. That scrawny old slice of oak protested my weight, whispered empty threats regarding a clean break at its midriff, with a promise to toss me into that murky drink.

"Don't be scared," she said from her perch on the porch. "It'll hold you."

I blurted, "Tanyon sent me," hopeful she'd acknowledge that name.

'Cept she didn't. Her blue-eyed gaze pulled a sideways looky-loo at me; a frown yanked at her pouting mouth. "How come you're made up like a boy?"

My fingers nervously fondled that glassine packet lollygagging in my pocket—when it should have been burning in a pipe. "Had to go someplace won't allow girls," I explained.

Her head went to wagging like I'd just confessed to being soft in the brain. "Ought to stay away from such places, a girl your age." She stepped aside, granting me entrance. "You can sleep in the front room, but you'll have to share space."

A kerosene lamp flung its awkward yellow haze against the low-slung ceiling. A pair of bare pallets loitered in the creeping shadows.

'Cept one of those shadows took to moving like a man, eased all casual into a puddle of light.

"Calls himself Moss," said the girl, nodding toward the offending party. "He's paid his, so don't expect me to kick him out."

A colored fella dark as Mississippi mud lazed on the biggest of the two pallets. His years stretched closer to thirty than twenty.

Even that blonde girl ran a fair piece back of him—eighteen, I'd guess.

"Ain't gonna be a problem, is it?" she asked, fixing me with that promise of a night in the woods should I say the wrong words.

My shoulders flinched a tight shrug, lent credence to some crazy notion that maybe a girl shouldn't mind sharing space with a fella she don't know from Adam.

I searched for something solid to rest my mind on, some sort of connection linking us all together. "How do you know Tanyon?" I asked the girl.

'Cept that split-tail knew nothing of links or solid ground. "I don't know the man," she admitted. "He give me some money, asked could I stash a girl for a night." Her fingers tugged nervously on the threadbare nightshirt concealing her thin body. "Only *one* night."

It didn't seem the sort of shenanigans for Tanyon to get up to, tossing me out to strangers. If he needed me stashed, why not just run me to home?

"I don't know if it's the law looking for you or some fella you double-crossed," said the girl, "but I ain't in no mood to be courting trouble round here." A sloppy two-step put her closer to the room at the back. "Come sunup, you best be on your way."

I kicked a-loose those muddy shoes from my feet, abandoned them near the door, tried like the dickens to ignore that packet pleading emancipation from inside my pocket.

That colored fella spoke up once we were left to ourselves. He told me not to fret over no bossy yellow-haired girl ain't got sense enough to move out of the swamp.

I pulled up caution, laid a decent space between him and me—just in case. "She stays here alone?" I asked.

"She made claim her daddy come around," he explained in a relaxed sort of pace, his words drawn-out and low. "She a squatter, you ask me. I'd bet drumsticks to thighs she found this place empty but for its ghosts."

I closed the gap, freed my head from the baseball cap, and took up with the smaller pallet. "Ain't no way *I* could stay here by myself."

Moss sat up, stretched his legs. A pair of dingy trousers, is all he wore. "They's another one back there with her," he whispered. "A dark-haired girl—not much older than you. Carry on like they married."

Curiosity wedged itself firmly between those two pallets, refused to step aside till something got done about it.

"How do you know?" I asked.

"Seen 'em today—through the back window."

"Seen what?"

Anticipation gave my belly a twist. That wide grin of his showed off a missing tooth right up front. "You wanna know bad enough, go see it yourself."

My fingers fished up that glassine packet, released it from my pocket. I thrust it into the narrow void running between us and announced. "I got this."

To see the man then and there—you'd have thought I just dumped a pile of gold nuggets onto the floor. The tip of his tongue traced his lips, toned that grin of his down to a fool's smirk. "That really hop?" he asked.

"Ain't got a pipe," I said, hopeful of my hint.

His knapsack practically walked itself out of the shadows and into that puddle of light. A rip along its bottom wore stitching called to mind some battlefield casualty, a reminder of one of those old-timers received their scars from the war between the states.

A wooden pipe gone smooth from use took center stage like a favorite old vaudeville star. An audience always cheers *that* moment. Just give us our money's worth, then dazzle us some more.

The colored man's fingers trembled, tamping our gold into the pipe's small bowl.

My gaze tripped up on those many pits marking his arms, the backs of his hands. I didn't pry—at least not yet.

A blue-tipped Lucifer met the floor with an easy swipe; its orange tongue licked at the bowl, set the night in motion.

Moss took that stem to his lips, drew short quick puffs. "That fella come pay for you—" He paused, holding his breath. "He your beau?" He meant Tanyon.

Sharp smoke cut into me, filled my head with all kinds of promises. 'Cept guilt trailed right behind. I mean, it didn't seem right, me smoking it down without DeShay.

But that stupid boy, he's the one took to running like a scared rabbit, left me alone to cover my own.

Left me with our prize.

"Ain't got a beau," I answered, reaching for the pipe.

That well-worn hunk of wood discovered my eager grip; its delicate warmth teased my blood in a single pull, set me on a notion where nothing mattered 'cept this very moment.

"Hey," I said, dipping into the smoke again. "How come you ain't asked my name?"

'Cept that colored fella, well, he'd conjured ideas of his own making.

His wiry shape shifted among the shadows, pooled like liquid cool onto my pallet, splashed against my limp bones. "Draw up on silence, girl," he whispered, tucking each word behind my ear. "Ain't no call for names out here."

Opium swirled inside my head, painted potential like dirty pictures on the backs of my shut eyes. Ideas I'd not yet dared consider showed off unbidden, barging into my mind like an armed intruder meaning to make a mess of things.

Suppose he expected more than simple good company?

A girl could find a bad time of it out where nobody knows.

"Ain't reason to fret," said Moss, like maybe he had means to ogle my thoughts. "I ain't much on action no more—though I *do* like me a nice look at a pretty girl."

"That why you peeked in on those two?" I asked, tossing a nod toward the back room.

"How'd you come to such a good piece of hop?" He cased that packet like a robber would a bank.

I put down a tableful of tales concerning that fat man, about how I had to get all gussed up like a Charlie just to see inside his place.

Though Moss didn't know Pig personally, he made claim to a familiarity with the same sort. "Gonna 'spect better than a sawbuck, you come to *his* steps again."

"Ain't going back," I promised, convinced of my own resolve.

"You will—you get them hungries. Ain't a thing sacred once *they* commence."

"That so?" I tipped back on my elbows, gave my courage a good kick in the backside, asked that one question I meant to know of the colored fella. "How'd you get them marks on your arms?"

Moonlight washed up silver across his face, like maybe the Creator

Himself took notice of Moss at that very moment.

"They's tracks," he explained, eyeing the pits as if he'd only just now figured them out. "Each one holds to a tiny piece of heaven."

I yanked myself aright, snatched up his left arm, had a good long gawk at the mess. "Don't seem like no heaven *I'd* want."

"These," he said, tracing fingertips over marks, "come from bad needles. I got real good ones now, kind don't show out."

"I hate needles."

"Ain't a thing to be 'fraid of."

"Didn't say anything about being afraid," I argued. "Just saying I don't like 'em, is all."

"A heap better than that old hop you smokin'."

"Ain't anything better than hop," I assured him. "Even corn liquor don't keep up."

Moss took up defiance like David's slingshot. "And you know this 'cause you tried some?"

"No. But—"

"Then you don't get a say—lessin' you took the needle."

Thwack! His point found its mark, burrowed past my forehead, dented up that armor concealing common sense.

"Yeah, but—"

"But what?" Moss laid a bump against my body, broke a-loose all sorts of sharp-angled urges, ideas sporting certain trouble. "Think it gonna kill you? Well, I done it a hun'red times. *I* ain't kilt!"

Moss worked his sell as if life itself couldn't get started without my having a go with that silver sliver. His canvas knapsack barged into the scene, vomited its contents at our feet, and placed demands on me no *boy* would get away with.

The nub of a candle rolled against my big toe. A dirty old spoon caught the moon by its tail, swung its shine into my lazy gaze.

His glassine looked nothing at all like mine.

"I don't know about this," I said, squinting at the accoutrements of my potential undoing. "Suppose it goes wrong?"

Moss sifted his pile, set his tools in the proper order of a man done this a thousand times, might could get away with it a thousand and one. "Can't go wrong, Pony. Once is only a taste."

A glass syringe came smooth and cool to my fingers. "My name ain't Pony," I said, though not in a snotty way.

He took back what belonged to him, and tucked a needle to it. "You gonna do this, or not?"

*   *   *

I can't lay claim to having ever been privy to any secret voodoo doings, but I ain't at all convinced they'd run too awful contrary to the rituals Moss conjured over his candle. The rules of it hypnotized me, coaxed me a-loose of my fears, made promise of certain peace.

That dirty old spoon danced a jig atop Lucifer's flame. The needle took in those cloudy leavings, filled the syringe with mystery.

"You fixin' to tie me down?" I asked, eyeing the rope biting into my biceps.

Moss grinned like that ancient serpent, tricking foolish Eve all over again. "Won't have to," he said, tracing my veins all swollen with life. "Gonna be a tiny poke, is all."

'Cept who wants to get stuck?

"Can't we smoke it?" I pleaded.

Moss laid that needle against my arm; the silver sliver pierced my skin.

"Wait a minute," I begged, stumbling recklessly toward full-on panic.

'Cept Moss, well, he knew nothing of fear.

"Time to go, girl," he whispered, sending the mixture into my blood.

My breath snagged hold on something inside my chest.

Angry bile stung my throat.

Moss tossed a hand to my back, aimed to steady me up, to keep my slumping body from tumbling ass-over-tea kettle into the void. His moving mouth conjured all sorts of sayings, though I couldn't catch a lick of what he meant to tell me.

I tried for speech of my own, anything to prove I still existed, 'cept all I managed drifted half-formed into the ether.

A wounded gray milk pail tucked beneath my chin captured my supper before it could soil the floor.

Peace got inside my bones.

A perfect peace…

It lapped up my marrow, made promises of nothing and everything all at once.

"Just be still," cooed the colored fella, even as the ocean reached my ears, and a rush of black butterflies blotted out the night.

*   *   *

Morning in that room tripped gray and grimy across the threshold like a mangy old mutt scrounging for the crumbs of yesterday's supper.'Cept nobody wants a wet tongue in their face at first light.

I ducked beneath the oily scrap of cheesecloth scarcely concealing my naked body, and plucked up memories by the handful, hopeful the vague pieces might fit together, disproving any shameful notions concerning the night before.

But something *did* happen; a girl can tell.

Incantations of a dark sort wandered in through the open door, stoked a fire in my belly, put me to my feet, and set me to gathering my clothes from all over the floor.

That big pallet lay empty.

Odd flickers of recollection jabbed wiry fingers of truth against my inner parts, though nothing certain made it through, no clear image I might take hold on and examine.

The yellow-haired girl barged in, caught a gawk of me taking up my britches. "Surprised you can stand," she said, "the way *he* done you."

Fire worked its boil in my blood. "Then how come you didn't stop him?"

She stepped up on me, poked a finger at my chest, put down the facts that even I knew to be true. "*You're* the one had your legs at ten and two; wasn't nobody but *you* holding 'em open."

A dark-haired girl no older than me came up out of the shadows like smoke from a bottle, took shape beside blondie, and said something or other concerning a body being ready.

"And *we* ain't killed him, neither," she flung at me, expecting I'd believe whatever she said. "Was the needle done him in."

Moss lay naked and wrecked on the front porch, just lazing away the morning—'cept for the purple along his back where the blood had settled. Those pits on his arms mocked me, promised to take me next, to put me as it put him.

"Never again," I whispered, my gaze lingering on that lifeless face gone blue in death, my fingers caressing the wound on my own arm.

"Hope not," said blondie, eyeing what remained. "Might could get away with it a thousand times, might take a thousand and one before it kills."

May as well have been me stretched lifeless beneath a bruised sky, strangers standing around gawking at my secrets, ciphering ideas over what needs doing.

I pulled in a breath, savored that heavy tang of ancient earth mingled with long-standing water, tried like the dickens to gain a clear thought, some little scrap of something telling me what's what. "Anybody call the sheriff?"

Blondie tossed about laughter like I'd just made mention of baseball-playing chickens. "Ain't no sheriff gonna come out here for this one," she said.

"Won't nobody miss him, neither," claimed the dark-haired girl. "So we'll just put him under."

I had to ask. "Under what?"

"Under the Atchafalaya."

Blondie circled the dead like a voodoo priestess, muttered another incantation meant to nudge his soul across whatever divide awaited him. Her gaze fixed hold on mine. "You got words need telling?"

I didn't.

Truth be told, I didn't even speak at Papa's burying. Besides, I hardly knew this man, probably wouldn't even recall his face outside of a week.

The dark-haired girl took to his shoulders; blondie got hold of his feet. Didn't take any big effort to roll his bones into the water.

A ruckus like that wouldn't go ignored.

Silent eyes split the dirty drink not more than thirty yards away, peeked up all cold and yellow, like a natural-born thing of evil.

"Suppose he ain't dead?" I said, already knowing the truth of the matter.

A bumpy green log turned up a murky commotion just below the surface, set the water swirling in a wicked frenzy.

I looked away before it took hold on its prize and stole away to the bottom. I owed Moss that much, at least.

A smile tugged at the blond girl's lips.

The dark-haired girl went sullen. "Such is life," she said, bowing her head in quiet consideration.

My time there had found its end.

I snatched up that pipe from among the colored fella's effects, tucked the smooth wood inside my pocket, right there beside a half-filled glassine, and laid out a line running straight for home.

*   *   *

"I didn't mean to leave you out there," Tanyon claimed, working his Chevy up to speed. "You gotta know that much, Emily Ann."

Familiar country raced alongside that narrow stretch of state road spilling out toward Rayford. If I never crossed the river again, I wouldn't be the least bit put off.

"What kind of fella kisses a girl full on her mouth," I said, eyeing the gray box wedged between us, "then leaves her with strangers?"

"They ain't strangers," he said, slinging us off the road toward a mingled gathering of oaks and pines and other hoodlum trees. "I've known that yellow-haired one for a spell."

I dipped into his space, demanded, "What's her name, then?"

The car went still in a spot most likely cleared by bootleggers.

Tanyon stifled his engine. "Got your dress from Bienville in the back seat."

"Don't avoid my question," I said, lifting a fresh pack of Lucky Strikes from his breast pocket.

"It's Teresa or some shit," he answered, grinning like in the old days, like he did while Papa still lived. "Or maybe Mary Beth."

"You're an awful liar," I told him, touching a Lucifer to a Lucky. I took up with that gray metal box, fondled it the way I would a birthday gift. "What's in it?"

Tanyon snatched the cigarette from my lips, traded it with a kiss called to mind a long-time lover in some romantic Hollywood picture show.

Would he still want to know me—even if he knew of the colored fella?

"Open it," he whispered.

'Cept I couldn't budge from our moment, from his taste on my tongue.

Tanyon swiped the box, popped its top. "It's your future, Emily Ann— *our* future."

Almost forty-eight hundred dollars, he claimed, that thick stack of green paper. Said he'd been saving, though even I knew better than that. Fellas like Tanyon Thibbedeaux spend it long before the ink has a chance to dry.

"This will get us to New York," he promised, "set us up in a nice place. Already got a line on a singing gig."

"Awful lotta money," I mumbled, mostly to myself, certain somebody somewhere might come to miss such a treasure before too long. "Ain't looking at trouble, are we?"

Tanyon's handsome head went to wagging against the absurdity of such a notion—even as those dark eyes of his ran to and fro across that quiet piece of earth. "Probably won't hurt to keep it hid, though."

Skittish, is a word came to mind.

He flung his door wide, grabbed my hand, dragged me along after him, the both of us traipsing recklessly through saw grass standing waist-high. He'd changed since Papa passed—and not just on account of him leaving me in a swamp all night, neither. Tanyon became a different man altogether.

He jabbed a thumb toward a long-dead tree resembled a girl squatting. "See over there, the one with the skinned knee?"

"Looks like she's making water," I said, drawing down on my pace. "What about it?"

"We named her Jenny, your daddy and me." Tanyon circled round the trunk, gave her barky bottom a swat. "And sweet Jenny here, she can keep a secret." That gray box snatched hold on my gaze. "How 'bout you, Baby? Can *you* keep a secret?"

Moss and that revenue agent stumbled hard against that quiet part of me, made a show of being there in the background, a place they'd forever stay.

My fingers went for that nick near my elbow. "I can keep a secret just fine," I answered.

Tanyon's hand searched that opening between tree-girl's parted legs; he tucked our new-found fortune away in her cunny. "We're the only ones privy to this, Baby—just me and you and Jenny. Understand?"

My head bobbled a nervous nod, put my balance in disarray. Breakfast and a bath, that's all I really gave two licks about. "How long till we leave?" I asked, meaning our promised run up north.

'Cept Tanyon, well, he didn't offer anything worth building upon. "Gotta bring the boil down to a simmer first," is all he said, nudging us back toward his dirty black Chevy.

CHAPTER TEN

Neesie took up real cozy with a bottle of Co-cola near to the icebox. She pulled down long draws from the thing like it might be the very last soda in all of Mississippi. Those dark eyes bit hard into some point of interest beyond that window framing the backyard.

Didn't take that Einstein fella to determine what had hold on her.

"What'd he do to you?" I asked, glancing through the newspaper spread across the kitchen table.

My words jerked the girl a-loose of her daydream. "What'd *who* do to me?" she demanded, sloughing away timidity like an old skin gone past its usefulness.

"That Injun boy you're gawking at."

Righteous indignation pinked up her cheeks real nice. "I ain't *gawkin'!*"

"All liars go the lake of fire," I said, making like the *Rayford Gazette* kept secrets worth finding out.

Aunt Frannie barged into our moment, oblivious to the colored girl's mooning. She let a little coffee into a cup, made eyes at me the way Neesie did Billy, 'cept without all that lust.

Reckon I'd call it guilt, that delicate flutter inside my chest. I mean, suppose she got word of the goings on across the river? Couldn't fully discount some fella from town seeing me over there.

"What did *I* do?" I asked, willing to take my lumps.

Aunt Frannie fell in behind me, lost to my sight. Her fingers combed through my hair as if ideas of a nasty sort loitered there. "Just picturing it long again," she said. "Think you might let it grow?"

Nothing concerning New Orleans came through. The woman couldn't get past my new look, is all.

I pushed a shrug up off my shoulders, muttered a thing about maybe buying a pair of trousers, a shirt and a tie. A joke, is all I meant.

'Cept Aunt Frannie is the sort who'd have a rough go at finding laughs in a Charlie Chaplin picture.

Her sigh came forced, exaggerated. "You'll have to grow up eventually," she said, pulling round to where I could see her. "People are starting to talk, Emily Ann."

I couldn't keep that smile away from my lips. "What's being said?"

Even the colored girl worked on a subtle grin.

"Facts are facts," proclaimed my aunt. "You'll always look like your mother—no matter *how* you wear your hair. Can't change *that* face."

Something akin to fire burned up my belly. I could hate her for that truth—almost.

Aunt Frannie gave no quarter to whatever argument I'd intended as a pithy retort; Bible study held greater sway than whatever denial I aimed to conjure.

"She say right," claimed Neesie, only after Aunt Frannie drove off. "You ain't look like no boy, a face pretty as *you* got."

I spun it right back on her, cornered that colored girl inside the laundry room, and set about having my say. "Suppose I ain't trying to look like no stupid boy?" I demanded.

Timidity made its return. Her arms dangled in limp surrender at her sides. She mumbled, "Was just sayin', is all."

She'd gone ripe for the picking, this one, and I aimed to pluck her nice and clean from the lowest branch.

"You tell Billy about my trips to New Orleans?" I asked, moving close enough to the girl to catch that hint of lilac on her chocolate skin.

"Ain't told nobody," she promised.

"'Cept *you* know—on account of you spied on me."

No argument there. The girl made habit of listening in on what belonged to other people.

Her cheek came warm to my fingers. "Trade me a secret," I whispered, stroking that smooth skin. "It's a fair proposal, don't you think?"

Neesie's eyelids fluttered in that way common to girls. "What kinda secret?"

My free hand searched my dress pocket, got hold on DeShay's dollar. "How much is Aunt Frannie giving you to spend?"

"My 'lowance? Dime a week."

"Suppose I give you this?" I fetched that piece of silver out in the open, let her ogle it a moment before pressing it to her palm, allowing her a touch.

Neesie's greedy gaze examined that shiny coin, speculated its worth to a girl from her station. "Tell you any old secret you want," she finally said.

'Cept ideas of my own making clamored for attention. Control, I'd call it—getting to be the one decides what's what.

Quick as fear, I snatched the dollar from her grasp, floated it teasingly in that narrow space between us, forced my intentions into vague little words. "Maybe I don't want you to *tell* me."

The colored girl's eyes held tight to that money, refused to turn it a-loose. She understood just fine the wherewithal needed to gain that coin. "You mean *show* you what Billy done."

My head tipped a nervous nod.

Funny how certain anticipations can turn a girl scared.

"Fine, then." Neesie took back what now belonged to her, fit that piece of silver down the pocket of her gray linen dress. "Won't do it in no kitchen, though."

"Course not." I stepped aside, granting the girl release from the laundry room. Every bone in my body rattled as though they meant to come apart with only minor provocation. "Go up to my room."

Neesie lit out without so much as a glance over her shoulder. I reckon to her, this was just a means toward extra candy, pretty ribbons for her braids, or whatever else she had a mind to spend that dollar on.

For me, well, it meant another curiosity cat would die.

Out back, Billy Blood's shovel tossed up dirt and manure, fixing a spot for still another shrub or flowering bush. Every now and again he'd set his gaze for the back door, eyeing that thin barrier, like just maybe he had a mind to waltz right past it and have a gander at the goings-on inside.

My fingers worked at the lock, slid the bolt into place.

Couldn't nobody bother us now.

∗   ∗   ∗

Peach-colored sheets concealed her body, though it didn't take no egghead college-boy to determine Neesie to be bare underneath. Her clothing lay willy-nilly across the floor like the leavings of some wild creature doing all it can to get caught.

My bed could easily accommodate the both of us, and maybe even a third—if we'd so been inclined to call on that Choctaw boy.

'Cept that's a different cat for another time.

Ideas filled my head like a million tiny dots, blotting out any consideration of the world outside my bedroom.

Do I kiss her first? I wondered, pulling off my own clothing. Or maybe Neesie ain't the type to want another girl's lips on hers.

I took down my underpants, scampered up under the sheet, and settled

in beside her. We traded self-conscious giggles, but said nothing amount-
ing to words.

Neesie's the one instigated that first kiss, shooing away any contrary
notions concerning another split-tail's lips on hers.

Liking this girl came easy as sipping iced tea on a lazy August afternoon.

Something familiar perfumed the air around us, sent up all sorts of
signals tugging us this way and that; the heady scent urged the colored girl
to take up on top of me.

"I do this—" she whispered, her soft belly pressed against mine, our
legs a-tangled like noodles in a cook-pot, "you g'wan give back?"

Such a contrast, our bodies, calling to mind unmingled coffee and
cream, two parts just dying to get mixed.

I swallowed hard at my fear. "Ain't gonna hurt, is it?"

Neesie's head went to wagging back and forth, tossing her braids here
and there, making promise that no harm would come.

"Then I'll give back," I swore.

"Well, then," she said, dipping her head beneath the sheet. "This what
Billy done."

*   *   *

Rowdy jazz raised a ruckus from a brand new Philco wireless bopping
atop that dour pine table. The tinny sound splattered Tanyon's parlor with
a tune I knew by heart; probably sang those words a hundred times before.
'Cept I really didn't cotton much to taking up with the song just yet.

I had blueprints of my own needed building.

"I want Neesie to come with us to New York," I announced, fitting
the remains from my glassine into that pipe.

Tanyon flopped down beside me on the sofa; his low belch reeked of
cheap corn liquor. "Can't go draggin' no pickaninny along with us, Emily
Ann," he argued.

Like a pendulum my anger swung too far in one direction to call it
back. Hostility took the form of words. "Don't you call her that!" I
snapped.

A thing like that goes against the rules—a white girl taking up for a
colored. There's been folks strung up for lesser forms of fraternizing.

'Cept Tanyon didn't lean toward those sorts of notions.

"Jeez, Louise," he said, eyeing me with suspicion. "Ain't gotta get all shoot-fire mad over some little black girl washes your dirty laundry." That Cajun twang twisted down low and conspiratorial. "Acting like you gone *sweet* on her or something."

Could he really tell such a thing just by sight?

Denials leapt from my tongue like watermelon seeds bent on winning a distance contest. 'Cept the words bumped one into another, falling into a pile there at my feet.

A crooked grin laid into Tanyon's countenance. "I believe you are a-blushing, girl." His arm fell heavy across my shoulder. "Ain't a big deal, really. Stuff like that happens plenty over the river."

I touched a Lucifer to my pipe, had a long pull, managed a lame, "Yeah, well…"

Tanyon knew.

He probably had a dozen dirty pictures working on his mind that very moment.

"Ought to stick with liquor," he said, ogling that smooth hunk of wood in my hand. "Hop will just chain you down."

I breathed off smoke right at his face. "Aunt Frannie smells hooch on me, I ain't *never* leaving that house."

The cap came a-loose of a second jar, which put Tanyon to his usual nosy meanderings.

"What'd you and her do?" He meant Neesie.

"Ain't none of your business."

That old crooked grin of his returned like a nuisance rash. "I got five dollars, you tell me what you done."

Scarlet heat warmed my cheeks, put me back beneath those peach-colored sheets with that colored girl. I didn't dish any details, though; I just gave Tanyon a sock to his shoulder, and told him to mind *his* and I'll mind *mine*.

'Cept Tanyon done-up on liquor calls to mind a snot-nosed schoolboy intent on gawking up a girl's dress. "You been with a boy yet?" he asked.

A subtle nod tugged at my chin, had me confessing misdeeds without doing much talking. I reckon I just couldn't conjure proper words for what that revenue fella did. And Moss, well—all those fragmented recollections I'd gotten hold on only pointed out my *own* culpability in the matter.

"It don't make me a whore, though," I said, more for my own hearing than his.

"No, it don't," Tanyon agreed, sucking on a Lucky. "Makes you more like your *mama*, though."

Smoke caught hold inside my chest, sent me to coughing like one of those fellas works over to the cotton mill. "What *about* Mama?" I demanded, once my air returned.

He took down half the jar in one long draw. "Just mean your mama had a whole other life apart from Rayford—before your daddy and you."

"And what do you know about *that?*" Truth be told, I'd caught whispers along my way to my current year—a word here, a line there. 'Cept nobody ever had the courtesy to just lay it out flat and allow me a regular old look-see.

Tanyon fidgeted like a bantam rooster tangled up betwixt a stump and an ax. "She wasn't much older than you when they put her right up front, that fancy ballet company she danced for. Took her to St. Louis, Atlanta, Chicago. I followed right after her."

I smoothed a wrinkle from my dress, screwed up a bellyful of courage. I needed to know. "Were you her beau?"

"Reckon you might could say that—but there *were* others. Norma Jean held no pretensions of settling in with just one fella."

An idea tickled my spine. "You think maybe that's why she did Papa wrong?"

Tanyon's head dipped a quick nod. "That'd be *my* guess." He fished a-loose a fresh cigarette, dragged a Lucifer across the pine table. "He's the one got her with child—which put a squeeze to her dancing. She never did want a normal life."

"You said I'm like her." I set that pipe on the table, fixed him good in my gaze. "How so?"

"Look just like her, act just like her." His hand found my cheek; his thumb caressed my lips the way an easy lover might. It's *Mama* he saw sitting there beside him. "*She* even took to a split-tail for a spell—a Creole girl from up near to Baton Rouge. Your daddy's the one put that little soirée to bed. Once *he* got in her blood, wasn't any room for the rest of us."

Tanyon carried a pull stronger than Valentino himself—and I ain't the only girl to say so. Could have been a Hollywood picture star—if he'd had a notion for that sort of life.

I leaned against his touch and pondered passing thoughts, those few-odd dirty glimpses I'd allow from time to time. "Then why'd she kill him?" I wondered aloud.

The glaze of his eyes made claim of too much hooch; loose words spilled oblong and misshapen from his mouth. "You got feelings for that colored girl, or are you just messin' around?"

My shoulders flinched a nervous shrug; I sifted my thoughts for a solid foundation, a definite answer to build upon. Just to *think* on the girl churned up a mess of minnows darting around the pond inside my belly— those silly tickles no boy ever coaxed.

"Can't say just yet," I admitted, though the words rang hollow to my own ears.

"Best figure what's what, then," said Tanyon, crushing his Lucky in the ashtray. "We can't afford to run no *fling* all the way to New York."

I straddled his lap the way I'd done a hundred times since memory could recollect, met him face to face. A simple wriggle of my bottom, and necessary secrets would just pour a-loose of him like a genie coming out of a bottle.

I put forth a question. "How'd you come to name a tree with Papa?" So casual came my squirm. "And why call it Jenny?"

Tanyon's cheeks pinked up real nice, like a schoolgirl's. Those large hands found rest at my hips. "We ran a numbers racket across the river," he confessed. "Did gangbusters for a spell; had money falling down like rain in April. Rydekker caught wind, demanded a cut—which he didn't in any way deserve."

Frank Rydekker controlled New Orleans, to hear Tanyon tell about it. And not just his own club, neither. The man had tentacles reaching every which a-way.

"A real parasite," he spat. "He expected *half* of all we got, in return for his blessing to work the city. Can't earn a living under another fella's thumb, so we found that tree, stashed our take in her hole."

I scooted my bottom down against his lap, asked about the name they chose. "Did you really know a girl called Jenny?"

Tanyon leaned in close; his lips brushed my ear. "You don't stop squirming your ass," he whispered into my head, "you and me might end up someplace we ain't never been together."

My heart kicked a ruckus back of my chest, mingled fear and excitement with my blood.

Jenny belonged to him and Papa—before Mama came along. A *shared* girl, he explained—Louisiana French, open to all sorts of unnatural considerations.

I'd gone lost in his eyes at the telling of it, at the notion of two beaus for one split-tail. Scandalous images flung themselves against the backdrop of my mind, put me warm and slippery where it counts most on a girl.

"Whatever happened to her?" I asked, pulling a-loose of him, settling my body, snug with the sofa.

Tanyon took up his Luckys, fished one free. "Put that shit in her arm, she did. It killed her. Your daddy's the one found her. I'd gone after your mama by that time."

Instinct nudged my fingers toward that faded mark on my own arm, put me to quaffing recollections by the glassful concerning that colored fella called Moss and that ritual we'd performed.

I reached for my pipe. "*You* ever take a needle?"

Tanyon wagged his head, swore only a fool would mess with sure death. "Be better off putting a gun to your head; it'd be a heap cheaper, and it wouldn't take so long."

Smoke swirled up like a charmed snake from that pipe, set me good and dizzy. "How'd Papa come to Mama?" I asked, drifting into that place between asleep and awake. "Did he steal her away from you?"

"Don't really matter anymore," he said, his voice gone distant from our shared moment. "Charlie Teegarten cost her more than just a career spinning round some stage; *his* sort of trouble cost your mama her father, her place in fancy society."

"Did you hate him for it?"

"Yeah," he said softly. "I would have killed him myself—if only I'd had the guts."

*   *   *

Angry words buzzed through the room like hornets evicted roughly from their nest, made threats with those barbed stingers.

Tanyon panicked. "I ain't took *nothing* from you, Frank!"

"Does five grand sound like nothing to *you?*" said Rydekker to one of his goons.

My hop-induced sleep lifted off like baby spiders carried away on the afternoon breeze. I remained prone on the sofa, though, hoping I'd somehow gone invisible during my nap.

'Cept Rydekker fashioned ideas of his own liking.

"Wake up, sleeping beauty," he said, dropping a heavy-handed swat against my backside. "We got business needs tending."

Two stocky fellas took hold on Tanyon, jammed his wiry frame in a corner. It's fear that pinched his face, distorted those handsome features, made me embarrassed just to see him.

Frank Rydekker yanked me upright, laid his arm across my shoulders. "Suppose you tell me where my money is, Jazz Baby?"

I tried for a snappy response, one of those impressive lines proving no fear in *this* girl. 'Cept all that stammering put me to stumbling over my very own tongue.

"Ain't gotta take up for Thibbedeaux," Rydekker claimed. "He ain't took up for *you*. Fact is—"

Tanyon tossed out denials well before any accusations made it to sound.

Two quick jabs to his belly put him up on silence—but for those ragged breaths he worked on.

My captor hugged me tight to his rigid body, let his foul words trickle softly into my ears. "Tanyon's the one made sure you ended up in that revenue fella's back seat."

I pulled a-loose of him, set my head to wagging my own denials. "A liar," I argued, "—that's all you are!"

Laughter seeped from those two keeping Tanyon in his corner.

Frank's grin called to mind a hyena I once saw in a magazine. "Oh, I had my own share in the blame for that little incident," he confessed. "I ain't the one wanted a kid on my stage, you understand. But Thibbedeaux—he can be one insistent cuss."

He made claim of that revenue fella ogling me during my tryout, of making me the upped ante to keep the club from getting shut down. That's when folks started itching, backs needed scratching.

Rydekker squeezed my shoulder. "Tan wanted you on my stage, I needed to keep the club open, and Mr. revenue man, well, he desired a sip of your nectar. That's what folks call a conundrum." His head dipped silly toward that corner. "But old Tanyon, he's the one dealt you in, made it come to pass."

My voice came low, strangled, my confidence all poked full of holes. "I don't believe you."

"Then ask him yourself." Frank's sharp nod dragged Tanyon from his corner, forced him to his knees center of the room. "He even got in on our friendly little wager, laid down a sawbuck claiming you still had your cherry." Rydekker's hand found the small of my back, put an easy pat to my bottom. "I bet against *that* notion—to my regret."

Tanyon's gaze fixed to some spot on the floor; he offered nothing to his own defense.

"You ain't been anything more than a meal ticket, Emily Ann," Frank announced. "A means to the big time—same as he'd once seen of your mama."

My thoughts went to swirling like sand caught in a dust devil.

I had to know. "Tell me he's lying, Tanyon," I whispered. "I'll believe you."

"Yeah!" Frank bellowed. "Go on and tell her what she wants to hear." He took up next to Tanyon, squatted low to the floor; his legs called to mind that tree named Jenny. "And then tell *me* what *I* want to hear—about my money."

Truth in Tanyon's eyes confessed his guilt in all that Frank Rydekker claimed. He capped that faraway stare so many boys picked up in the Great War.

In that airless gap in time, all I'd ever known had fallen away.

I begged one last plea to Tanyon. "Won't you say *some*thing?"

Rydekker leveled his own question. "What can he say that wouldn't be a lie?" A glint of silver met sunlight in his right hand. The hammer snapped back real crisp and businesslike. "Is five grand worth your life?"

That short barrel nuzzled the side of Tanyon's head.

"Don't!" I pleaded, my fingers stopping my ears against that moment.

Frank squeezed the trigger.

A crimson spray lingered midair before painting its gruesome pattern along the hardwood floor.

My eyelids fluttered; my gaze rolled up somewhere inside my head.

Gone.

CHAPTER ELEVEN

A sore ache of loss gnawed on my bones and lapped up my marrow like a starving dog; it put me in a mind where Papa himself had come back to me only to die all over again.

'Cept Tanyon, he'd never sit in Papa's place.

Certainly not now.

Thoughts came at me disassembled; some expected to be left undone, while others demanded immediate reconstruction.

Had I really seen that moment as it happened, or did my own eyes miss where Tanyon got hold on the gun?

I tossed onto my back, kicked a-loose of those peach-colored sheets, and stared into the canopy above my bed.

Mama's the one started all this killing business. If I had *my* say in what's what, I'd lay all the blame for everything bad across her grave. Tanyon's demise and that revenuer's back seat—it all belonged to Mama's account. Every murder and every forced girl would be *her* personal doing—that sin that labeled her wicked before God.

The new Eve, a female Cain.

Rydekker's specter confronted my thoughts, sent them to scattering like spooked birds taking flight. "I can get you anytime I choose," he promised before fading like last night's dreams.

Neesie wedged herself into the void Frank's departure left behind. I pined for that colored girl in ways a split-tail's only supposed to pine over boys. And did she feel the same for me as I felt for her?

I couldn't just ask her, neither; not with Aunt Frannie fluttering about like some loony Florence Nightingale, constantly checking up on me, determined to know my state since Sheriff Dantley came by with news of Tanyon's "suicide."

That's what they were calling it—as if Tanyon did it to himself.

'Cept I knew the truth.

Neesie's scent lingered in my sheets like a delicate dream, lured me away from damaged ideas concerning Tanyon and his mess. My eyelids drooped low as if I'd taken to the pipe that very morning. I breathed in the colored girl; my mind stirred up recollections of the time she shared my bed.

'Cept nosy Aunt Frannie breached my threshold, barged right on in where I really had no need for her. A hand found my forehead, searched out the remnants of a passing fever—or some other notion likely to unravel a girl like an old worn rug.

"I ain't sick!" I argued, hoping to come a-loose of her suffocating sympathies. "And you don't need to skip your Bible study, neither."

An easy smile softened her features, made her look even more like Mama. "Someone's here to see you," she whispered.

"Who is it?"

"Come see."

I tossed my feet to the floor and followed after her, traipsing dutifully down the stairs, dressed in a white cotton nightshirt that scarcely pulled a hint of protest from Aunt Frannie.

That meant Jobie Pritchett lurked somewhere in the house.

"So," I said, aiming for cute and funny, "you fixin' to try and pawn me off again?"

My humor missed its mark.

Aunt Frannie spun hard on me like a top that's lost its center, shoved me back a step or two through sheer force of will. "Stow the sarcasm, young lady!" she growled through clenched teeth.

Sure enough, Jobie occupied space on that black velvet loveseat once belonged to my grandparents. He sported that familiar forlorn look I'd come to expect from the boy. And that shy blue gaze of his, well, it tackled his will, drew down on a good long gawk at my bare legs beneath my high-riding nightshirt.

Truth be told, I appreciated this seldom-seen side of the preacher's son.

"Gonna go to hell," I said, "you stare too awful long."

A warm girlish blush pinked his cheeks at getting caught—though he never did divert his gaze. My fingers took hold on my hemline. "Ain't wearing any underpants," I teased. "Wanna see?"

Jobie's pink went full-on scarlet.

Aunt Frannie barked, "Manners, child!" before leaving us alone to our own devices.

'Cept the boy's the one tossed off all sense of manners and such.

Hands struck quick as a copperhead working on a mouse, latched onto my nightshirt, and yanked it belly high.

A grin played up the sides of his mouth. "All liars go to the lake of fire," he announced. "Revelation twenty-one and eight."

Jobie dipped down on one knee, took hold on my left hand.

"Get up, boy," I demanded, knowing full well the nature of his intent.

"Gonna do this right, Emily Ann."

"Ain't nothing ever gonna be right."

A shiny band, simple and silver, fit snugly around my ring finger. A mark, really; that outward sign telling all who sees it that I belong to the preacher's boy.

"I ain't asking you to change, Emily Ann." His voice came soft, soothing, like just maybe everything would come out as planned.

'Cept whose plans were we working on?

I tugged my hand free from his and eyed that ring. "I won't quit singing jazz," I swore.

"You wouldn't be you if you did."

"In speakeasies."

"I'll be in the front row every night."

His face fit perfectly in my hands. "Can't be in no speak if you're gonna preach," I told him.

"I'm an artist," he said, "not a preacher."

"Your daddy's gonna hate me. He'll tell all of Rayford how that old jazz-singing Jezebel done corrupted his boy."

Jobie took to the loveseat, swept me up on his lap, and whispered directly into my head about how he'd taken a job over to the grain elevator, rented the rooms above the general store, and how there'd be no turning back.

"What's done is done," he promised. "Are you gonna say yes?"

I didn't have to.

For all his troubles, all those sneaky preparations he'd been conjuring behind my back, I honestly owed this boy nothing.

'Cept my head tipped forward—though I wouldn't quite call it a nod.

Jobie demanded more, something solid to rest his future upon, like pilings sunk deep in the muck meant to keep the pier above the churning black water.

"I need to hear you say it, Emily Ann."

I worked the word against my tongue, savored its smooth contours. If it took to sound, that would be it. Can't take it back once it's been given.

"I still want New York," I blurted. It needed telling; can't go building off a lie.

"You ain't expecting it tomorrow, are you?"

My head went to wagging left and right. "Maybe not tomorrow," I told him, holding his gaze with my own, "—but I won't put it off forever, neither."

"Fair enough," said Jobie.

"Then yes, I'll marry you." The words hurt like the dickens coming a-loose of my mouth. And it had nothing to do with Jobie Pritchett, neither. He'd make a right fine husband to any girl in all of Mississippi.

It just meant I'd never be free of having to answer to someone who ain't me, myself, or I.

"Well then." Pride laid a shine to the boy's countenance like a fine new pair of shoes. "Shall we go see where we'll stay?"

*   *   *

We gained those rickety stairs rising along the back of that old red brick building situated where every busybody in town would be privy to our comings and goings. And they'd talk, too, the way they always do when a boy and a girl hitch up. Didn't matter a tinker's damn that *this* boy happened to be a preacher's son; they'd still toss gossip on how far along I am.

From that rear porch I found Aunt Frannie's house two blocks away, over to where that colored girl stayed.

It ain't cheating if it's with another split-tail, is it?

Jobie's key slid slowly into the lock, like just maybe second thoughts took to poking at him, trying to nudge him toward the shame of what really lay behind that door.

"Ain't much to brag on just yet," he said, "but I reckon a girl's touch…"

He'd called it *rooms* back at Aunt Frannie's place.

'Cept there were no *rooms* to be had on the second floor, only a single space with an icebox to the rear and a lonely mattress up front.

"We have a water closet," he claimed, jabbing a thumb at a closed door along the wall. "Has a commode *and* a bath tub."

I passed inside, smoothed the fib of a wrinkle from the pale blue sundress I put on just for this showing, and allowed my gaze to stumble through the tight, bare space.

Jobie's hand found the small of my back. Funny how natural his touch felt.

"Got room to make my drawings," he said, letting that hand linger. "Can even draw *you?*"

"Without my clothes on?" I teased.

He didn't say anything at first; he just sort of gawked at me the way boys will do when they're conjuring ideas of what a girl looks like under her dress.

A few nervous steps put him center of the room. "I ain't sinless, Emily Ann," he confessed, putting his gaze to the floor.

I trickled in like a slow leak, pooled at his feet, took hold on his hands, and waited for details.

In his silence I caught glimpse of the man inside the boy.

"Been down to Biloxi a few times," he admitted, "over to a coloreds speakeasy. Ain't nobody gonna know me in there." Jobie went to dishing secrets like he'd got them two-for-one from some stand along the side of the road.

He'd gone down there a dozen times.

He'd smoked cigarettes and drank corn liquor while there.

Danced to jazz.

Drew pictures of a colored girl.

"Did she have any clothes on?" I asked, holding off a curious grin.

"She didn't," he answered, unable to meet my eyes.

"You do more than just draw her?"

"Ever notice how there ain't no coloreds in my daddy's congregation?" He shook a-loose of me and drifted to the window looking down on the street out front. "How's *that* a godly notion?"

My feet shifted beneath me; I couldn't keep my words from making sound. "I ain't a virgin," I blurted.

Jobie's smile came warm and dreamy, like maybe that corn liquor he'd got into the night before last had only just now gone to his head. "Neither am I," he promised.

"And I've been sneaking over the river, too."

"Singing?"

I dropped a quick nod in that space between us, blabbed on about the Crescent Club, smoking hop, Tanyon's grand plans for New York City.

Jobie's gaze caught mine. "Then why'd he kill himself?"

My spine checked up real straight. "He didn't."

The boy wouldn't dig any deeper—at least not where Tanyon's demise lay buried. He closed up that space, ran those long fingers of his through my hair. "How come you to cut it?"

That revenue fella, his back-seat doings—it all gushed out like blood from a stuck pig. "I didn't want fellas noticing me anymore."

His kiss came soft and warm, full of secrets I'd be privy to in no time at all. "Still look like Baby Teegarten, you ask me," he whispered.

"You gonna take me to that speak?" I asked, leaning on his strength.

His fingers turned a-loose of my hair and took to tracing those too small nubs at my chest. "Suppose I do?" he said, showing all sorts of hunger in his eyes. "What's in it for me?"

I flinched a shrug, told him if I got it he could have it.

'Cept Jobie didn't have a make on what I'd figured him to covet.

"Get me some of that hop you been smoking," came his request.

"Gotta go across the river," I said. "Ain't likely to find any in Rayford."

"I'll take you over."

There were secrets involved, secrets didn't belong to me. "Can't go in with me," I told him, "—and it ain't *my* say-so, neither."

Jobie understood. He dropped down on that mattress, took up Injun style, like he'd gone back to being a schoolboy all over again. "How much can we get?"

I settled beside him, fingered that silver ring on my hand, contemplated its very intentions. "There's a man called Pig…"

Laughter spewed from somewhere deep inside the boy, laughter like I'd never heard out of Jobie Pritchett. "Kinda name is *that?*"

Something akin to anger burned in my belly. "Why do you want a lot anyway?" I snapped. "You can only smoke so much before you nod off."

"Ain't looking to smoke it," Jobie confessed. "I'm fixin' to sell it down at Biloxi. I can make twice what I spend on it."

"Pig won't want *money*—least not from me."

Couldn't nobody call Jobie slow; the boy caught hold on my drift and rode it directly to the shore. "That how you got yours?"

"Ain't done it yet. He just *give* it to me last time."

"You willing to make such a trade?"

I went back to that silver ring.

Jobie took my hand. "Ain't married just yet."

"How come you wanna sell it, anyway?"

Jobie Pritchett conjured some big idea meant to put enough money in his pockets to tide us over until folks might come around where his drawings were concerned.

"Those nudes I did," he said, perking up to the notion of it all, "—got twenty bucks for a pair!"

"That colored girl?"

"She's Creole. Speaks perfect French."

Didn't need both eyes to see through to Jobie's true feelings.

I went back to that ring, fought against the pride demanding its immediate removal from my finger. "Is she the one you've been with?"

Jobie's head did a quick bobble. "She's real sweet, Emily Ann."

I can't recollect for sure where the sadness came from, that bitter sting that crept up the back of my throat. I mean, it's not as if he'd been my long-time beau or anything. We'd only just now got engaged.

I picked at a loose thread on my dress, framed my question with the proper words. "Why am I here, Jobie?"

"Because we need each other, Emily Ann."

"Don't seem that way to me."

The boy shifted his position, took to his knees directly across from me, met me with that cool blue gaze.

I could easily learn to love him.

"How'd you talk Frannie into allowing you over the river?" he asked, already making his pitch.

"I didn't—you know that."

"She'd lock you in a closet, she ever found out. Wouldn't she?"

A *threat!*

At least that's the way *I* heard it.

I yanked back from the boy, tried like the dickens to read his meaning, to be awful sure I understood his gist. "Are you holding that over me?" I demanded.

Jobie's eyes narrowed. "I'm doing no such thing, Emily Ann." He jerked me back into his grasp, held me fast. "I'm only suggesting a thing to the benefit of the both of us."

The way that boy told it, he, too, had been sneaking around—same as me. 'Cept Jobie's wanderings put him in Biloxi the last few weekends, had him making claims to his folks of fishing trips with Tommy Letts.

"Which really ain't a lie," he explained, "since me and Tommy really were on about fishing when we found that speak in the first place."

Voices fluttered up from the sidewalk out front, folks gathering for afternoon gossip over cold Co-colas bought from the general store. They could hear our talk just as sure as we could hear theirs.

I brought my tone low. "You ain't gotta marry me to get out of your father's house."

"Appearances, Emily Ann."

"You're a grown man now, Jobie Pritchett; just quit trying to please him."

The boy had ways he wouldn't easily be turned a-loose of. "If we're married," he promised, "you'll not have another soul to answer to ever again."

I reckon that's the part had me in all the way.

His hand found my cheek, laid on a caress meant to bend me to his will. "It'd be only us, Emily Ann," he whispered. "And I'd bet dollars to dirt they'd be thrilled to have you sing down there in Biloxi."

I leaned into his body. "And what of New York?"

Jobie stroked all my proper spots. "We'll get there, Baby. I promise."

*   *   *

That shiny tan Packard crouched low in Aunt Frannie's usual parking place and glowered at me like I'm the one didn't belong there. It's cooling metal popped and pinged, mocked my minced steps.

I crept along the back of the house, searched for that Injun out among the shrubs and roses. 'Cept the day being a dingy gray made promises of rain before lunch; Billy Blood wouldn't be over until sunlight split the cover above.

Stupid boy—to be out gadding about when a girl had real need of him!

I pressed my ear to the rear door, drew off a quick listen, caught little more than the low hum of the motor keeping that fancy new icebox cold.

The door gave against my gentle nudge, put me inside the kitchen.

Familiar voices drifted in from the parlor, easy conversation, like old friends playing catch-up on the doings of years past.

I snatched up a paring knife from the counter where Neesie meant to carve potatoes, concealed it in my hand, and let it take me to the parlor, toward that useless banter.

"And here she is," said Frank Rydekker from that loveseat once belonged to my grandparents. "Been waiting for, what, an hour almost?"

Neesie dropped a nervous nod from her perch beside the man, fixed her eyes to the floor like she's the one did wrong and had to give answer for it.

Rydekker's meaty hand rested on the colored girl's shoulder. "This little pickaninny, she's been a right fine hostess. Hasn't she, Jimbo?"

One of his goons let go a grunt from a spot halfway up the stairs—as if he had all the rights in Mississippi to be sitting there, sucking on a cigarette.

'Cept I'm the one had authority in that house. "Get out!" I demanded.

"Ain't very hospitable, Miss Teegarten." Rydekker gained his feet, made a show of that pistol at his waist. "Or is it Mrs. Pritchett by now? He's in love with a colored girl, that boy you aim to wed. Been sippin' her honey down to Biloxi."

The knife came high, yanked my arm up with it. "I'll tell what you did to Tanyon," I blurted before considering my threat, the situation. He could kill us both, Neesie and me, and be long gone before Aunt Frannie ever found us.

I backtracked from my own foolishness, lowered the knife. "Just leave us be and I won't never say a word."

Rydekker's easy laugh made it seem like I just sang some funny little ditty had nothing at all to do with the moment. "Ain't here to negotiate, doll face. All's I want is my money."

Squatting Jenny came to mind, that small fortune squirreled away in her cunny.

Frank had nothing to prove it belonged to him.

"I don't know anything about no money," I said, forcing my spine upright.

It's greed that gets us to lie like that. And greed can come awful heavy, like a wet wool blanket, suffocating, snuffing out the light.

Rydekker's gaze bit down on me, threatened all sorts of venom for my blood.

"Ain't gonna just forget about five grand, girl." He gained space a bit too close to me, worked up a grin set my belly to water. "I could put you on your back in one of my houses over the river—get mine with interest."

My fingers went tight around the knife's handle. "Can't give you what I don't have," I said, keeping up my end of the lie.

His sharp angle scooted me nice-as-you-please into a corner 'neath the staircase, cut off my retreat. "Your mama killed your daddy; ain't that how it went?"

"What's that got to do…?" My words fell dead and brittle like oak leaves in fall. Why'd he have to bring Mama into this mess?

Frank's fingers slipped under my chin, raised my gaze up off the floor. "I saw her dance a time or two, back when she traveled with that ballet company. You look an awful lot like her. Be a shame you end up same way she did."

A lonely tear breached my will, splashed hard against his hand.

Rydekker's lips brushed my ear. "Come back with me, Emily Ann. I'll take care of you—and it won't be like that cheatin' preacher's boy you're intended to."

My fingers reminded me of the knife they retained within their grasp.

"Get out!" I ordered, pushing the blade against his stomach.

His hands shot up in mock surrender, though his grin called my bluff. "Your say-so, little girl." He backed away, motioned his goon down from the stairs. "Like I said, I won't forget about my five grand."

I waited until that tan Packard hit the street and raced off toward the river before attempting words of any sort.

"You ain't hurt, are you?"

Neesie's head went to wagging left and right. "'Cept that one on the stairs, he been in your room."

"Won't find anything in there," I said, taking perch on the sofa.

"Where you hide it?"

"Who says I have it?"

"Can just tell, is all." She dropped down beside me, took hold on my hand the way I imagine a lover might. "You really g'wan marry that Pritch-ett boy?"

My chin tugged a-loose a nod from my head. "But that don't mean, you know, me and you can't still…"

Confession to our secret wouldn't come just yet—not out loud at least. And it had nothing to do with shame, neither.

Neesie's giggles came girlish and reassuring, as if the threats of Frank Rydekker carried no real weight in her little corner of Mississippi.

'Cept Billy Blood saw to it that nothing could get done between me and that colored girl.

"I ain't interrupting, am I?" he asked, barging into the moment like it was just a natural thing for him to be there—like maybe he'd even been invited.

"How much did you hear?" I demanded.

"Enough to know the man won't let this alone."

"Is that all you heard?"

Billy dropped down beside me, pinned me tight between him and Neesie. "Just give it back, Emily Ann. A man like that might hurt his own mama for that kind of money."

I fixed on those dark pools he called eyes and considered taking a dip. "I won't be here long enough for him to know anything."

"Pritchett won't go for no New York," Billy said, certain of his own proclamation. "You'll never get him out of the state."

I pushed out from between the two, smoothed the wrinkles from my dress. "You can't say what Jobie might do," I told that Choctaw know-nothing. "When we're married, we can go wherever we want."

"Stubborn," he grumbled, "—always have been."

"Take me over the river."

That dark Injun-gaze took hold on me, searched my bones up and down like I'd only just now appeared from the ether, a dream or a specter looking for something solid to rest upon.

"Fine then," he said, gaining his feet. He jammed his hands into his trousers pockets, angled his chin like pride had got to him. "Gonna cost you ten dollars—up front."

*   *   *

Couldn't see Jenny from that narrow dirt road curling around the woods; I'd have to go through the trees to find her. And Billy, well—I didn't see much need for him to meet the old girl, bother her where she squatted, made water.

"Wait here," I told him, hopping down from his truck.

The boy's head dipped toward a lane running straight through that stand of trees. "There's others," he said.

A black Model T Ford skulked in the tall grass beside the lane.

"Bootleggers," I said, pushing his door closed. "Ain't none of our business."

"They think we're spying, it is!"

"Then just ignore them."

I broke through grass high as my chest and caught the woods fast as a rabbit.

Blackbirds overhead squawked warnings against my intrusion.

My head swiveled atop my neck in controlled desperation, tossing my gaze here and there, searching for the one promising an easy way out.

A skinned knee, I recalled—and red bark.

Rough red bark.

Couldn't miss a squatting girl, though. Right?

'Cept everything familiar mingled with the background, took up real nonchalant, like maybe it meant to confuse me, to keep a girl from finding what fell into her lap.

Muddy earth swallowed my shoes.

All those noisy blackbirds shut off their alarms, scattered silence thick as deep water into the air.

"Where are you, Jenny?" I said aloud.

And there she stood—or squatted—making water in a clearing at the center of the woods.

I pulled a-loose of that Louisiana muck and met the girl concealing my dreams inside her privy parts. I stroked her bottom, patted her thigh. She'd be an Injun if she were real.

"Let's have it," I whispered, reaching deep between her legs.

That grey box found my eager hand. I twisted it left and right, tugged and yanked until it came free from captivity.

A soul might walk down an entire lifetime and never set a peep on that much money—at least not all in one neat pile.

Wasn't no five grand, though, not by my counting.

I ran through it a second time, landed again at the same crisp figure: $4,620. I reckon there ain't much difference between two such sums once you take after numbers reaching that high.

'Cept where could I hide it all? I mean, only a fool would traipse about waving a stack that thick, just daring some old bootlegger to brave an idea. And Billy Blood had no rights to any of it, neither. He got his before we ever crossed that river. Ten bucks, he said. A deal's a deal.

But it wasn't any Choctaw boy tracking that line running directly at me.

That greasy-headed fella moved with the hobble and scoot of a man overly familiar with predetermined escape routes.

His Cajun twang nicked the silence. "Whatcha got there, girlie?"

Nervous tension spiked my blood, had me chasing panic through my veins. I could outrun him—easily. 'Cept my legs betrayed me, refused an urgent order to just go.

"Leave me be," I said, wedging my words between ragged puffs of sticky breath.

His toothless grin put that gimpy man in charge of the moment. "Won't nobody hear you, you work up a fuss out here."

I took up a sure stance, a thing meant to declare my capability to handle trouble of his sort. 'Cept this fella, he waded through it all, caught hold on me back of Jenny. Fingers gripped tight those delicate hairs at the scruff of my neck.

"Let go!" I screamed.

He jerked me upright, set me like a puppet on my tiptoes, moved my body here and there and wherever else he had a mind to sway me.

It's that scuffle put my green paper to light. Flung it high like lanky butterflies discovering only just now they possessed workable wings.

"Give it back!" I demanded, clawing at the puppeteer's arm.

Bony knuckles kissed the side of my head, knocked me face-down against the earth, drove all common sense from my mind.

"Take that ass while I'm at it, girlie," he said, snatching handfuls of green butterflies.

Cool silence pressed hard against the trees, turned a-loose reminders of that revenue fella, of what all could happen when nobody watched.

'Cept somebody saw this time.

"Won't a soul miss you, I put a bullet through you." Billy Blood circled around Jenny, cut a dark figure in the midday light.

That Cajun thief fixed his droopy gaze to the pistol in the Choctaw's hand. "Best go on and mind your own business, boy," he spouted, like just maybe he still maintained his charge over the situation.

Billy read it his own way. "This girl *is* my business!"

I gained my feet, gathered up what belonged to me, though some bills fell casualty, lost to the mud or tucked away in the Cajun's pockets.

But the bulk found comfort in my hands.

Billy moved on Jenny, on the thief hunched at her backside. "If I catch even a glimpse of you in my mirror..."

He left his threat dangling like a loose thread on a favorite shirt.

The Cajun understood just fine: Don't tug on it and it won't come all undone.

"Here," I said, pushing a hundred note into Billy's hand.

'Cept that boy's grip let him down, wouldn't take hold on his reward. "It's tainted, Emily Ann. All of it."

"Still spends just fine," I said, climbing up inside the truck.

Billy slid in beside me and turned the key. "And what about Tanyon?" His thumb jammed at the starter button. "Ain't nothing but trouble, girl."

My gaze fell to the pile in my lap.

"That's all you're ever gonna know," he said softly, "until you get rid of it."

CHAPTER TWELVE

Folks scarcely make a noise for me in church—at least not in the way they do across the river. The best I might squeeze from Rayford's Baptists is a knowing nod, maybe a wink and a smile. Usually it's tears, though—all those stone-faced old gals spilling their salt over the likes of "Amazing Grace" or "Love Lifted Me."

Bet they cheer over to the colored church.

Bet *Neesie's* a star in *that* congregation.

I took up with Jobie in a pew up front once I finished my song, let him hold my hand while his daddy splashed the walls with hellfire and damnation. Just to read the boy showed he hadn't yet made known all those big-deal alterations to a no-longer intended life in the pulpit.

Even as Pastor Pritchett tore down sin, harangued the nightly drunkard, and castigated those lust-filled fornicators, Jobie squirmed in his seat and sought refuge behind a growing pile of guilt.

That boy sure carried an awful heavy burden.

"Just say you ain't called to preach," I told him while waiting outside for Aunt Frannie. "He's not gonna hate you, Jobie Pritchett."

"It ain't that easy, Baby." Those blue eyes of his lured me in, shook me a-loose of all I'd meant to say.

Aunt Frannie stumbled out the front door, shaking hands and sharing gossip from here till next Sunday.

Jobie yanked me between two parked cars. "Come out with me to-night, Emily Ann."

"Where?"

Secrets swirled around us like spirits of the dead looking in on sins of the living.

His voice dropped low, conspiratorially. "Over to N'Orleans."

"Good luck with *that*," I said, straightening my navy skirt.

'Cept Jobie Pritchett couldn't be put off his trail. "You just leave Frannie to me." The devil's very own grin curled around the corners of his lips. "After all, I'm the preacher's boy, right?"

My body tilted toward his. "I have money, Jobie. You ain't gotta sell hop."

"It's not always about money, Emily Ann," he said, cutting a line toward Aunt Frannie.

I climbed inside the Pierce-Arrow, watched from the front seat as my aunt's head bobbed her permission to a boy had no idea what might happen across the river.

"He's going to take you to dinner!" she exclaimed, sliding in behind the wheel. "To that fancy French place up in Jackson."

"And you said yes?"

"Why wouldn't I?"

My shoulders flinched a shrug. "Awful long drive for us to be alone."

A smirk, I'd call it—that thing on her mouth. "You blew that good-girl routine long ago. Besides, you'll be married in another month. Why should I give a care if you get an early start?"

My eyes went wide as silver dollars. "Lord a-mercy—"

"And don't act all offended, either. I'm not dumb, Emily Ann." She punched the starter button, found first gear, and rolled us into Rayford's usual Sunday morning hum.

I fingered a button on my blouse, contemplated how deep I aimed to dig.

'Cept Aunt Frannie snatched my shovel. "I found the cigarettes in your room," she said, digging the hole for me. "And I'm almost certain you've never spent a night at that Markley girl's place. I don't even need to know *where* you really stayed. Just like your mother, you are."

"Is that why you're marrying me off?"

"He'll do you right."

"Make me proper, huh?"

She twisted the wheel, floated us into the dirt lot beside the general store. "Don't sass me, girl. You've been a smart aleck since you first learned to speak."

What could I say? I reckon she hit on a truth of some sort. Besides, sounded to me like she'd already since turned me a-loose.

"I still love you, though," she said, sifting through her purse. "It's just your time to grow up."

I snatched the two proffered nickels from her hand, flung my door wide, and stomped off for the store.

I can't make claim to being overly angry with her. At least she wouldn't smother me any longer.

Nola Patterson sat perched atop a tall stool back of the counter, ogled the morning's *Rayford Gazette* spread before her.

"How's God this morning?" she asked.

I slid the cooler door open, plunged my hands inside, plucked up a matching pair of Co-colas. "How am I supposed to know?"

A grin softened her features. "You're coming back from church, ain't you?"

Nola used to go to my school, though she ran a full five grades ahead of me. It's her folks own that store, keep it open come Sunday since ain't a Patterson one had any use for God or church or religion in general.

A whole family of unbelievers.

"Got a letter here for you," she said, holding that envelope between her fingers. "Well, not for *you*; it's addressed to that Negro girl stays with you." Nola squinted at the name scrawled in black ink. "Nessa?"

"Neesie," I corrected, stealing it away.

"It's been here since Friday past."

I tossed the nickels on the counter. "Guess we just were busy, is all."

"Daddy says you and Jobie are taking the room upstairs."

I offered a nod, slipped that letter in my skirt pocket.

She'd be pretty if she lost her baby fat—even with hair as red as hers.

"Just remember to shut that front window," she hollered at my retreat, "or everyone coming in here's liable to hear you two coursing."

"That's okay," came my retort, my foot kicking wide that heavy front door. "We do most of our coursing in his back seat."

The certainty to Aunt Frannie's scowl carried promise of a full morning's worth of discontent. "Have you no *shame*, child?"

I don't reckon she expected anything by way of an official response. It's what Papa would have called *rhetorical*, meaning a fool asks a question she thinks she already knows the answer to.

Anyhow, I suppose the woman would forever douse me with the same gray disappointment she poured over Mama the final thirteen years of *her* life.

I climbed inside the car, handed her the extra soda, and took mine apart in one long pull.

'Cept I couldn't hold that burp down.

"Manners!" she scolded.

My butt raised up off the seat; the air passed through *that* end this time.

Aunt Frannie's nose went all wrinkled, as if she herself had never been capable of such functions. Her words came neatly tucked under her breath.

"Just like your mama."

I'm the one saw that Choctaw boy sneaking out our back door like some fool thief forgot to carry anything away. Aunt Frannie, she'd gone too busy yammering another long-winded spiel concerning proper behavior to take notice of the doings happening right beneath her own roof.

I broke a-loose of Frannie's gravitational pull and took up real quick to that tiny room just off the kitchen, Neesie's room, before all evidence evaporated and certain sins remained forever hidden. In an awkward silence I watched her through a crack in the door, standing at her dresser, naked as that morning she lay in my bed.

Neesie made no frantic effort to conceal all those parts left uncovered—even after I breached her threshold and gave myself away.

Her gaze tried to pin my gaze down, hold me accountable to *her* will, to see things the way *she* would have me to see them. 'Cept my eyes, they roamed that girl's raw outline, those narrow hips, her small breasts, that sweet spot where her legs came together.

I pushed the door closed and perched on the foot of her cot, lost in her familiar scent. "What'd he do to you?" I asked, my tone low, kept softly away from Aunt Frannie's ears.

Neesie offered me her back, that bare bottom, so perfect and round. "Ain't nobody done nothin'," she said, scarcely bringing her words to sound.

"Then why are you bare?"

She spun on me, brought it so close, that girlish crease. "I'm in my *own* room, ain't I? Can't I change from my Sundays clothes?"

"I saw Billy."

"So?" Defiance raged behind that one little word. "Gonna tell on me now?"

I'd never tell. Even if they tossed me in the murky Atchafalaya. "Do you love him?"

Such a subtle nod, but it still claimed all sorts of ground.

My hands fell to my lap. "Has he stuck you yet?"

"You mean is we coursin'?" Her head waggled left and right, sent her braids swinging. "Ain't ready for *that!*"

My fingers combed my pocket, dredged up that letter. "This came for you," I said, handing it to the girl, knowing full well she lacked sense to read its telling. "Envelope says it's from over to Alabama—Selma."

Neesie relieved me of my charge, let it slip inside the top dresser drawer. "Can't know about it just now," she said, reaching for her gray linen dress lying on the cot. "Maybe you might could tell it to me later on, you think?"

I would. Couldn't name an awful lot I'd not do for that colored girl. "Ain't mad at me, are you?"

Neesie's head went to twisting again. "Ain't mad."

I gained my feet, watched her wiggle into that dress. "Are you sorry for what *we* did?"

A smile tugged at the edges of her mouth. "Truth to tell, you do it better than even Billy."

The doorknob laid cool against my hand. I had to know. "What of that boy you claimed waited for you in Alabama?"

"Ain't no Simp for real," she whispered, dodging Aunt Frannie's racket in the kitchen. "Said it so nobody 'spect me and Billy."

"Then who's that letter from?"

Her easy sigh relinquished control, set me back to my charge. "May as well read it now, find out what they's sayin'."

She fished that envelope up again, brought it to me as if she carried an invitation from King George himself, and took to her cot like some sort of fever laid into her.

Ain't nothin' but nervous gumption puts a girl all loopy like that, breathing fractured ideas in her ear, convincing her it's sure to read *no* when all she really wants is a simple *yes*.

A woman called Hatty affixed her name to this piece of news, thereby painting herself either mean or wonderful, depending on whichever way the bones came together.

I asked, "Who's Hatty?"

"My grams. Read it."

Thirteen words, that's all Grandma Hatty saw fit to toss over state lines.

My gaze fondled each word individually, smoothed away all those rough edges had the makings to wound this girl.

I lowered the page and met her gaze. "Are you expecting something specific?"

*   *   *

Can't say I recognized the shiny black truck creeping up the front drive, but I most assuredly knew that blond-headed boy back of the wheel.

Jobie Pritchett angled his fancy new piece of machinery in behind the Pierce-Arrow and sounded the klaxon.

Aunt Frannie flung none of her usual commands concerning proper behavior for a young lady, made no demands regarding a reasonable curfew. She didn't even bother with a goodbye.

Fine by me. I'd gone good and well past needing some other soul looking after something I could see to myself.

I climbed the driver's running board and had a look at Henry Ford's latest. "Who'd you swipe *this* from?" I teased.

Jobie gripped the wheel as if some old thief just might take up a notion to snatch that entire rig right out from under him. "Borrowed it from work," he claimed.

"What's wrong with *your* car?"

"Can't chance being seen in N'Orleans, Emily Ann."

"Why not? Don't seem such a big deal for a full-grown man."

The boy ignored my dig, passed a quick gawk over the tan blouse and green skirt I wore. "Where's those *Charlie* clothes you fussed on about?"

"I didn't *fuss*," I assured him, coming a-loose of that running board. "Pig's just awful peculiar, is all."

DeShay's grubby overalls and dingy T-shirt posed like fugitives in a dark corner of the garage. Hiding out, they were. Just waiting for another run.

I grabbed them up, shook 'em for spiders, and bolted for the truck in a grand escape.

Jobie eased us down the drive, set us toward the river. "Why dress in those?" he asked, pulling a sidelong glance at the costume on my lap.

"Pig likes boys," is what I said, leaving it at that.

He squeezed the shifter into third gear, had us rolling along like the devil himself gave chase. "How come you call him Pig?"

"I can't get a whole lot from him," I said, ignoring his question. "He only gave me a small glassine last time."

Jobie let on a better understanding of such things than I'd have figured him to know. "He didn't get anything from *you* last time. It's *gotta* be more—right off the top."

Can't say I'd call it nerves, that annoying twinge laying roots inside my belly. Of course I wouldn't call it excitement, neither. That last time, his rough touch, those naked words—I'd be a liar to deny I felt *some*thing.

I studied Jobie's profile in the dying daylight. "What do you reckon he'll want from me?"

"If he likes boys, well…" He slowed back, put the truck on the state road leading out of Rayford, had us outrunning the devil again. "Billy Blood still working for Frannie?" he wondered.

"Yeah. 'Cept he wrote a letter to Neesie's grandma asking for her hand."

Jobie's gaze slid into me like a rogue wave. "What's he wanna marry someone's grandmother for?"

I socked him in his arm. "He asked for *Neesie's* hand, boy."

"And what did granny say?"

My belly went tight, though it had nothing to do with Pig this time. "They're leaving for Alabama next month, getting married before winter settles."

Jobie moved the truck to the side of the road, brought us to a stop.

A colored fella sprouted from the cotton and yanked my door wide. "This the girl?" he asked, taking no means to deny his hungry stare.

Jobie tugged me across the seat, gave the man my spot. "This is Nestor," he told me, getting us back up toward the river. "He's a friend from Biloxi."

Conversation floated back and forth above my head, words and telling gone way beyond my knowing, fixing on plans thought of long before we plucked up that stringy black man from a roadside cotton patch.

A gap finally opened between vowel and consonant, a muted void inviting me to wedge myself into the mixture, get my own questions in the ether. I asked that colored fella, "How'd you come to be sitting in a field?"

He jostled against me, took his voice low. "What you gonna give me if I tell you?"

Jobie's the one answered, said, "I put him there."

My hands rested on those overalls still folded in my lap. "How come he's coming along with us?"

Jobie said, "Quit worrying, Emily Ann," and skipped us like a flat stone across the river.

He and Nestor conjured a plan of some sort, a thing I meant to get hold on, to examine its workings.

I hugged my Charlie clothes to my chest, reminded Jobie to pull over someplace private before we hit the city.

He brought us down to second gear, slowed our pace to little better than a crawl. "How come we gotta pull over?"

I poked a glance at the colored man, tossed my gaze back to the preacher's boy. "So I can change my clothes."

Stupid boy! He spit off a chuckle, spilled my secret to Nestor, told how I had to pretend to be a boy if I expected a full glassine.

The black man snatched those denim overalls from my grasp, held them aloft like he meant to study them for clues. "Gotta wear these, huh?" he handed them back. "Well then, put 'em on!"

Giggles tucked neatly into the nooks and crannies of my words. "I can't change in *here!*"

Nestor pulled back, gave me a long gawk. "Ain't shy, is ya?"

Jobie cackled like a loose goose. "Ain't a shy bone in *this* girl's body."

A silver flask found the black man's hand. "This Pig fella might 'spect you get bare; what then?" He dangled the drink in front of me.

'Cept Jobie's the one grabbed that hooch. "Ain't no *might* about it," he said, twisting the cap a-loose. "And there's nothing she can do gonna get us all we need."

Nestor stole his flask back, returned it to his pocket. "Gots to be *straight*, a job like this."

I went to the preacher's boy for answers. "What's he mean?"

Jobie took us off the road just shy of the city, set us alone in a field beside a stand of mulberry bushes, snuffed the engine's growl.

The colored man's the one did all the talking. "If they's mor'n one fella inside that house, you come right back on out. If this Pig the only one, we comin' in ten minutes after."

Facts jabbed me hard. "You aim to *rob* him?"

Nestor fished a pack of Chesterfields from his breast pocket, shook one a-loose. "What Pig gon' do, he gon' take your lily-white ass and give you a measly *piece* of hop in return." He dragged a blue-tipped Lucifer across the dash, dipped his cigarette into its orange glow, pulled up a grin to make the devil himself proud. "Now, if you're so shoot-fire *curious* about such ways, well then, when this job is done, you want, I'll tap that backside for ya, teach you what's what."

Jobie didn't tend to jealousy, wouldn't even defend what's supposed to be his. The boy just tossed a nod toward those lonely bushes, narrowed his lazy gaze against mine, and said, "Now get along and get changed, Emily Ann."

*   *   *

Distance collapsed underneath itself like sand gone through an egg timer, settled that borrowed Ford on a corner of Pig's very street, left us only a block away from the fat man's crooked shack.

Nestor's the one ran his mouth like a whippoorwill's ass, ticked endless instruction from the tip of his tongue, made clear to anyone listening he—not Jobie—had charge over *this* trip. "Let this Pig fella do his mess, his sweet-talkin', whatever," he said, kicking his door wide. "We gon' come save you before he gets too awful far."

I hopped a-loose of the truck, followed the black man onto the sidewalk. "You won't hurt him, right?"

He took up DeShay's blue ball cap and fixed it to my head. "Ain't nobody gonna get hurt," he said.

"Promise?"

Something about that man didn't quite fit him. It's almost as if he only played at being colored.

He sucked on his Chesterfield, held on to its smoke. "You sweet on this fella?"

"Just don't want anybody getting hurt, is all."

He tossed that cigarette, stamped it under foot. "I give you my word, baby girl."

Jobie Pritchett added nothing at all to our moment. He stayed back of the wheel, kept apart from me and Nestor, as if second thoughts like a sharp stick poked and jabbed at the familiar boy inside this strange new man.

"Ten minutes," Nestor repeated, "—then *we'll* take over."

My shoes worked up a nervous rhythm against the sidewalk.

Long shadows like dirty fingers reached out from between darkened houses forever been empty.

Wouldn't nobody hear a girl scream on *this* block.

Does he expect that coded knock? I wondered, finding Pig's place exactly where I last left it.

Henry Ford's machine mingled with those dirty fingers somewhere down the street. They wouldn't just leave me to my own, would they?

On wobbly legs I gained that rickety front stoop; its rotting lumber squealed like tortured rats beneath my meager weight. My knuckles drew wood, tapped a knock not so coded.

A space opened between door and jamb. The moon-faced man took his time to gawk.

Fatty Arbuckle—*that's* who Pig called to mind.

He pulled the door wide, scattered his gaze to the scene at my back. "Didn't bring that monkey, did you?"

"Uh-uh," I said, already gone warm and slippery where my legs come together.

"No talking, Charlie boy," he said, tugging me over the threshold. "Give a nod or a shake, I ask a thing needs answering."

Fire milked an orange residue from a candle burning somewhere in back. Fresh bacon leavings scented the air with a casual recollection of home, of Papa.

My conscience stumbled between contrary notions either begging my immediate rescue or hoping Jobie and that other one just might leave me be for a spell—long enough for curiosity's sake, is all.

Pig's heavy hand perched on my shoulder like a menacing bird. "How about we smoke some?" he said. "Just a taste."

I tipped a quick nod—just like he said.

'Cept Pig tossed in a nod of his own, a subtle thing that landed on those stairs. "Go on up," he ordered. "I'll be along in a sec."

A breath caught in my throat, nervous and tight. DeShay's warning about snakes and spiders crawled through my mind.

"Uh-uh," I said, backing away.

The long hiss of a frustrated sigh slipped through the fat man's lips. "Monkey said something, didn't he?"

I offered him nothing, no nod, no shake; I just stared up at him, trying like the dickens to read him in the dark.

I never realized how soft his gaze could be.

"Fine then," he finally said. "Got another room in back." A case of the hurry-ups got into him, like maybe he knew others had makings on this moment. "Come on, now; ain't got all night."

Kerosene fed the hungry flame in a lamp atop a modest kitchen table. Wasn't any clutter at all in his eating space—but for a cast iron skillet reckoning its next service at center of a crouching potbelly.

Mama never kept her kitchen so clean.

Pig's hand found the small of my back, gave me encouragement toward the tight space he meant for us to share. "Go on and sit down," he ordered, nudging me closer to a fancy sofa tucked beneath a lonely window.

Moonlight spilled in, splashed everything with its silver shine.

Pig whispered, "Don't want your money, understand?" His hand fell lower, grabbed my bottom, squeezed at it like it was so much biscuit dough. "This back here is what I want. Even trade. You up for it?"

Uncertainty swallowed whole that curiosity I'd foolishly dared sport with. A familiar recollection took up with the resulting void, spun memories of that cool glass stem Mama used in taking my body's temperature during childhood bouts with fever and whatnot.

Would it be like that? I wondered.

And what of Jobie Pritchett and that other one?

Pig lowered his bulk against the sofa, pulled me deep into his atmosphere like a helpless chunk of ice caught up in the sun's draw. A full glassine shined in his hand.

"Just a taste, mind you," he said, pinching a small piece into a smooth wooden pipe.

The flash of a Lucifer gave me a start, had me looking past the kitchen, looking for those other two.

Smoke came easy to my lungs, a good long pull, enough to put heat in my blood.

I handed the pipe back, waited for Pig to have his own go with it. 'Cept Pig, he ain't one to partake in the things he sells to common folk.

"Ain't getting *me* hooked on that shit," he explained, sliding the pipe beneath the sofa.

My head took on air, filled itself full of nothing and everything all at once—the way a good piece of hop will do a person.

Pig's voice came soft as his brown-eyed gaze. "I'm gonna let you talk some, Charlie," he said, tossing an arm across my shoulders. "I got a question needs answering."

My mouth had gone dry, sweet. I swallowed against a word, managed a low, "Okay."

The fat man leaned closer, his lips brushed my ear. "Do you catch lickin's?" he asked.

That brief taste of hop set my mind sideways, had me conjuring ideas of chasing *chickens*.

'Cept Pig didn't say "chickens."

"Caught my fair share," I admitted.

"What for?"

"Sassing, mostly."

Pig's tone dipped husky, conspiratorially. "Who's the one does it?"

My own voice slipped on a whisper. "Mama, usually—'cept Papa tanned me once."

Even a few years removed, that shame *still* gave my belly an awful twist. I mean, I'd only swiped a piece of penny candy from the general store, but to Papa, well, it didn't carry much difference from robbing a bank. A thief is a thief, he'd said.

Pig's finger slipped beneath my chin, brought my gaze to meet his. "How'd he know you stole it?"

"Nola Patterson," I mumbled. "She told on me."

Words soft as cotton tumbled a-loose of his lips. "I wanna dish you one."

That ten-minute count had long since ticked away, and still only me and Pig stood company in his neat little space.

I said, "A lickin'?" Just to be sure.

"Ain't no negotiations going on here, Charlie." He laid an easy tug to my overalls, said, "Take 'em down."

That's all he meant to do?

Dish me a lickin'?

There's one of every kind in New Orleans.

My fingers fussed with those twin brass clips keeping my britches up. Jobie and that other one, they'd come soon enough, I figured, stretching time like taffy.

'Cept those hurry-ups, they got into Pig again, put him to clutching and clawing at those denim overalls till he had the things—and my under-pants—down around my ankles.

He put me on my feet, spun me ass-backward to his face, took my bottom in his meaty grasp. "Awful provocative," he pronounced, "—for such a skinny collection of bones."

Heat flushed my blood hot, set me to trembling for something had nothing at all to do with fear.

"White as fresh milk," Pig proclaimed, his fingers tracing the crack of my butt.

My voice trudged recklessly from a tangle of words caught in my throat. "Do it already," is what I said.

But even as he took me over his knees, steadied his hand for this new curiosity, I heard those footsteps, the whining cry from ancient floor-boards.

Its Nestor's voice broke the spell. "What's *wrong* with you, fat man?"

Jobie Pritchett traipsed in behind the colored fella, a shiny silver pistol in hand. Both intruders sported red handkerchiefs about their faces like train robbers in a Hollywood picture show.

I went quick at my britches and refastened those dull brass clips. Time shrugged off a tick or two of stone silence, just long enough to get my breathing close to a normal rhythm.

Nestor fixed on Pig. "Let me get this straight," he said, sounding more a white man than black. "You mean to *whip* this girl?"

Jobie had part in this, too. "Kinda shit is *that?*"

'Cept pig didn't flinch. "Kinda shit to get your head broke open, you don't get gone from my house."

I stayed near to the fat man, played like he and I shared equal in this mess, like I, too, held a victim's stake in the offending matter.

The colored man breached the doorway, squeezed into that small room.

Pig rose up from that sofa. "What you wanna do, monkey?"

The preacher's boy lured my gaze, dropped a nod. "Get outta here, kid," he said.

'Cept it's anger that got up in me. "I ain't no *kid!*"

A soft laugh came to Jobie's lips, as if maybe he'd had a pull on that flask after all. "Whatever," he said, letting his gaze slide away. "Just get going."

I could read it in his eyes, that disdain for all I lacked beneath those overalls; the idea that I could never be a big-boobed colored girl with a wide bottom.

I'd never be Jobie's favorite flavor.

Pig's hand found mine, pulled me down on the sofa behind him. "You ain't gotta go anywhere," he told me. "I'd never let anybody hurt you."

He cared for me; couldn't fake a thing like that.

Nestor's laugh came a-loose of him like a hoarse bark. "Got plans, do ya?"

"Gonna watch over her, is all," Pig said softly, dropping down beside me. His body leaned into mine; his lips brushed my ear again. "Got a nicer place than this, Charlie. I can take care of you real good."

My heart sunk low for what we meant to do to the man.

Jobie stepped closer, fixed me in his angry blue stare. "I said get *out!*"

Papa's voice issued from that stupid boy, got me on my feet and moving toward the door.

'Cept I held my ground in Pig's tidy kitchen, tucked myself away in gathered shadows.

Nestor spewed demands thick as black smoke, took up the stance of a fella intent on having his own way. "We'll take all the hop you have, fat man, and whatever else you've derived from the poppy."

Pig's voice came almost jolly, excited. "Sounds like you might be an *educated* monkey, huh? Well, learn this: You won't be long for this world, you take from *this* house."

I crept closer, moved up behind the preacher's boy.

Nestor tucked his hands in his pockets like he had a mind only to talk fishing or maybe the weather with the man. "And you're gonna do what? Sit on us?"

'Cept Pig, he knew the situation better than the rest of us. "Ain't *me* you gotta worry about."

From beneath that fancy sofa he slung a-loose a knife long as my arm.

Stupid Jobie, he's the one panicked, raised that silver pistol before Pig ever set his charge, squeezed down on the trigger.

The pop of lead shoved the fat man against the wall, dropped him on his backside like a punch from Jack Dempsey himself.

Nestor snatched the gun from Jobie's hand, hollered, "What's wrong with you, boy?"

The preacher's boy offered no response; he just gawked, is all, wide-eyed and terrified at the bloody mess he'd not allow himself to soon forget.

Pig's the one needed help, though.

His words came weak, stunned. "Don't let 'em kill me, Charlie."

I tumbled into the scene, took up beside the wounded man, and turned on that colored fella. "You *promised!*" I screamed.

Nestor's head went to wagging easy denial. "I'm not the one who shot him."

"*You're* the one promised he wouldn't get hurt!" I spat.

Pig's head raised up off the floor; he tugged me into his sad gaze. It's that unspoken accusation called betrayal that did him more hurt than any old bullet.

Jobie's mumbled words unstuck the moment. "Help him," he said, "before we *all* get the chair."

"*Help* him?" I ogled that hole in Pig's right shoulder. "And what am *I* supposed to do?"

'Cept Jobie meant Nestor. "*You're* the doctor. Do something."

I gained my feet, steadied my trembling body. "You're a *doctor?*"

"Two years shy," the colored man argued.

Didn't matter to Jobie. "Close enough," he said, snatching the gun back into his own hand. "See what can be done before he bleeds to death."

"Save *your* ass, you mean." Nestor yanked the handkerchief from his face and squatted beside the man. "Needs compression to slow the flow."

'Cept Pig had ideas of his own. "There's a phone in the front room," he told Nestor, taking hold on the handkerchief. "Send for a *real* doctor." He turned those soft brown eyes to me. "You broke my heart, Charlie. I only liked you, is all."

My lips moved, tried for something, for anything.

Pig tossed up his hand though, hushed me. "What you came for, it's under a loose floorboard in the closet," he said. "Now take it and get the fuck gone."

I dropped a nod, searched for an apology.

But Pig, well, he couldn't be sold on it. "A thief is a thief, Charlie boy."

Chapter Thirteen

I twisted and tugged at that shiny gold band attached to my finger, the new ring, the one making claim of my last name having gone from Papa's Teegarten to Jobie's Pritchett. And it wouldn't come a-loose, neither. The stupid thing, it bound me in fetters to a boy had as much use for me as Sunday morning hellfire does a Saturday night drunk.

I reckon you might label it regret, that long-toothed rodent of an off feeling gnawing its way through my innards.

And that preacher's boy, he saw no need at all to soothe the bite; he just blathered on about how maybe we'd find a house in Biloxi, one big enough to allow that *other* girl in with us. "Tell folks she's our cleaning lady, is all," he explained, aiming his car toward that very town. "Won't cost much. Three of us in one house."

I offered nothing of the four grand lollygagging beneath a loose floorboard back to Aunt Frannie's place. It's *New York* shined my dreams, not Biloxi.

My gaze wandered lazily among passing fields of standing cotton or leaning trees, whatever that piece of Mississippi meant to show of itself. "What am *I* supposed to do while we're down here?"

Jobie grabbed third gear, took an unlit Lucky between his lips. He spoke as a friend rather than a newly hitched husband. "Nestor's keen on you, said he'd take you to that speak."

We hadn't even consummated our nuptials and already he meant to push me off on another.

I smoothed a wrinkle from my skirt, pondered all my varied and scarce options. "Think they'll let me sing?"

The boy flinched a shrug. "Might not cotton to a white girl on their stage."

"Shouldn't matter—so long as I can carry a tune."

"True enough. But it's all colored down here."

I swiped the Lucky from his lips, dragged a Lucifer across the dash. "Shoulda seen me sing over the river," I told him, tossing rings of smoke against the windshield. "Folks love me in New Orleans."

Jobie's sidelong glance fondled me gently. "Folks love you in *Rayford,*

Emily Ann."

"Ain't the same, singing so old ladies can weep." I sucked that Lucky again, held on to the tails of its smoke. "Why do you suppose they cry?"

"Does it bother you?"

It did—though I'd never confess to such a notion. "Singing's meant to put people *happy.*"

Wisdom burned soft blue in Jobie's eyes, had me almost sorry I'd not be in *his* bed this night. "Ain't nobody always happy, Emily Ann; we're just not made that way." He pulled down on our pace, set us on a narrow run of dirt luring us toward the dipping sun. "Watch those faces sometime, when you're up there singing; there's plenty of sadness in those speakeas-ies."

A white clapboard mingled among ready cotton in a field just a toss from town. The little house sported airs of a petulant child demanding a treat despite its turn of naughty doings.

A colored girl gained the front stoop. Straight black hair washed over her shoulders like spilled ink.

"Is that her?" I asked, trying awful hard not to gawk. 'Cept this partic-ular girl, she's the sort *expects* all those loose-eyed stares, might even take offense should a soul look away.

Jobie's old Ford tilted in the girl's direction as if he no longer held sway over his own machine. "Her name is Della," he announced.

I flung the door wide, tossed my feet to the dirt, and held my ground through her curious looky-loo.

"This the new Mrs. Pritchett?" she asked, working a slow circle around my tense body. "Awful scrawny, you ask me."

I took my say. "Ain't nobody asked you."

Jobie meant to put us right. "Emily Ann's got a great voice for jazz."

'Cept Della could give a tinker's damn about such things. A grin curled around her full lips like a lazy cat settling in a puddle of midday sunshine. "Sassy, young, and white; guess you got it *all* in your hip pocket, eh?"

Jobie breathed off a sigh. I reckon he had expected a clash of sorts, bringing his wife along to meet his girlfriend.

We drifted inside the house like so much flotsam wandering away from the actual wreck. Electricity fed the lamp atop a table next to a fancy tan loveseat. The tinny sound of jazz escaped the tall radio skulking in a dark corner.

Della helped herself to another dig. "Got indoor plumbing, too. So you ain't gotta step your dainty ass in no ordinary privy."

Jobie grabbed up my suitcase and drew me to a room back of a kitchen free of the sort of mess I reckon I'd expected to find. "She's real sweet," he promised, "if you only give her a chance."

"Sweet as vinegar," I retorted, tossing myself against that wide brass bed. Box springs squealed beneath my weight. "I take it I'm sleeping here?"

The preacher's boy tipped a quiet nod. "Water closet's the next door down." He meant me to sleep alone—or at least not with him.

I had to ask. "Suppose I, you know…meet someone?"

Jobie read me right. "Ain't *my* business what goes on in here."

Dueling voices modulated up front of the house. A tangle of words unraveled into a sturdy line guiding the colored fella to that back bedroom.

Nestor peeked past the door. "Well look at you," he teased, eyeing my legs beneath that green skirt. "Up for a wild time tonight?"

"Always," I assured him, dropping back on my elbows, allowing my hemline to crawl toward my knees. Couldn't nobody snatch that smile from my lips—not even Della.

The Creole girl filled the doorway, attached her dark gaze to Nestor, made some utterance in the French tongue.

I sat bolt upright, gained my feet, made demands of interpretation.

Laughter filled the space between me and her.

Nestor's arms fit easily around me, hugged my body tight to his. His lips brushed my ear. "How about you and I go have us a time over to the Honeysuckle Club?"

*   *   *

"What's it gonna be?" I asked, tramping a path called to mind a fresh scar scratched straight through that stand of trees back of Della's place.

Confusion laid into the colored man's features. "What's *what* gonna be?"

The darkening sky rumbled like an empty stomach gone without more than just one meal. Jagged silver flashes jabbed the coming night over against the horizon.

"The way you talk," I said.

"What about the way I talk?"

"Sometimes you talk black," I explained, "and other times you sound almost like a white fella."

Nestor's pace slowed; his head dipped in mock shame. Nonsense flourished behind his gaze. "You know my secret," he confessed.

Those black shoes on my feet halted on a scrap of earth at center of those woods. "What secret?"

"Shoe polish."

I scratched a vague itch on my arm, tried like the dickens to read the man. "What about shoe polish?"

"Ain't really black," he whispered. "I use shoe polish so I only *appears* colored."

It's his laughter got me riled, put me in a mind to sock him in his shoulder, demand something closer to the truth. "And no teasing this time," I ordered.

That grin of his softened into a genuine smile; his fingers found my cheek, caressed my skin. "I studied medicine in England for a spell," he admitted.

"So you really *are* a doctor!" I exclaimed.

Nestor's countenance tumbled into a dark thing. "I quit with two years remaining."

"Quit?" I pulled away from his touch, studied that darkness leaking through him. "Why on earth would you quit? I mean, a *doctor!*"

"You sound like my father," he said, fishing a pack of cigarettes from his breast pocket. "So easily impressed by a fancy title."

I snatched that pack from his hand, shook a-loose a pair of Luckys. "A title brings respect," I assured him, accepting his proffered Lucifer.

"Not in Mississippi, it doesn't." He took a Lucky to his lips, drew down on an anxious suck of smoke. "Just be an educated nigger around here, is all. Ain't no white man gonna ask me to tend to his wounds."

"But you could help other coloreds."

"Not if it ain't my calling."

That preacher's boy came to mind, brought all sorts of notions concerning callings and such. 'Cept Jobie had drawings to fall back on.

I dropped that Lucky in the dirt, snuffed it under my foot. "If not a doctor, then what?"

"Gonna own my own club, is what." Nestor took up his pace again, shuffled along toward a song I knew by heart. "Ain't gonna be like no Mississippi speakeasy, neither."

"Plenty of money to be had in a speak—don't matter *where* you put it," I said, lending one ear to Nestor and the other to those delicate notes seasoning the night.

"Can't always be about money, baby girl. I've been to clubs in Paris; I know how it can be."

My gaze sifted that colored man like a handful of loose pebbles. "Paris, *France?*"

An easy chuckle left his lips, put our moment right. "Doesn't matter over there—your skin color, I mean. Me and you, we could share a hotel room, and nobody would bother to take notice."

Saxophone rose high on a warm breeze, sprinkled us with its familiar tune. I could sing that song in my sleep.

Our legs broke eager across a clearing showed off a heap of old lumber piled into the fixings of an ancient barn. The music seeped from its cracks and crevices like a determined scent. Cars of every make lay willy-nilly along the dirt yard.

Nestor pulled up short. "Might take some talk to get you inside."

"Tell 'em I wanna sing," I said, certain of my prospects.

"Ain't gonna happen—at least not tonight."

"Why not?"

We gained a patch of shadow up tight to the barn. That joyous cacophony behind its walls sent a tremble through the black soil beneath our feet.

Nestor touched the door with a knock. "Don't you say a word," he ordered, his voice a harsh bite.

The colored fella inside, he wasn't anything special; nothing distinguished him from any other doorman in a thousand speaks from here to New Orleans—'cept that nervous tick he had, the one set his peanut head to waggling left and right. "Nuh-uh!" he barked. "She ain't gettin' in *here!*"

Nestor knitted wisdom to logic. He strung a fine bunch of words together, lines carrying enough sway to spring a condemned soul from a death owed.

But that doorman, he couldn't be persuaded. "Can't do it," he swore, looking me up and down like I'd gone sour in the sun. "*Won't* do it."

I sought to plead my own cause. "Why not?"

Nestor wedged himself between me and that peanut head. "How about I give you this?" he said, allowing bribery its own plea.

The doorman swiped that glassine for his own purpose, held it against the pale light dripping from a lone bulb above. "Tell ya what," he offered, sniffing at his payment. "Bump gonna be done in a short piece. You two wait outside, I'll see to it he comes talk with you."

Nestor dropped a nod, tugged me back into the shadows.

'Cept that doorman, he conjured a secondary notion meant to pink my cheeks. "You could always leave the girl with Ruthie," he hollered, holding his post. "She's right now up in the office."

Nestor waved him off, hid us in the unseen.

"Who's Ruthie?" I asked, snugging up against the barn.

The colored man called up his flask, coaxed the cap a-loose, took down an easy swig. "Ruth is sister to the owner."

I waited my turn at that liquid heat, my eyes catching colored folks wandering in and out of the club. "She could get us in, can't she?"

Nestor breathed off his easy laugh. "Ain't a thing about *us*; it's getting *you* inside gonna be tricky."

That cool flask met my waiting hand. I introduced it to my lips, drew off a double portion, welcomed its burn into my blood. "Let's talk to Ruth."

"She's too complicated."

"How so?"

He stole away the drink, sneaked it back to his pocket. "Ruth is gonna expect from *you*, not *me*. Understand?"

I understood just fine. Ruth likes girls, that's what he meant to say.

"But if she can get me in…" I said, almost committed.

Nestor's eyes rolled in his head like a pair of dark marbles. "Bump's the one has say over who takes to his stage. It's *his* band up there playing." He fished a Lucky from his pocket, dipped its tip in a flashed Lucifer. "Besides, I can't sell that hop without his blessing."

"Bump plays?"

"Piano," said Nestor. "Made a fortune in New York."

I leaned into the barn, accepted that proffered Lucky. "Then how come he's back in Mississippi?" I asked between puffs.

That's when the man himself divided the shadow, yanked me and Nestor into his glow. He raised that glassine in his hand. "Dew says you give this to him."

Nestor managed a quick nod, said, "Got plenty more."

The fella called Bump worked me over with his liquid gaze. "Ain't it past your bedtime?"

I searched for a sass of some sort, a thing meant to put me right. 'Cept nothing clever found my tongue.

Bump laid a tilt to a gray fedora atop his head, took up real close like he aimed to study my potential. "How come you want in my club?"

A tangle of words caught in my throat, shriveled my confidence like night crawlers on a hot sidewalk. "I—I sing jazz," I stammered.

"White-girl jazzes, huh?" He swept a stray wrinkle from his pinstripe suit—the same smoky gray as that hat he sported. A nasty notion bent his lips. "You meet Ruthie yet?"

A bead of sweat like a lover's fingertip traced my spine beneath my blouse. "Just wanna sing, is all."

"Not in *my* club," he bellowed before ditching me for Nestor. "Can't have *you* selling hop in my place, neither. Take what you got to the bunkhouse and give it to the Chinaman. You'll get yours when it's gone—minus my cut, of course."

*   *   *

"Used to be slave quarters, that bunkhouse," Nestor explained, traipsing us deeper into the night. "Bump bought it all, the whole plantation—including the big house on the hill."

My legs moved double against his, just to keep pace. A million questions grew wild like toadstools in the damp darkness inside my head. "He made all that money in the clubs up to New York?" I asked, plucking at the important ones.

"His band made some of those phonograph records, performed on the radio a dozen times. But it's all those other folks singing songs Bump wrote put the most money in *his* pockets."

"I gotta get to New York," I said, toeing that narrow path.

"Ought to consider *Paris*," claimed the colored man, his fingers loosing from his waist the money belt concealing Pig's stolen stash.

We fell into a puddle of dirty yellow light at the foot of an oblong building butting against a quiet field. An up-tempo number splashed through an open window, dared my feet to tap out its rhythm—Bump's tune, that sweet ditty spinning reckless from Edison's Victrola.

A short, slanty-eyed fella caught us at the door, made no bother to wait for a knock, like just maybe he knew to expect us. Foreign words issued from his thin lips.

French, he spoke. 'Cept how's a Chinaman know French?

Nestor waved that money belt like a white flag of surrender, spat out a retort in that very same foreign tongue, cut his line toward the door. "Wait out here, Emily Ann," he ordered, disappearing inside.

By all rights I had a share in this deal, seeing's how I'm the one led him to the stuff. That alone entitled me a say in the matter.

'Cept I really didn't want a say—not the way we came into it.

The colored man darkened the doorway, found me loitering in the shadows. "You up for smoking some?"

No need to ask *me* twice. Besides, smoking it ain't the same as stealing it.

I followed him inside, squinting through a dim haze coming off candles set here and there. Four narrow bunks stood sentry along the west wall; four others took up with the east. A quiet riot broke a-loose around a pair of tables hunkered at the center of it all. Some fellas took to the pipe; others tipped liquor jars, played cards. One lonely figure consorted with Morpheus atop a corner bunk; a dirty spoon and bloodied needle riding the nightstand did little to conceal the slumbering man's secret.

At one table a dealer shuffled a loose deck. His slippery gaze attached itself to me. "How 'bout a run at naked draw?" he asked, grinning like a grim wolf.

My shoulders tugged up a shrug. "Don't know how to play," I confessed.

Nestor tucked in real close; his breath warmed my neck. "Strip poker," he whispered directly into my head. "And the way these ones cheat, you'll be buck naked in only a few hands."

A burst of giggles stirred my belly, mingled with a thousand butterflies. I put down on a chair nearest to the dealer, received his proffered pipe, drew off a long pull. "Suppose I do play?" I said, reaching for a half-empty liquor jar. "Do shoes count?"

Truth be told, I had no intentions of fooling with the sort of game could make me bare before strangers. 'Cept all those oily eyes, red-rimmed from opium and cheap whiskey, came silently open, took notice of *me*— that's what worked my curiosity to a higher pitch.

"Shoes ain't never count," said the dealer.

Nestor and that Chinaman fed each other hushed lines in that foreign tongue, tossed gawks at me like I'm the one might cause the biggest commotion.

I tipped the jar to my lips, took up my cards, swiped a lit Lucky from the dealer. "How's a Chinaman come to speak French?" I asked.

The Injun boy directly at my right made claim the man came up in a place called Indo-China; the French just marched on in and stole away that corner of the earth. "Same as the white man took *my* people's land."

The dealer, himself a colored, managed a solemn nod, a means of solidarity with this brash Choctaw. "Stole more than just *land* from *my* people, he did."

Their words conjured images of a vulgar being, singular in nature, traveling the night sky, laying claim to whatever people and places happened to come under his wrinkled white sole.

'Cept it ain't my place to offer up apologies; I'm not the one did all that taking.

"I ain't playing no games gonna make me lose my clothes," I said, double dipping in the nearest jar.

Heads went to wagging; complaints made it to sound.

That Injun boy set down a calculated measure meant to leave me sticky with guilt. "She drinks our liquor, smokes our hop, and still she won't share any of that lily-white skin hiding beneath her skirt."

I sucked on a Lucky, tossed smoke in his face. "You say it like I'm sure to lose." My bottom shifted against the chair. "Might could be *you* coming a-loose of your coverings."

He leaned in close, like he aimed to tell me all he understood concerning God and life and how hot the sun could get, said, "Ain't chicken, are you?"

I met him in the space between us. "Ain't scared of anything," I assured him. "I just won't play that sort of game with strangers, is all."

A fine collection of names tumbled into my lap, five in all—minus that snoozing heap of bones, of course. 'Cept with a rush of excitement at catching so much attention, combined with opium and hooch flushing warm in my blood, I could not retain a single moniker those boys flung at me.

My elbows took up with that wobbly table; words ran into one another leaving my mouth. "Can we do a few practice hands?"

That Injun came off awful eager, impatient. "Nobody *practices* poker!"

"Fine then!" I huffed, shoving away from the game. "Can I at least use the privy first?"

Wicked grins curled tightly around serpentine lips; forked tongues tasted the air. To tell it in a fairy tale: a mouse had wandered into their nest.

"Privy's out back," claimed the dealer, gathering loose cards, making a show of his shuffle. "Check for snakes 'fore you sit down."

I pulled up on shaky legs, stumbled toward the rear door, fooled with an image of those boys cheating me down to nothing but my scent and a pair of scuffed black shoes.

Nestor and his Chinaman loitered just outside, trading secrets I'd never come to decipher on my own.

The colored man broke a-loose of his foreign talk, took to following after me like he had a mind to join me in that crooked outhouse. "You see how they look at you, don't you?" he said, keeping step with my pace.

"See just fine," I assured him.

He stopped me short of the privy. "They won't play you fair, Emily Ann. Ain't a one gonna settle for only a gawk, either."

Might have been the opium. Or maybe all that bootleg whiskey is what shook me free of my own center. Whatever. All's I know is urges came to me. Even a simple insinuation of being shared put me warm and slippery where it matters most to a girl.

My body went light in its tilt toward Nestor's; my voice came low, giddy. "You going jealous on me?"

Righteous indignation of the Baptist sort etched its very presence on his countenance. "I'm not jealous!" he insisted, leaning closer, pushing my tilt back to an upright stand. "I'm just saying you ain't like that, is all."

"And how would *you* know what I'm like?"

To read the man's face, you'd have figured I spat on his mama. "You're absolutely right, Emily Ann," he concurred, drawing back from me. "I *don't* know you." His feet swept up that path cutting through the middle of the woods, carried him from my immediate line of sight.

"Hey!" I hollered, peering into the dark. "Where are you going?"

Nestor sent nothing back, not even the sound of retreating footsteps.

"Shit!" I whispered, setting my legs in motion. Through the inky black, along the scarred-earth trail, I ran, scampering toward the one I'd determined to stay with.

Mosquitoes big as birds swooped and dived like bats from a belfry, fixing on the warm-blooded one moving through their feeding grounds. Owls taunted from high trees. Saw grass reached across the path, tugged angrily at the hem of my skirt.

I dropped into a gully; my feet stumbled against rising ground. Just ahead, beyond a nearing incline, an orange glow opened the night. Gasoline-tainted smoke choked the air, cleared the mosquitoes from their hunt.

I gained that hill, fell to my knees, tried to hide in the rich soil.

Must have been more than a dozen, those fellas in their starched white robes, those silly pointed hats, all gathered around Salvation's cross, alive with the fires of hell.

Hateful words clawed at the sky, opened wounds in the air meant to fester and kill with their poison. I knew plenty of these sorts, living among the rest of us like they belonged, as if they somehow did noble service to our towns, our state, our families.

Blood rushed through my ears like hot wind, blotted out the devil's clamor. My heart beat and banged against the bones of my chest.

Fingers, like the fangs of a spooked cottonmouth, sank deep into my ankle; a strong arm yanked me down that short hill with one sharp pull.

Panic pinched my words, forced them through my lips. "*I didn't see!*" I cried.

Nestor's meaty hand covered my mouth. "They stringing somebody?"

I shoved his hand away. "Just burning a cross, is all." The tight, angry ball of my fist connected with the colored man's chest. "Don't you *ever* sneak up on me again!"

Tears stung my eyes as I yielded to his hug.

"*My* house," he whispered into my ear. "It's closer than Della's."

'Cept Nestor fell blind to the pointy hat jabbing the air at his back. He couldn't see how close our necks stretched toward a rope-fitting in those awful woods.

"Please," I pleaded, the word thick in my throat.

The colored man spun on the interloper and froze, unable—or unwilling—to take up the silent challenge.

That lone figure stood tall and menacing in the dying orange haze. Dark eyes haunted his skull through narrow slits in his headgear. I'd been this close before, back at Rayford. Only last time I knew the shape belonged to Sheriff Dantley—though he never did speak.

Voices called out back of that incline; their hooting and hollering mingled with smoke and evil particulates, caught a breeze like the hounds of hell racing toward heaven.

My bladder went a-loose. All that liquor I'd meant to leave in the privy rushed hot with fear down my legs.

The Klansman's hooded head took to wagging back and forth as if it had ideas to twist free of his neck. Something akin to laughter broke through that heavy linen. Like a benevolent specter from the netherworld he eased back into the inky black.

"Git gone," he whispered, "—the both of you."

*   *   *

"Sorry, I don't have a regular bathtub," said Nestor, touching a blue-tipped Lucifer to a kerosene-soaked wick. "I have an old washtub, though."

I tossed him something shy of a commitment, allowed my eyes to wander the bare space of his shotgun shack. "What if they come *here?*" I asked.

The colored man knew better. "If they'd wanted us, they'd have taken us out there."

His lamp ran off the lingering spooks, put a comfort in the room, a thing claiming we'd be just fine through the night.

'Cept I still wouldn't sleep.

The gray washtub he spoke of huddled with a water pump in a rear corner, conjuring an image of a chubby lady and a skinny fella trading whispers concerning the pee-smelling girl wandered into their private gathering.

"Water's bound to be cold," said Nester, taking perch atop a stool squatting center of the floor. "But if you wash quickly—"

"Why do you suppose he let us go?" I asked, holding my ground between the man and his tub.

"I don't know." Contemplation worked fervently along the edges of his face. He had ideas, theories on the matter, though nothing concrete presented itself for a thorough examination. "Maybe he's following Daddy's footsteps—he just don't have a taste for it."

Shades concealed the only two windows up front.

I drew water from that hand pump, filled the tub to halfway.

Nestor offered me his back.

"Ain't gotta look away," I said, unhitching my skirt. "You're a doctor, ain't you?"

He watched me undress in a puddle of light coming off his lamp; those dark liquid eyes swore to memorize every part of me.

I rinsed my underpants in the cold water, draped the white cotton garment over the side of the tub. I didn't mind at all, him having a look. "The sheriff over to Rayford is Klan," I told him, easing into my bath. "Only he don't think I know."

Nestor shifted on that stool, kicked a-loose the shoes from his feet. "Go on and tell it then," he said. "It's *your* story."

"Ain't much of a story, really; he just caught me skinny dipping once. I came out of the pond, and there he stood, on the dock, in robe and hat—like that fella we saw tonight."

The colored man came off his stool. "How'd you know it to be the sheriff?" Bare feet brought him closer, right beside the tub.

My cheeks flushed hot scarlet; a hushed tone wedged itself between my words. "It's the way he stood, is all."

Nestor crouched low; his hands gripped the rim of that metal tub. "Did he touch you?"

Didn't matter, the water being so cold; all my secret parts went warm with anticipation. "Only gawked, is all. An awful *long* gawk, you ask me."

"Can't blame him," said the colored man. "You're nice to look at, Emily Ann." Long tapered fingers stroked my cheek, caressed my neck. "Were you really gonna play strip poker with those yahoos?"

Truth be told, I don't know *what* I would have done had we gone back inside that oblong bunkhouse.

I didn't tell that to Nestor, though.

"I ain't scared," I assured him.

"How far have you been?"

I wouldn't call it pride exactly, that ringing in my tone. Couldn't confuse it with shame, neither. "All the way," I answered. "I'm *not* a baby."

"May not be a baby," he said, letting that slippery gaze of his fall into the tub with me. "But that don't mean you're all grown up, either. Do you suppose you might ever fill out more than *this?*"

I dropped a weary glance over what I already knew of myself, capped a rough anger pulling pressure inside my chest, and hollered, "Does it even matter?"

"Does—to that Chinaman."

"What's *he* got to do with it?"

"He's the one has the money."

I raised my bottom out of that cold water, took to my legs; that anger found release like sticky sweat seeping from my pores. "I ain't *coursing* with no dirty-minded Chinaman for a few lousy dollars!"

Nestor's cocky grin slid sideways across his lips. "Nobody said a word about coursing, Emily Ann."

I climbed from the tub and accepted his proffered T-shirt. "Suppose you tell me what you're going on about," I said, wiggling into that dingy gray covering.

Nestor's wide hands rested on my shoulders. Something about that colored man called to mind Papa—it's that gentle quality, I reckon. "Do you trust me?" he asked.

"You fixin' to rob the Chinaman, too?"

Even his soft laughter stirred reminders of Papa. "Nobody gets robbed this time, baby girl. It's a plan beneficial to everyone involved." He dragged his stool over to the window, took perch—his way of saying we'd not be fooling around tonight. "Besides," he said, touching a Lucifer to a Lucky, "a dog never shits where he sleeps."

Chapter Fourteen

We made it back home to Rayford as Sunday evening milked the last bit of daylight from its purpling sky. Jobie Pritchett offered only spare scraps of conversation during our drive home—'cept when he thought to remind me from time to time that naked pictures done with a camera had nothing at all to do with real *genuine* art. And it didn't matter a pig's ear that Nestor's Chinaman promised a hundred dollars for just ten images.

"He'll make copies of those pictures," Jobie argued, "and sell 'em for ten bucks a pop. Make *himself* a fortune, he will."

I lugged my own suitcase up those rickety steps climbing the rear wall of the general store, tried like the dickens to sort through all the boy meant to say. "Ain't making money the whole idea behind such pictures?"

Jobie fit his key in the lock; he flung the door wide on its squeaky hinges. "There'd be hundreds of those things littering both sides of the river, Emily Ann."

"*Littering?*"

"Do you want strangers pointing at you, saying, 'Ain't she the French postcard girl?'"

I found a loose thread in his reasoning and took to pulling on it. "Doesn't seem all that different from you drawing *Della* without a stitch and selling *her* likeness."

Exasperation boiled over in the boy. "It's all the difference in the *world*, Emily Ann," he huffed, yanking me across the threshold into our quiet, quaint space. "What *I* do is *art*. Mine is one of a kind."

"You can still tell it's Black Della from Biloxi."

"You *ain't* posing for him."

I challenged him. "Says who?"

He countered. "Says that ring on your finger."

I gave that shiny gold band a twist, but it still wouldn't come a-loose. My own frustration bubbled at the surface. "And what good's a *ring*," I hollered, waving my hand in his face, "if you won't even consummate me?"

Panic, this time. It's what put him to searching the yard for nosy neighbors from high atop the stairs.

When Jobie spoke again, his voice came low, tight. "I thought we had an arrangement, Emily Ann."

I hadn't meant to unravel him like a useless old sweater; I only hoped to make known my own urges.

I pushed the door closed, leaned against it like I intended to keep the world—or at least Rayford, Mississippi—at arm's length. "What exactly is *my* part in this arrangement?" I asked. "What do *I* get from pretending we're happy newlyweds? I've seen the ways of the world, Mr. Pritchett, and I know an arrangement means *both* sides are supposed to get something."

His eyes burned a warmer brand of blue; fully-formed ideas came to the boy in the guise of peace. "Nestor says they wouldn't let you sing in the club."

I corrected him. "Wouldn't let me through the front door."

Jobie gathered himself at the little oak breakfast table Aunt Frannie gave for a wedding present. Like a perfectly adequate ballerina he pulled lazy pirouettes behind the true bones of my discontent. "I suppose Della could talk to Bump, sort of smooth things over. She *is* his cousin."

'Cept blood wouldn't count for a whole lot in *this* particular matter. You put a young white girl in a colored's speak, and all sorts of bad elements have a way of poisoning the moment.

"She doesn't even know me," I said, drifting toward him like smoke. "Can't say she likes me much, neither."

Jobie took offense at that. "Della likes you just fine. She opened her home to you, didn't she?"

I took to his lap, straddled that boy face to face, determined to bend his lust to my very own will. "Nobody's gotta know what we do up here, Mr. Pritchett," I promised, easing a subtle squirm against his lap.

He couldn't retrieve that low moan of hunger once it got out. "I know, Emily Ann," he whispered. "I know."

"Won't be a sin, neither."

'Cept that stupid boy, he went and ruined everything. "But I made a *promise*, Baby."

"Promised what?" I demanded, tasting anger behind my words. "Promised you wouldn't lay with your own *wife?*"

"I'm sorry," is all he could manage.

But I knew the truth. "She's jealous of me," I proclaimed.

"How so?"

My hand waggled that piece of gold in his face. "She'll never get to be Mrs. Pritchett in *this* lifetime."

His angry shove separated me from the very one who swore to love and honor me till death puts one of us under. I reckon a stupid old promise counts more than a vow before the Almighty—or so some seem to believe.

"At least *Della* understands our arrangement," the boy grumbled, gaining his feet. "I only wish *you* did, too, Emily Ann."

*   *   *

Footsteps on the stairs outside, is what yanked me from my daydream—a dirty little smudge I'd conjured while lying in bed.

Lemon-yellow sunlight splashed against the pulled shade, gave shape to the boy on the other side of that locked door. Wasn't no Jobie Pritchett, that much I could tell. This one here, he ran too short and too skinny to be the one called himself my husband.

Gave me ideas, though.

I allowed a second round of knocks before gathering myself from the privacy of my early morning fiddling, scavenged my nightshirt from the floor, and composed myself at the door.

The shade snapped high.

Tommy Letts offered his crooked grin.

I parted the door a crack, already certain of the direction we'd be traveling. "Jobie's at work," I told him.

"I know that, Baby," said Tommy, leaning hard against the doorjamb. Jobie's best friend, this one. "Come to see could I take you to breakfast, maybe."

I cast glances like rune stones over the boy's shoulder, reading to see if we truly were alone. "Already ate," I said.

"Got some Co-colas in the car—"

I blurted, "Teach me to drive?"

Tommy Letts ain't exactly the most handsome sort to gawk at, but even homely fellas sometimes make amends for it with simple charm. "Sure thing, Emily Ann. Driving's an easy enough task."

I took up a baby blue sundress from my closet, pulled a quick change in the bathroom, and followed the boy down the stairs to his car.

"How 'bout I drive us out of town first?" said Tommy, sliding in behind the wheel.

Small talk filled gaps between drawn-out slabs of silence—mostly ideas concerning the rattling Packard's clutch and gear system, and could I reach the pedals with my legs being so short. Tommy's the one had the most to say about that, using the moment to pat my bare knees as often as he would.

We made it to Mr. Norprin's cotton fields, just beyond the schoolhouse, before Tommy had us standing still.

"Ain't a thing to be scared of, Emily Ann," he assured me, switching our places lickety-split. "Just do like I say."

My left hand took hold on the wheel; my right grabbed the shifter. I'd watched this act a thousand times, that delicate balance between clutch and gas, and still the temperamental machine jerked forward and shut down. It did this two or three times, until whatever needed to catch finally caught, flinging the car and us toward no place in particular.

I discovered second gear all on my own, set that growling engine to nipping the morning air like some wild beast had a taste for warm flesh.

I didn't even mind Tommy Letts sitting so close to me, his arm tossed across my shoulders, that curious hand stroking my knee. Every now and again he'd pour instruction directly into my ear, talking me into third gear, reminding me to check my side mirror, make sure the law hadn't sneaked up behind us.

Driving came easy to me—that feeling of being in control.

I put us onto Posner Road, felt the condensation of the last few months settle on my skin like a sweaty sheen, luring me out to where I'd first drawn breath.

"You sure you wanna go there, Emily Ann?" Tommy asked.

My foot stepped on the clutch; my hand took us back to second gear, first gear; my arms twisted that wheel, pointed the Packard up the dirt drive.

Weeds had come up along the sides of the house, obscuring the flowers me and Mama put down just this past spring.

I snuffed the engine's growl, leaned against Tommy. "Where's those Co-colas you promised?"

'Cept Tommy had yearnings for a thing warmer than a cold soda pop. "Gotta make a trade, Emily Ann," he said, tilting his head closer to mine. "I mean, learning someone to drive don't come cheap."

That curious hand crept boldly beneath my dress.

My voice fell low, hushed. "What about Jobie?"

The boy's tone mimicked my own. "We both know he's not fooling with you—you ain't even his type."

Tommy's slow kiss swallowed my retort; his hand sported mischief down below. Blind fingers of something unclean breached my very center, slipped easily inside my secrets, searched with a certain determination for that pearl of great value.

My breath escaped soft and moist, a sinless sound, a thing almost pure.

'Cept it couldn't be like this—not outside where any old fool might see, lending credence to our intended iniquity.

I shoved that offending hand into his own lap, made a show of straightening my hemline, told him we ought to go inside. "Won't be seen in there," I said, tossing the driver's door wide.

"But you don't live here anymore, Emily Ann," Tommy argued.

"I can still get in."

"That's trespassing. And you *know* old man Kuiper would just love to sic the law on us."

I gained footing on the dirt drive, scattered a quick look across all that cotton coming up around the house. "Mr. Kuiper ain't gonna say peep," I explained, sweeping a wrinkle from my dress. "That dirty old man used to watch me skinny dip all the time. And he knows I know."

Tommy fell in to the proper order of things, snatched up those promised Co-colas, and followed me around to the back of my former home.

Lilacs scented the warm air; honeybees droned their busy song while picking over those late-summer blooms. Mosquitoes planned attacks from the overgrown grass.

My feet took to the porch with a notion of hesitance. My hand brushed the aged railing, contemplating that brief stretch worn smooth where I'd straddled the raw plank a hundred times before, my own secret pony, riding away lazy afternoons; my bare legs would kick like a waterborne frog, working in quiet desperation to achieve that slippery tickle.

Sounds of life had long since faded from our tiny wooden box. Didn't make a lick of sense to encumber that particular patch of ground with its rickety stature any longer.

"Ought to just tear it down," I said, leaning into the loose door.

Tommy agreed. "Ten years ago."

The barrier gave against my meager weight, put us inside the sorry space. My belly went tight with an expectation that would never again find fulfillment.

My voice fell low, soft; a thing meant for just me and God to hear. "I would give anything…"

Tommy whisked through the kitchen, set out for the parlor, for the bedrooms beyond. "Ain't so cluttered," he hollered, "—not like it used to be."

Aunt Frannie had got at all the good stuff—or at least those sorts of things she deemed worthy of rescue. Everything else, well, it'd be right here, waiting on the next tenant.

Tommy took to snooping, first through my bedroom, then on to Mama's.

'Cept it's Papa's old rocker that had *me* intrigued, the way it lazed in its familiar corner, just waiting for a return to what once had been.

I don't know if I expected that ancient thing to skitter away like some poor fraidy cat, but I approached with something akin to caution, as if one wrong move and I'd never set eyes on it again.

I offered it my back, settled my body gently against that smooth oak chair, got a feel for its perfect rhythm, the familiarity of creaking wood.

I whispered, "Anything at all…"

'Cept stupid old Tommy barged into my moment, the dumb dripping thick from his words. "Still got the beds here," he claimed, moving into the parlor. "Course yours ain't big enough for two. But that other one—"

"Come here," I ordered, gaining my feet. He was too small to be Papa, but he'd do in a pinch. "Sit on the chair and don't talk."

The boy's brow furrowed as if what little bit of smarts he may have had just leaked out his ears.

"Why?" he asked.

"Just do it," I demanded.

With a huff he obeyed, took his place right where I needed him to be.

I climbed on his lap, mingled his warmth with mine, took his arms around me like that's where they were always meant to be.

"Rock slowly," I said, closing my eyes.

For a moment I was there. *We* were there, me and Papa, like times before, back when this sort of thing stood for something.

'Cept Tommy Letts ain't Papa.

Those hands of his, bigger than a boy his size had a right to, found my breasts, took to squeezing on them like he had a mind to mash 'em even smaller.

"Stupid boy!" I hollered, slapping at his arms. I broke a-loose of him, gained my feet, fought like the dickens against those tears stinging my eyes. "You ruined it!"

Oblivion murked his gaze. "Ruined what, Emily Ann?"

Couldn't blame *him*, though; what did *he* know?

My legs carried me inside Mama's room, drew me into that dark space where I'd first came alive. It looked the same as it ever did—'cept for that missing dresser; another one of Aunt Frannie's takeaways.

Atop the bed lay a jumble of white linen—the last sheets they slept on together.

"Why don't you pull up the shades, get some light in here," said Tommy, sucking on a Lucky near to the door.

"Where's that Co-cola you promised?" I asked, finding perch on the foot of the bed. Their mingled scents had faded from the space, replaced by the musty smell of neglect.

The boy returned with those sodas and a fresh Lucky between his lips. I cringed just to watch him pop their caps with those near-perfect teeth of his.

"You mad at me, Emily Ann?" he asked.

I shook my head, accepted the proffered drink, took it down in three long pulls.

Tommy's body dropped beside mine on the end of the bed; he stubbed that Lucky against the sole of his shoe, tossed the spent end in a corner. "You okay?" he asked.

"Course I am," I countered, trying awful hard to recollect the last time we were really a family. "I don't think they were happy—Mama and Papa, I mean."

Tommy agreed, drawing a final sip off his Co-Cola. "Happy folks don't do those sorts of things."

My eyes sifted through shadows congregating around us, hopeful for one last glimpse, something I could savor, maybe even take with me.

I said, "I was born in this room."

Tommy set his empty bottle on the floor beside mine; his narrow body took a lazy lean toward my direction. "We didn't come out here just to ponder old times, did we?"

I rose on shaky legs, kicked a-loose the shoes from my feet. I knew to expect it might go this way. Truth be told, it's the only reason I agreed to traipse around with the boy—though I'd never admit to such a notion to the likes of Tommy Letts. And given me and Mr. Pritchett's *arrangement*, this sort of thing wouldn't even count toward cheating, would it?

"Shut the door," I ordered, peeling away my socks.

Tommy's brow arched. He said, "Who's gonna see us, Emily Ann?"

That baby blue hemline came to my fingertips. I hiked it belly-high, held it there against the inevitable. "You fixin' on tellin' Jobie about this?" I asked.

The boy shoved the door closed, worked up a look meant to convey a negative opinion concerning the stupidity behind such a notion. "Are you gonna talk me tired, girl, or are you gonna get naked?"

My dress graced the floor with a pale blue splash called to mind fallen sky; discarded underpants conjured visions of a puffy white cloud.

Tommy grew eager; he sloughed away his own clothes like they were an unnecessary second skin. Ideas of a wicked sort cavorted with devils behind his bold gaze.

I'd get no say in this particular doing.

Fine by me.

That wiry frame of his stirred easy recollections of Jobie Pritchett— though the one calling himself my husband stood a head taller, strolled leaner, wore confidence to a near-perfect fit.

'Cept Tommy, he owned that certain hunger a girl sometimes won't mind feeding.

I waded slowly into that familiar parental bed, floated lazily at its calm center, worked up a study of the boy's muscle and sinew, contemplated the way that silly appendage of his thought to draw attention to itself by reaching toward me with impressive determination.

The lay of my knees fell butterfly-wide.

When Tommy spoke, his voice came soft, almost unsure of itself—a watery sort of thing, really. "*Damn*, girl," is what he said. "Jeez *Louise!*"

And just what did he mean by *that?* I wondered, squeezing my knees together. "You act like I'm the first naked girl you ever seen before."

That brow of his arched again. "You saying I'm a *virgin?*"

A nervous giggle slipped a-loose of my lips. "Might could be, for all I know." 'Cept I knew the truth of it. Wasn't just rumors tying him to Esther Prowse a few summers back. Folks tend to talk when a girl disappears for most of nine months.

"Guess I got something to prove, huh?" he said, gaining advantage over top of me.

I wouldn't call him rough—though neither could I claim him to be gentle. Determined, is the proper word, I suppose, the way he got my legs to part again.

My breath caught and my eyes scrunched shut when his body pressed into mine.

"Beginner's luck, I reckon," he teased, sinking it to the root.

I breathed, "Lord a-mercy." That's all the sayings that came to me. "Lord a-*mercy*."

Those big hands of his got hold on my wrists, yanked me this way and that, held me fast against those squeaking bed springs, taught me lessons in rag-doll etiquette.

I can't put a proper name to it, that slippery tickle that seeks its beginning between a girl's legs, works itself into her belly, heating her blood like a fever gone rabid. I'd known it a time or two, though, at my own hands—and that once with the colored girl.

'Cept Tommy—that boy just plain worked harder for it.

His sticky voice dripped softly inside my ear, spilled words of the dirtiest sort meant to bend even a saintly girl to his own personal predilections.

My legs went easily around his waist; the toes on my feet curled under with intentions of hiding themselves away.

I wouldn't call it love, though, coursing my veins; Tommy just possessed a sense about him I yearned to keep all for myself. A thing I'm certain Jobie could provide if he was of the right mind.

The boy's rhythm caught a hitch; his muscles went tense like a loose string suddenly pulled tight. Inside my body, that mess of his let go; the stuff meant to leave a girl damaged, lost.

Tommy searched for his breath, tossed a-loose of me, dug up a fresh pack of Luckys from his shirt off the floor. "Gonna steal you away, is what I'll do," he said, dragging a Lucifer across the old oak headboard.

I sat up, snatched the lit cigarette from his fingers. Underneath, my body cast out his leavings, taking care his plague wouldn't leave *me* the way it left Esther Prowse. A girl can't get in a way if nothing remains, can she?

The boy's body leaned into mine. "Gonna have to grow your hair long again, though," he said, searching for secrets. "Did you really cut it short for some fat fella had a mind to dish you a lickin'?"

Smoke rings fluttered a-loose of my lips. "Who told you that?" I asked.

"Jobie."

"Jobie Pritchett don't know anything."

"Knows enough to keep you from dirty old Chinamen."

My gaze searched out the ripest place to draw blood. "It's only a few pictures," I argued. "No different from stuff that boy draws."

Tommy's fingers stroked my thigh. "Ain't like you *need* the money, right?"

"Hundred bucks is a hundred bucks," I said.

"A mere pittance, compared to that nest egg you got squirreled away."

I shoved his hand from my leg. "I ain't got *nothing* squirreled away!"

"I wouldn't call five grand 'nothing', girl."

Panic breathed silent threats at my neck, made promise that only dark shades of bad would ever come from this shared moment. "I don't know anything about no five grand," I swore, firm in my conviction.

'Cept Tommy, he somehow knew better. "Just give it back, Emily Ann; he just wants what's his."

"I didn't take it."

"Thibbedeaux did; you're the one holding it."

"Maybe Tanyon spent it."

"It don't make you rich, Baby Teegarten. You're still just Mississippi white trash—always will be."

I gained my feet beside that bed, searched for proof of that stupid boy's error. "If I'm just trash," I argued, "then how come *you're* here with me?"

The devil grinning at Eve, is what he called to mind. "Ain't nobody ever said trash can't be beautiful."

"Fine," I confessed. "I got it. 'Cept there's only three grand left."

Tommy pulled up straight, trimmed away the space between me and him. "Where's the rest?"

My shoulders managed a quick flinch. "Tanyon spent it, I reckon." I backed away from his grasp. "But why should *you* care about it?"

"Because Frank Rydekker *pays* me to care about such things."

The muscles in my body tensed up. Something akin to rage worked smoke signals down in my core. "You saying you work for the one killed Tanyon?"

That boy's grin washed away like chalk drawings left out in a spring rain. "I don't know nothing about no killing, Emily Ann."

"*I* do," I assured him. "Saw it with my own eyes."

I don't know that I'd call it fear, that dark mask obscuring his natural features—at least not fear for himself.

Those hands of his caught my wrists again, jerked me closer to him. "You ain't told anybody, have you?"

My head waggled left and right. "Not yet, at least."

"Forget what you saw," Tommy warned.

"And what of Tanyon?"

Quick and easy, the boy yanked me across his lap, like just maybe *he* intended to finish Pig's job and dole me that lickin'; an exquisite thing meant to draw down my deficit. "The flesh is weak, Emily Ann," he pronounced, tracing the crack of my bottom with a stray idea. "Where you got this money hid?"

Amazing, the delicate approach of his singular touch.

Goosebumps clothed my bare skin.

Damp breath mingled with my words. "It's hid at Aunt Frannie's," I whispered. "We can go there now—if you want."

'Cept Tommy Letts, he fixed on a notion of his own design. "Ain't no need to rush off, Emily Ann."

That big hand of his laid hard against my backside.

The sting of skin on skin set fire to my blood.

The smart girl might have gotten up and gone. 'Cept sometimes, well, I ain't exactly the smart girl.

*   *   *

I ticked off three grand and kept the rest back to myself. Twelve hundred, it shook down to—plenty enough to put a girl in a faraway place like New York. The way I reckoned, I'd gone through too much trouble to turn a-loose the whole pile to some stupid boy didn't have sense enough to step around dark fellas working both sides of the river.

Didn't bother Tommy any; he snatched up what I offered and turned tail after Rydekker's specter—supposing a stack of green paper might endear the boy to a new station in life.

Awful foolish notion, you ask me.

Some folks are just too keen on messing with snakes.

Aunt Frannie pulled a long gawk from the loveseat. Her silence pricked the sticky air, made it bleed. "Why are you here?" she finally asked. "And what sort of trouble have you gone and dragged Neesie into?"

The colored girl spied on us from shadows gathered like hoodlums just inside the kitchen.

She didn't blab on what we did that one time, did she? I wondered, trying to read the situation.

"I ain't dragged nobody into nothing," I assured my aunt, holding fast near the front door. "What'd she say I did?" I came off awful defensive for someone claiming innocence.

"Neesie hasn't said a word." Aunt Frannie gained her feet; her presence crowded my space. "A man called Frank did all the talking." Mama's voice, all her disappointments, is what I heard coming from my aunt's lips.

The back of my neck tensed against her accusation. "Frank who?" I demanded, offering heaps of righteous indignation to the one person not foolish enough to accept it.

"Give it back," she ordered.

A jagged piece of something stubborn caught in my throat, a thing some might call pride. "I ain't the one took it," I argued.

"But you're the one who has it."

The colored girl cleared that mob of shadows, fastened her dark-eyed gaze to mine. "Mista Frank only wants *his*," she explained. "Give it to him so he don't come back."

"Already did," I said, fiddling with naked recollections of the girl. "That's why Tommy Letts brought me here."

Even a mongoose couldn't sidestep Aunt Frannie's quickness in wrath. Her hand caught my throat; sheer strength slammed me hard against the wall, forced all the breathable air from my body. "You hid stolen money in *my* house?"

"I ain't done anything wrong," I cried through a narrow voice.

"You gave place to that son of perdition." Her slap rang loud in my ears; my cheek throbbed at the suddenness of it all. "Get out!" she screamed, turning me a-loose, turning her back on me. "And don't you *ever* come back here."

CHAPTER FIFTEEN

A subtle tilt put my body flush with the doorjamb. My thoughts swayed with Jobie's determined rhythm of razor and strop. Glimpses of Papa gathered along the edges of past recollections, of mornings spent watching him shave in our cluttered kitchen.

I'd never know him this way again.

Suppose he'd lived? And Mama, too. I wouldn't be stuck watching Jobie Pritchett scrape fictitious whiskers from that still-smooth face of his, that's for sure.

I'd still be caught in Rayford, though.

My bare feet breached the threshold. New York daydreams lured me farther inside the water closet.

The preacher's boy took notice of my company; he pinned my gaze against the mirror. Tommy Letts had gone blabbing to him, told all about our doings of a few days earlier.

A cautious grin softened his features. "You look awful pretty in that dress," he noted, dragging a razor along his jaw. "Got plans, have ya?"

"Already said I'm sorry," I scolded. "I shouldn't even have to say *that* much—the way you carry on with your colored girl."

Jobie's grin faded beneath a frothy lather. "Thing is, Della ain't your best friend, Emily Ann."

"And why should that matter? I ain't even your type. Remember?"

Words failed the boy. Couldn't hide a thing like jealousy, though. Feelings have a way of taking root—no matter how faithful our aim to pluck them up.

Like quiet smoke my body settled into that narrow scrap of space. My bottom found perch against the claw-foot tub. All those near-naked angles laid Jobie Pritchett more a man than a boy.

"I'll quit if you'll quit," I promised.

"Quit what?"

"Fooling around."

He relinquished his razor to the cool porcelain washbasin, took up a towel for his face, met me at the tub. "It ain't that easy, Emily Ann."

"Says who?"

He flinched the sort of shrug meant to free the boy from whatever rope of guilt had him tied up, had him tethered to me. "It just ain't," he said. "Besides, nobody's saying you gotta quit fooling around. Just saying find someone ain't Tommy Letts, is all."

It just seemed the most natural thing in the world, my body pressing against his. "Got any suggestions?"

Jobie pulled a-loose of my heat, gained his feet, and fixed himself for work. "I don't want to know about it, is all I'm saying."

I took to my own feet, blocked his escape from the water closet. "Why you acting jealous all of a sudden?" I demanded.

"I ain't jealous!" he hollered, incredulous over such a notion.

'Cept *I* knew better than he did. "Don't you go complicating situations," I argued, "setting me up to be something bad before God and Mississippi. *You're* the one decided on some stupid arrangement."

"But I ain't the one told you to take up with—" Any idea of a fancy retort just sort of came unraveled like life itself, leaving the boy with blank spaces he'd never fill up. "Do what you wanna do, Emily Ann," he said, shoving past my blockade. "I don't give a damn anymore."

"Liar," I muttered, though my word fell soft and short against his retreat.

Silence sprinkled the room with its ancient dust once Jobie had gone and left me to myself. Fragmented thoughts dared to bother me, those common whisperings meant to lay a shine to a girl's guilt, leave her naked in her shame.

'Cept the trouble with shame, it scarcely lingers long enough to conjure much change in a soul—at least in *my* experience.

The moment that colored girl laid knuckles to my door, Jobie Pritchett and his mess faded like last night's dreams.

Neesie held aloft that china doll she'd once coveted, said, "I brung you this," as if Stella no longer held sway with the girl.

"I didn't mean for you to give her back," I told her, waving her inside.

"Ain't g'wan need her, I git married."

Stella came comfortable to my hands, like taking hold on a hundred memories. "Who you gonna sing to, then?"

A pale scarlet flush pinked her up real nice. She'd thought about this on more than a few nights. "Git me a real one soon enough."

Ideas of a filthy sort cavorted back of my eyes, called to mind that Injun getting at her the way a boy will. And though it made not a lick of sense to draw off a jealous notion, there it stood, between me and the girl.

"You sure you want that sort of thing?" I asked, propping Stella on the table.

Neesie's nod tipped real subtle; a seed took root, its fingers spreading deep into that part makes a girl conjure dreams of escape. "Does it hurt?"

"Like the dickens," I assured her. "And he'll want at you probably five times a day—maybe more, him being Injun and all."

Second thoughts took up on Neesie's shoulder, promised better days if she'd only reconsider.

I gathered myself close to the girl, breathed in her natural scent mingled with the Ivory soap of her morning bath. "You don't have to run off with the first boy who asks," I assured her.

Her voice came soft, full of warm air. "Suppose I love him?"

My fingers stroked her cheek, her neck, found that small swell of breasts pushing at her dress. "You could come to New York with me."

"And do what?"

"Whatever you please. You could live with me and Jobie—"

"And wash your dirty drawers and clean your house? Uh-uh. Billy Blood say I don't gots to be nobody's wash girl no more."

A slow breeze carried me back to the table, stirred up notions on how to get my own way in this. "Gonna need money to get by," I said, dropping down on a chair. "How do you aim to live?"

Nervous fidgets hummed through the girl like mosquitoes at dusk. Thing about Neesie: something sweet or soft or shiny always comes along needing to get bought. Couldn't sit still on a dime, this one.

"Billy g'wan git work," she proclaimed, certain of a Mississippi Injun's prospects in a white man's Alabama.

'Cept I knew better than she did. "Maybe *I* could give you some," I suggested, reaching for my pocketbook. "Enough to get you started, at least."

"*Stolen* money?"

"Spends just the same."

Defiance needled her stance, drew that Ivory-scented girl nearer to my reach. "Billy won't take no stolen money."

"Ain't giving it to Billy," I said, making a show of all that green paper.

Greed shined its candle in her dark windows.

A person can usually count on that particular emotion.

The lilt in her voice ran low and delicate, a thing not at all confident in itself. "How much you givin'?"

"Hundred, maybe."

"What you 'spect back?"

My tongue went dry as toast; my tone cracked against the quiet air. "Same as last time."

"Ain't natural, two girls doin' them things."

"Didn't much bother you when *you* were the one getting," I argued, biting hard against the bitter taste of shame.

Neesie's shoulders fell loose and timid in that submissive sort of way. Another easy defeat for a girl not used to winning.

"You g'wan pay first?" she asked.

A confederation of varying denominations gathered all neat-as-you-please atop the table, daring that dark girl to snatch up the pile and stake our deal.

She went at her dress instead, yanking that gray linen uniform above her head, taking careful measure to drape it over the back of Jobie's chair.

Would that stupid boy count *this* an act of betrayal?

Neesie came close enough to touch. Her fingers tugged those underpants a-loose of her hips.

Just to gawk at the bare girl put me all agitated in that peculiar sort of way. Ideas wandered willy-nilly through my mind, conjured notions I'd not considered till this very moment.

"Awful nice to look at," I told her, my voice running low, conspiratorially. "Just wish I could draw you the way Jobie Pritchett might."

An odd tilt laid against Neesie's head; a grin took up with her lips. "Don't nobody wanna draw *me*," she said softly.

I whispered, "Come to New York with me. I'll take care of you. I promise."

"And how you g'wan do that?" she asked.

'Cept long about the time I meant to spend the details of my grand idea, some old busybody took to banging at the door.

Neesie's eyes went wide as supper plates. She yanked up her drawers and scampered for the water closet.

I drew up on calm, parted the door just a crack. "What do you want?" I demanded of this intruder.

Nola Patterson flung her gaze over my shoulder like she might somehow have a part in the goings-on up here. "You got that colored girl up here, Emily Ann?" she asked. "'Cause if you do, she'll have to leave."

My body shifted in the doorway, crowded that girl's nosy view of the space behind me. "Says who?" I argued, certain I cold fend her off.

'Cept Nola crowded right back. "Says my father." Bigger than me, this one; squeezed herself between me and the doorjamb; gained entry without much effort. "Folks might think we're running a flophouse for coloreds, if we ain't careful."

I fought like the dickens to keep my posture from taking that same timid dip common to girls of Neesie's station. "Jobie pays the rent," I said. "Shouldn't matter who we have for company."

"*We?*" Nola Patterson's gaze sported with Neesie's gray linen dress as if the lazy garment were some sort of flag, a thing to be captured. "Looks like *you're* the only one has company this morning, Emily Ann."

Half a dozen arguments traipsed through my mind, not a one suitable enough to push against her insinuations.

"We'll go someplace else," I offered, hopeful she'd leave us be.

But Nola had already turned a-loose stingy ideas of her own conjuring. "I ain't stupid with what's going on up here, Emily Ann." Neesie's dress came to her hands like a won prize. "And since Jobie ain't touching you, you gotta make do somehow, huh?" A crooked grin left the girl lurid in her appearance. "But ain't that sort of thing a sin? I mean, two girls—"

"We ain't done anything," I argued.

"You're a terrible liar, Baby Teegarten. I mean, why else would you keep a naked pickaninny in that water closet? She must only be bathing, huh?"

Anger flushed my blood with a rush of heat, laid my fists like two heavy stones meant for violence. "Don't you call her that," I warned, scarcely concealing my intentions to put her right.

'Cept girls like Nola Patterson—they can't be put right.

"Uh-uh, missy," she said, stepping close enough for a whisper or a kiss. "You don't get to tell me what's what. I own a share in *this* little secret."

I mumbled, "Ain't got no secret."

Nola knew better, though. "You just keep believing that, Emily Ann," she said, making for the door. "I got my eyes on you, girl."

Whether she'd take it to the gossip vine or keep it for threats, it didn't matter anymore. Just one more prod to get me gone from Mississippi.

After Nola's retreat, Neesie trickled in like a slow leak from an old oak barrel. Without a word, the girl wiggled into her dress and stood sentry by the table, right near that Rockefeller-sized pile of money.

I pulled up tight against her back, leaned my weight into her. I still controlled *this* situation. "You ain't done anything to earn all that," I said in her ear.

Her voice fell confident. "You got someplace else we might could go?"

We slipped away without anybody taking much notice. Just two girls, we were, going for a walk. Even Nola left us to our own, kept herself hidden inside the general store—probably deciding on what all she'd blab, given the chance.

The colored girl lollygagged back of me a step or two—as if old Jimmy Crow himself might be watching. The soles of her shoes slapped a syncopated rhythm against that hard dirt called itself Posner Road. Even her voice mingled well with the thumping cadence of her walk. "You suppose that girl saw to our aim?"

"Nola?" I wondered aloud, pulling down on my own pace. "Ain't did anything for her to see. Besides, the shade was drawn. Only thing nosy Nola's sure of is you were out of your dress."

"Could mean anything, that."

"Uh-huh."

"Could mean we was darnin' a rip in it."

"Yup."

'Cept Nola understood it right. Couldn't get a-loose of that simple fact. And the means to her silence would probably come steep.

We cut across the front yard, stirred up a mess of yellow butterflies hiding in the tall grass. Must have been a million of 'em, loitering in that sparse patch of ground Papa used to tend so neatly.

Neesie slowed up short of that rickety house like maybe ghosts had got to her. "This where you was brung up?" she asked.

My gaze followed after hers, searched out those blank windows. "You got shame for what we're fixin' to do in there?"

If I hadn't caught her in a sideways glance, I might have missed that nervous flinch meant to be a shrug.

"Okay," I said, picking harder at that scab. "Suppose I just give you the money—all of it—and you ain't gotta fool around with me. Would you take it and go?"

She took a while in pondering such a notion, as if the very idea had been hers alone without any prodding from me.

I reckon I knew her response even before that lovely head of hers tipped its subtle nod.

"Well it ain't gonna go like *that*," I assured her, breaking for the familiarity at the rear of the house. "Ain't a thing comes to us for free."

'Cept that swirling dust along the horizon stole away my attention, the way it floated on the breeze like a menacing smoke signal foretelling some grand doom to anyone fool enough to wait around for it.

I fell back of Mama's lilac bush, squatted low to the ground.

Neesie took up right beside me, her dark eyes reading the same signal. "Who you reckon it be?" she asked.

"Did I ever tell you about the man and woman come fetched me to Jackson the morning Papa died?"

A shiny black Ford pitched left onto the driveway, trundled toward us at its own leisure. Wasn't no Eunice Spatch this time.

Tommy Letts proved recognizable in the back seat. Couldn't hide a goofy face like his. But those two apes up front could have been anybody—or no one at all.

A nervous proclamation issued low and soft from my mouth. "I'll just give you that hundred dollars; we ain't gotta fool around."

A door flung wide, coughed up a tall fella in a pinstripe suit. Big as a barn, this one, all full of muscles.

Neesie leaned in close; her lips brushed my ear. "What gots you so spooked, then, huh?"

A thing of dark proportions coursed my blood like a spilled river ain't sure where it's supposed to go.

"If I say run," I whispered, "get you to the middle of that cotton field and lie flat to the earth."

Neesie wondered aloud, "Don't you know the boy in back?"

My gaze shifted to Tommy. "Thought I did."

The big fella plucked a cigar from his breast pocket and took it between his teeth. Blue eyes, he had—though not at all that warm sort of blue common to nice boys like Jobie Pritchett. His weight settled against Henry Ford's machine like maybe he could move it by strength alone—if he gave any real thought to it.

Tommy Letts offered a struck Lucifer through a rear window. "Girl at the general store claims they came this way," he said, touching that orange tongue to the man's cigar. "I'm betting they're inside the house."

Big Fella breathed off a heavy gray cloud, paid no mind to the stupid boy babbling nonsense from the back seat. Those cool blue orbs of his strolled through the scene, searched for signs of life. "Come clear," he announced, "and let's get this sorted, Emily Ann." Said it just like a lawman might.

Tommy's door yawned like a waking fool.

His feet slapped the dirt driveway. "Nola Patterson made claim those two split-tails might be Sapphic." Tommy moved toward the house, near to where me and Neesie held cover. "I'd pay good money just to watch a thing like *that*."

The crack of pistol fire tore the air from top to bottom. Its very suddenness tugged a gasp from somewhere deep inside the colored girl. Blackbirds raised a ruckus in their immediate retreat from ancient willows long familiar with man's sore sense of judgment against one another.

Tommy's body toppled at the edge of the grass.

Fingers scrabbled hard at the dirt as if searching for life itself, like just maybe he could drag himself to it.

He saw us then, me and the colored girl, huddled behind Mama's lilacs. Those eyes of his, failing in the afternoon light, fixed on mine like maybe he meant to send his passing thought from his own head directly into mine.

Only thing indicating he'd once been a living soul was that twitch in his left leg. Nerves, is all that was—like a rabbit shot clean in its head, though its feet haven't yet realized the futility of such useless movement.

Panic laid into Neesie like the fires of hell, put that girl to running as if the devil himself showed up to take stock of the situation.

The silver pistol shined with that high sunlight. Big Fella raised it steady, fixed its intentions against the colored girl's back. "You don't stop," he hollered, "I will shoot you dead."

'Cept Neesie got wise, heeded my words, fell low to the ground, found cover at the center of all that cotton.

Big Fella tossed a nod to the man behind the wheel—a boy, really— and ordered him to go retrieve that runaway colored girl before she crawled away.

Short and skinny, this one, but he wore that same cool blue stare, like maybe he and the bigger one were kin of some sort.

"You want her beat?" the boy asked.

My own panic got to squirming like a tin of fishing worms.

Big Fella drew on that cigar, contemplated the boy's offer. "Just bring her in, is all," he finally said.

I coulda run, bolted for the swimming hole out past the cotton. 'Cept

Neesie meant more to me than my own escape.

Big Fella ambled over to where I stayed squatting, got hold on those short hairs back of my neck, gave a good enough yank to take me away from Mama's lilacs.

"And you—" His meaty hand caught me hard upside my head, knocked me ass-over-tea kettle onto the dirt drive. "This ain't no game, girlie."

My body lay sprawled for the taking.

Every thought inside my mind tipped sideways and unruly. My own eyes failed to recognize the true horror of Mississippi sunshine sparkling in that lazy crimson puddle gathered beneath the dead boy's head.

It could be…beautiful somehow, that lonely, disfigured image.

Big Fella snatched me up, shoved me toward the car. "Get in the back seat," he ordered.

The boy returned with Neesie in his grasp.

Somehow the girl had gone smaller, even more vulnerable than she'd been only minutes before. Tears stained her cheeks; snot glistened above her lips.

I'm the one got her into such sorry straits.

I gave my voice a try. "You can let her go," I said, searching for conviction. "Rydekker has no truck with Neesie."

Big Fella squeezed in tight like he intended to take a bite out of me. "Get in the back seat," he repeated. Quick as a cottonmouth he latched on to the colored girl's arm and laid that cigar against her wrist.

Her scream is what broke me open, had me pushing fingers in my ears and singing spirituals to no one but me.

Neesie's body fell against mine in the back of that Ford. The tremble of it lured my heart into the very same rhythm.

"It's gonna be okay," I promised, wrapping the girl in my arms. "We'll see this through."

'Cept Neesie knew better. Even her sobbing had drawn up on silence. "Won't nothing be okay," she whispered. "Won't nothing be okay ever again."

*   *   *

We crossed the river just past noon. All those smells and sounds common to the city no longer came at me in their once-welcoming way. Truth be told, I never hated a place as much as I did New Orleans that particular

Wednesday afternoon.

Storyville's cathouses rose in the sticky heat like a gaggle of voodoo hoodoos bent on conjuring spells and stealing souls.

Didn't mean a lick to me. I'd gladly lay up in any one of those rickety old places if it meant Neesie could get back to Mississippi, back to her Injun.

A dark Victorian on Marais Street cast invisible hands toward the Ford, lured us nice and snug against the curb out front. Big Fella jerked us from the back seat and ordered Neesie and me up the stoop.

"Get on inside," he bellowed, herding us like a pair of wayward lambs. "Got folks mighty eager to make your acquaintance in here."

A familiar knowing saturated my bones, got in deep to the marrow. I'd been here once before.

Rose Thibbedeaux separated herself from a loveseat gone to tatters after a lifetime of reckless endangerment. Like a chintzy duchess, she crossed the sparse parlor, coursed a slow circuit around me and Neesie, read the both of us from head to toe with all the makings of a schoolboy's crush.

Would she remember me? I wondered.

And where were all the other girls, like that Abigail?

Rose took up with Neesie first, dipped a finger beneath the girl's chin, dared a gaze inside those dark eyes. "Lovely," she proclaimed. "though I can't use a Negro at *this* house."

She got to me next, brushed stray strands of hair away from my cheek. "Now *this* one—I can do quite well with a girl like *this* one."

If she recalled our past meeting, she offered nothing by way of recognition.

My voice came tight and high, dappled with hope. "I came here once with Tanyon. Remember?"

Rose Thibbedeaux leaned in close, wrapped her words in a whisper almost too delicate for a woman of her size and station. "I understand you are no longer in possession of your virtue, Emily Ann. Did that no-'count brother of mine relieve you of it?"

A familiar dark figure slotted himself tight against the kitchen doorway, sucked lazily on a cigarette, flung his own take on the subject of my lost virtue into the mix. "Agent DuShelle got at her," said Frank Rydekker, murderer of Tanyon Thibbedeaux. "Payment for not shutting me down, it was."

Rose's spine checked up real straight. "Coulda brought her to *me* first," she argued, confident in her business sense. "A thing like that won't go for cheap."

Rydekker nudged a low shrug. "DuShelle likes 'em fresh."

"So do fellas with deep pockets," Rose retorted.

Did she even know that this was the very man who killed her baby brother?

The cigarette fell from Frank's fingers; his shoe crushed it against the hardwood floor. "Let's get on with this, then," he said, holding me hard in his gaze.

"Take 'em around back," said Rose, nodding in the direction behind Rydekker.

Rough edges of panic pricked my soul. Half-formed ideas tried to gain shape inside my head. "I'll pay you back," I blurted, hopeful still.

The man's laughter shrank me down to next to nothing. "And just how do you intend on managing *that?*"

"I'll sing in your club," I promised. "Every night—if need be."

A smirk most evil bent his lips. His voice came low, cold. "Ain't enough songs to be sung gonna pay down what you took. Besides," he said, plucking a shiny knife from the kitchen table, "how you gonna sing after I cut out your tongue?"

Pleadings issued from me like some broken verse. "I got most of what's left—twelve hundred. I can sing away what remains."

These angry hands got hold on me, pinned me hard to the wall. "And what of the ten large," he hollered, "that boy of yours stole off me? How do you mean to square up *that* difference with a song?"

Big Fella stepped into the fray, took ownership of the colored girl as if answering some unspoken command.

I sifted my words, hoped for time enough to decipher this new accusation. "What boy?" is all I managed.

Neesie's posture went limp, like all her bones had clean dissolved away, leaving only her skin to make due with standing.

Rose Thibbedeaux wouldn't help us—or maybe she just couldn't. The big-boned woman bowed out of this dying moment, shut the kitchen door in her retreat.

My gaze fixed on Rydekker.

A threat spilled from my lips. "I'll tell Rose you killed Tanyon."

Frank's grip found my neck. "You talk too much," he growled, squeezing down on my air. "Got Tommy Letts killed, you did, telling him about my business."

Promise and panic mingled with salty tears, had me flip-flopping on myself. "I won't tell another soul," I swore.

That grip relaxed against my throat, became almost a gentle thing, like a lover's touch. "You're gonna spend a few days over to Earl's," he said, "getting acquainted with the needle. It'll put you in a mind to do all Rosie says."

Rydekker dropped a nod so subtle I can't say for certain I actually saw his head give a tip—or if I only imagined it. Didn't really matter, I guess. Big Fella saw and honored the cue. His heavy-handed toss met with Neesie's belly; plunged that long, shiny blade to its haft; laid the colored girl flush with the floor.

Crimson gloss seeped through dull gray linen like a horrible parlor trick.

My own legs gave beneath the weight of it all, flung me to the floor beside the fading girl. "*Help her!*" I cried. My hands pushed frantically against the source of all that blood, tried in vain to stanch its flow, to put it back inside that jagged hole. 'Cept a thing like that—only *Jesus* could manage such an act.

Neesie's body stiffened, offered a sacrificial twitch to the last gasp of life.

Couldn't collect *that* breath, though—not even with a jar.

Angry butterflies in black crowded my sight.

A sudden ruckus tore at the brief silence.

My fingers, warm and sticky with the life of the colored girl, filled my ears again, tried like the dickens to quell a racket long in the making.

'Cept how does a girl blot out a thing that comes from within?

"Shut her up!" Rose Thibbedeaux hollered, barging back in on our changing scene. "She's liable to have the law in here, a scream like that."

It fell upon me all at once: Papa and Mama, Tanyon and Tommy…

And now my Neesie.

Frank Rydekker snatched me limp from the floor. A hand like raw meat covered my mouth; greasy fingers pinched down on my nose, stifled my air. "Quit your screeching," he ordered, "or I'll suffocate you right here."

Still, Neesie didn't move.

The shine had gone from the colored girl's lovely eyes. Couldn't nothing but a miracle bring it back again.

CHAPTER SIXTEEN

Something dark stained the edges of Wednesday's remains—though it couldn't ever come black enough to hide me away from certain bad intentions. I found my voice in it all, though, took up a soft spiritual in the back of Big Fella's Ford, sang it as my last. Maybe I'd been foolish, thinking to get to New York someday.

Big Fella's boy ran a frantic pace through the gears, flung us to the center of Storyville as if all their wicked plans might go to dust if we got there too late.

Big Fella himself watched me from the passenger seat up front; he sucked on a cigar, tossed stray smoke rings into the sticky air. "You have a way with song," he pronounced, sliding his gaze against me. "Shame nobody cares."

That boy got on me in the mirror, pressed me hard with those same blue gawkers belonged to the man on his right. Father and son, I'd bet. "Earl Mouton's awful eager to have you back again," he said, supposing to add to my distress. "Claims you and him got on like religion—till them other two barged in like they done."

Limp words dropped from my lips in a mumble of uncertainty. "Don't know about no Earl Mouton."

The boy pulled down on all those gears, tucked us neatly to a curb I'd walked before.

Big Fella yanked me a-loose of that back seat, dragged my body stiff with fear up those familiar rotted steps.

All my tears and sobbing did nothing to turn the man.

Pig's round face separated door from jamb. "Hello, Charlie boy," he crowed like a doting uncle. "Glad you made it back."

Big Fella shoved me across the threshold, drew down on his cigar. "Rydekker says don't lose the girl; she's got work to do over to Rosie's house."

Pig's heavy left arm—the one not in a sling—fell on my shoulders, hugged me tight against his bulk. "This lovely young cunt ain't going nowhere," he announced, awful sure of the situation. "Me and her, we got some unfinished business needs tending."

Big Fella's nod dropped with a subtle knowing. "Just don't ruin her," he said, taking his retreat. "Make her need, is all."

Pig slid the lock in place once he had me to himself; the whole of his weight rested against the door. "Won't do just to give you a lickin' *this* time," he swore, fixing me hard with his dead-eyed glare.

A thing like panic swelled up inside me, threatened to swallow me belly first. "Why'd you claim we took ten grand?" I asked, hoping to lure him from whatever intentions he'd meant.

Whining floorboards warned of his lumbering pursuit.

Didn't matter how fast I moved to avoid his grasp, I just couldn't get away.

Plump fingers wrapped themselves with the hairs at back of my neck. Pig gave a hard jerk, put me on my tiptoes. "All that hop you and those other two swiped up out of here," he growled, "belonged to Frank Rydekker." His weight shifted, pinned me tight to that rickety staircase. "You were just stupid enough to leave behind all that cash."

Didn't take no Einstein fella to figure up *this* score. "You still have it, don't you?" I asked.

Pig's answer came with an angry yank that set me to dancing at the end of his arm. "And who you gonna tell?" he bellowed, traipsing my body here and there like a skilled puppeteer. "Won't nobody believe no miscegenatin' little cunt."

I spat a promise I had no mind for keeping. "I won't tell a soul," I hollered, latching onto his arm, trying like the dickens to come a-loose of his grip. "I'll say I took it, and just work it off."

Pity, it might have been, that hint of something warm in Pig's brown eyes. "Gonna take a lot of coursing to scratch down ten large," he surmised, settling me at the foot of those steps. "You'd belong to Rydekker for *years*—supposing you even last that long. A whore's life gets used up awful quick."

An idea of sorts teased me up with a taste of hope. "Suppose you just give the money back?" I suggested, moving closer to the man. "You could tell him I took you to where I hid it—make like you forced it out of me."

A familiar grin took to his lips; that same particular smirk Tanyon used to conjure whenever notions meant to raise his own station got in his head.

'Cept that's where any similarities between the living and the dead fell straight away.

"Take a thick-headed fool to let go that kind of money," he announced, backing me up those stairs.

The myth of that room up there hung heavy in the stale air, recalled recollections of that colored boy's words.

Spiders, he claimed.

Maybe even snakes.

"I'll let you have your way," I blurted.

"Gonna have it anyway," he replied, trudging on with intent.

"Please!" I pleaded.

'Cept Pig, he just twisted my arm behind my back, and marched me toward those sorts of things no rational girl wants touching her skin.

We both tumbled into a dark space situated directly beneath the roof. A loft, folks might call it—a place for hiding stuff from the light.

Pulled shades blotted out the glow of a gas lamp from the street below.

My gaze stumbled over shadows stacked high in low corners, caught hold on a claw-foot tub at the center of it all. Didn't have any spigot, no logical way to draw water into it.

"You making gin up here?" I asked, holding my ground near those stairs.

Pig's hand found my back, gave me a shove. "Go on and have a seat on the bed," he ordered.

It took a short spell to get my eyes acquainted with all the clutter meant to be a lonely man's life: a busted stool, a battered nightstand, that brass bed with a sag in its middle.

The fat man dragged a Lucifer across a low table, touched off the nub of a candle, and set about working that familiar ritual of spoon and flame.

But even I could tell he'd made too much.

My bottom dropped onto the bed like a heavy weight. "A fella called Moss *died* from less than *that*," I said, almost certain of Pig's intent.

"You ever done this before?" he asked, sucking those cooked leavings into a glass syringe.

I managed a single finger. "Once."

"Then you don't know." His tossed nod landed somewhere between that tub and a husky bureau. "*Those* will kill a person," he assured me. "Especially with you being so small and all."

My gaze fixed on those glass liquor jars lying lazy atop that bureau. The blunt force of panic twisted at my belly. "What's in them?" I dared ask.

Pig's grin came cold, dark as that space beneath his roof. "Fiddle-backs," he said. "Brown recluse spiders. About a dozen, I reckon."

I could feel them almost crawling up my legs, skittering down my back, searching for the softest place to feed on.

Pig ambled over like we were fixing on only having tea and a talk; he dropped down beside me and put that loaded syringe on the nightstand. He took hold on my left hand, fingered that shiny band. "Is this for real?" he asked.

"It is," I assured him, wondering if that stupid preacher's boy even took notice I'd gone missing.

Pig's touch wandered delicately along my arm, tested the veins for ripeness. "Where's he at, then?—this husband of yours."

My voice fell small, vulnerable. "Home, I reckon."

"And where exactly *is* home?"

"Back over the river," I confessed.

The fat man let go a snort. "Mississippi white-trash, huh?" That one good hand went to creeping, tucked itself beneath my chin, raised my gaze to meet his. "This boy of yours," he whispered, leaning close enough to kiss me, "—he's the one shot me, ain't he?"

Fear stole denial right off my tongue, left me mute as a soft-headed girl without a lick of sense.

Pig's wide grin claimed satisfaction; he knew the score. "You got a way to fetch him over?"

My head went to wagging this way and that. A jumble of protesting meant to plead Jobie's innocence came a-loose of my lips, fell to the floor, scattered into nothing worthwhile.

And Pig, well, he had notions of his own to consider.

"You ever had a real good look at a fiddleback?" he asked, gaining his feet.

"It wasn't Jobie," I swore, pulling all my pleadings into a straight line. "He wouldn't shoot anybody. He's a *preacher's* son."

Pig demanded, "Then who'd you bring in here?"

I lied, claimed I didn't know them, said, "They just followed me, told me to go along or get shot."

"Better me than you, huh?" He offered that one good hand, said, "Come on; let's go have us a look."

"I don't *wanna* look."

"They can't get at you," he promised, "—exceptin' I let 'em out first."

My voice stretched high and tight, like a string pulled taut. "And how do I know you won't?"

'Cept Pig took no inclinations toward explaining himself. That meaty hand of his snatched hold on my neck, jerked my bones a-loose inside my skin, put me upright on my feet. He growled, "You don't get a say in this!"

I tumbled ass-over-tea kettle at the back end of his slap, landed hard on my bottom near to that claw-foot tub.

"You're gonna tell me how to get at that boy of yours," he swore, sifting through shadows gathered in a corner. "And I want that monkey, too—the one claimed he's a doctor."

My head hummed and whirred like a busted radio can't get a fix on anything sensible. The salty taste of blood met my tongue.

Pig had determined to draw this moment out.

He squatted beside me on the floor, set a jar between my knees. "Thing about fiddlebacks," he explained, giving the lid half a twist, "they're awful partial to warm, dark holes."

It eyed me with malice, that ugly brown spider.

I knew of a boy from school got one in his ear. It wasn't no brown recluse—or even a black widow. It just crawled in there while he slept and laid a batch of eggs.

It took a special doctor from over to Jackson to scrape it clean.

Could they crawl into other places? I wondered.

Pig nudged the jar closer, supposing to add to my torment. The smooth glass came cool to my bare legs—the inner part, high up, where skin is always soft and warm, white as fresh milk.

"Gets its nickname from that fiddle mark atop its head," he explained.

Dark brown against yellow, that peculiar shape. A thing belonging more to the devil's chaos than the Almighty's order.

"Ain't gotta get it so close," I complained, weary of its lustful gaze.

Fat Earl gave the lid another turn. "Your boy's called Jobie, huh?" he asked, coaxing my hemline belly high. "Bet that's pet talk for Job—like in the Bible, I mean."

His spider drew up a fuss inside the jar; the vibrations of its fit coursed clean through my body like a lover's touch.

My eyelids fluttered over the confusion of it all; every word I pulled only proclaimed Jobie's hands clean in the matter.

'Cept Pig yearned reprisal for that shoulder of his.

"Always *someone* gotta suffer, Charlie boy," he said, fetching that lid away. "Now get out of them clothes and climb in that tub."

Instinct jerked my body up off the floor—like the fires of *hell* got on me. That lidless jar came a-loose of me, rolled into a rich puddle of darkness near where I meant retreat.

Wherever that spider got off to, couldn't neither one of us tell.

Pig scanned the floor in search of his runaway. His voice came low, distracted. "Ain't no reason to be scared, Charlie boy."

My own words fell shaky and clipped, though still determined. "Stop calling me Charlie boy!"

The man didn't cotton to no split-tail giving him sass—especially under his own roof. Fellas like Earl Mouton, they need to be the big boss—if only to their *own* reckoning.

'Cept notions like that, they too often come attached to angry burdens.

Pig sprung quick on me, got those long fingers of his tangled up with my hair again. Smoky black rage flung me willy-nilly across the loft. That old oak nightstand gave ground against my body's collision, cleared space enough for a ruckus to commence.

"Awful fresh mouth you got," he huffed, lunging at me, "for a *dead* girl."

His open hand caught my cheek, dropped me to the floor.

A girl my size could never hold her own against a fella like him—no matter her determination.

Pig squatted low; his body straddled mine over near to the stairs. His voice came harsh, rough, like sand had got mingled with his words. "I ain't gotta keep you alive. Understand?"

"Frank Rydekker said—"

That one good hand of his fell upon my throat, pinched down on my wind, my warning.

"Frank will see you dead just as quick as I will," he said, squeezing tighter.

My legs took to kicking and stomping beneath him; my fingernails opened angry wounds along his arm.

Couldn't nothing move that fat man to turn me a-loose.

Inky black butterflies gathered in loose confederation along the edges of my sight, whispered threats of putting out what little light remained.

I took after that hole in his shoulder—the same one Jobie Pritchett conjured up for him. My eager fingers tore away his bloody bandage as if the thing concealed a certain wish any girl might hope to find on her birth-day.

Pig's howl split the moment wide open. *"You cunt!"*

His grip went limp, came a-loose of my neck.

My own hands scrabbled at the filthy floor beneath me, searched after anything to draw this matter even.

That slim glass tube came warm to my touch.

I pleaded one last time. "Just let me go."

'Cept Pig meant to see it through to an ending of his own making. "Can't do that, Charlie boy; we're both in too deep."

It ain't a thing I thought on—not with time folding in on itself like a blank square of paper brought tight and tiny. Couldn't stir up a workable notion even if I tried.

I grabbed up the syringe from where it lay, brought its shiny silver sliver hard against the soft pink flesh at Earl Mouton's neck…

Pressed down on the plunger…

Pig said nothing, offered no protest. Those soft brown eyes of his shot wide for a moment, as if caught in a thought, some wild idea of escaping that narcotic's rush, before the lids fell low and the very life ran dry in the man.

*   *   *

I went left where Marais Street crosses Bienville, kept to the sidewalk under splashes of gaslight promising both safety and exposure all at once. Any old fool driving past could pick me out of a crowd—even a fool with bad eyes.

Those black shoes had my feet slapping urgent, restless rhythms meant to discourage drifting shapes of smoke and fog from sporting after me with dirty ideas no longer capable of making me blush.

Giggles from girls gone silly with drink fluttered a-loose of open win-dows.

Coulda been me in there, lying in a bed ain't my own, with a fella I only just met, sipping whiskey from his flask, all the while drawing good money into the pockets of Rose Thibbedeaux or Frank Rydekker.

I eased back on my pace, took to squinting at all those worn façades lining either side of Bienville.

Couldn't tell one place from another in that corner of Storyville.

A collection of colored boys shared a jar of liquor atop the front stoop of a tiny scrap of house gone dark with night. The whites of their eyes fixed me tight, followed my awkward flow along the street they considered home.

I'm the one out of place, I reckoned.

Nasty promptings came at me like so many hungry mosquitoes. Ideas drew themselves unbidden from vague notions conjuring smoke inside my head.

I dared to breach that dirt patch of a yard, allowed my feet to carry me closer. Rayford, Mississippi—that's all I really wanted.

A wiry boy came a-loose of the porch, caught me face to face beneath that low-hanging summer moon. Dark eyes read my features like maybe this one here had never seen a split-tail up-close before.

Sixteen, I'd reckon—nosy as a heated tomcat.

He leaned in close, drew a slow breath. "Won't nobody pay for it," he whispered, "—not here, at least."

I pulled back from the boy, tried to square his angle. After Pig, I wouldn't scare so easily. "Pay for what?" I demanded.

His grin came straight and neat—the way he'd likely smile for his own mama. "All kinda cathouses up and down Storyville, a fella need to *buy* some."

My gaze tripped past him, fell against those other two still on the stoop. They weren't much older; stupid boys, is all.

I gave my voice a try. "Anybody know a fella called DeShay?"

The tall one on the stoop set his head to wagging. "Don't nobody by that name stay here."

I wouldn't call it courage, that notion nudging me forward. More like necessity, I reckon.

"Maybe we could trade," I said, determined.

The tall one came off his stool, joined our little soirée at center of the yard. "Sorta trade you 'spect?"

I could do it—so long as it brought me home. "Take me over the river," I told him.

"Mis'sip?"

My head tipped a nod.

That wiry boy perked up. "What *we* get?"

Sweat took to my body like a late spring rain. "You get *me*, I reckon."

"All of us?"

I glanced around, counted just the three, tossed up another nod.

That tall one took charge of the matter, worked toward the particulars. "How far you 'spect to get inside Mis'sip?"

"Rayford," I said. "Just up from Biloxi."

Cloudy ponderings got hold on the tall fella's countenance. "Have to wait till sunup," he explained. "Won't catch *me* in no Mis'sip with a white girl after dark."

The one on the stoop shifted against his stool, bit down hard on me with his gaze. "What you want with DeShay?"

That wiry boy let go a hiss sounded like all the air had gone out of him. "Come on, Mellie—we *this* close."

"Can't be no *friend* of his," claimed the one on the stoop. "Friends know where friends stay."

I squeezed into the gap, drew closer to the boy. "I only went there a time or two. Can't find it in the dark."

He fished a pack of Luckys from his pocket, shook one a-loose. "DeShay don't stay with his granddad no more," he said, dragging a blue-tipped Lucifer across the porch railing. "Got his own place now."

The wiry boy chimed in. "But he don't got Mista Frank's blessin' yet."

Fella on the stoop breathed off a silver cloud. "Means he can't earn a livin' till that blessin' comes."

The tall one laid open space between me and him, as if only now did he finally recollect the one speaking with him. "You're that girl sings jazz," he said, "—the one robbed Mista Frank."

Suspicion turned the sticky air fearful—like just being *near* me might put them on a list somewhere.

Silence, heavy as baled cotton, fell in around us, blotted out the happenings going on up and down Bienville Street.

Atop the stoop, that other one pitched his Lucky and made for the front door. "Go on and *walk* across that river, you so quick to get away," he said, vanishing from the moment.

The two lingering boys just sorta scuffed at the dirt, contemplated their options.

My feet put me closer to their huddle; my tone came low, hushed, leaking words meant only for their hearing. "I got money to home. I'd pay real good to get back over."

'Cept the tall fella pulled out his own retreat. "Can't nobody here take you over," he said, leaving me alone with that wiry boy.

I conjured one last plea. "Don't suppose *you* still wanna do a trade, huh?"

His smile broke nervous. "Won't cross Mista Frank," he said, hiding himself among those long shadows. "What you do, you go on up Villere Street. Number twenty-one. That's where you find DeShay."

*   *   *

"Pig's dead," I blurted. "I think *I'm* the one killed him."

DeShay snatched hold on my arm, yanked me across his threshold. That dark-eyed gaze of his absorbed the motions of the street behind me. "Anybody see you come here?"

Though I wouldn't have sworn it a thing most certain, I convinced the boy I'd kept to the shadows. "Just the way you showed me."

He shut the door back of me, slid its lock into place, fixed my body snug in a corner. "What you mean you *killed* Pig? How?"

The story just sorta fell a-loose of my lips, all those awful goings-on from over to the fat man's place. Couldn't go back and undo what already got done. "Think he hates me now?" I asked.

A deep furrow got tangled in the boy's brow. "*Pig?*"

"Uh-uh. God."

He found it written on my countenance, a thing steeped in fear. "Ain't no way he can hate you for this—'specially him knowin' all Pig been up to. Besides," he continued, granting my release from the corner, "might could be Pig ain't even dead. He do a *lotta* that stuff on his *own.*"

I drifted through his tiny parlor like a slow trickle, took perch against a fancy black loveseat called to mind the one belongs to Aunt Frannie, helped myself to a half-empty pack of Chesterfields lying atop a low table. "He meant to kill *me* first," I said, dipping my cigarette into the orange tongue of a lit Lucifer. "Had notions to put me in a bathtub with a mess of fiddlebacks."

"*Told* you don't go upstairs with him." DeShay fell in beside me, got hold on a jar of corn liquor he untucked from beneath that sofa. "Anybody else know what you done?"

Smoke, like twin phantom snakes, curled lazily from my nose. Demons, they were, peeking through for a curious gawk at what lay ahead for me.

"Only you and God knows about happened," I said. "And the devil knows."

DeShay tipped the jar at his mouth, pulled down on a long gulp. Nothing in the boy had changed from the last time we were together.

That jar came cool to my own hands; its liquid heat set fire to my blood before it ever reached my belly. "They killed Tanyon," I said, intending to tell *someone* all I'd seen. "Killed my best friend Neesie, too."

'Cept DeShay wanted none of that business. "Don't tell me 'bout no killin'," he argued, snatching that jar from me.

"Well *we* ain't the ones swiped the money," I huffed. "Me and them other two, we only took *hop*."

"Frank Rydekker thinks *I'm* the one put you to it. Can't get his blessin' if he 'spects I *robbed* him."

Funny how news of Tanyon's demise did nothing at all to stir surprise in the boy.

I sucked hard on my Chesterfield, held its harsh smoke in my lungs. "Did you know about it before they got to him?"

That dark-eyed stare of his tugged at all my notions. "You don't know the *half* of it, girl," he explained. "This thing with Tan, it go way back before you even come to this world."

"What about Tommy Letts?"

"The boy talked too much. Everything was a joke with him."

I picked at the scab a little more. "Did you know they were fixin' to grab *me?*"

The colored boy's breath came slow, uneasy. "Reckon so," he admitted, "—but that don't mean I had say in the thing. Couldn't *nobody* change Mista Frank's thinkin'."

My hands found the jar again; Jobie's shiny ring played hard against the glass. "Suppose I pay him back?" I offered. I mean, Aunt Frannie might help—if she didn't hate me for Neesie. "The whole amount. In cash."

DeShay's head took to wagging. "If it was just 'bout money, you'd be dead already."

"Then what's this about?"

"A girl."

"What girl?"

"The one Tan and your daddy got at together."

My spine pulled up tight. "*Jenny?* The one they named a tree for?"

"Jenny *Rydekker*," claimed the colored boy.

Frank's baby sister, to hear DeShay tell about it. And Papa's the one took all the blame for putting the girl to the needle.

'Cept I knew Papa better than that. "My daddy didn't fool with that stuff," I assured him. "Ain't no way on God's green he'd *ever* do such a thing."

DeShay leaned in close to me, drew up all sure of the things he said. "You don't know *what* that man got up to before you come along."

"You don't know Papa."

"I know what I heard with my own two ears."

"Frank Rydekker's a liar!"

"Ain't Mista Frank done the talkin'." He grabbed up those Chesterfields, shook one a-loose. The thing about DeShay, that boy had a way of laying grease on a fire. "*Tan's* the one told tales outta school. That's why he stole that money—to get on up someplace won't nobody know him."

I pulled away, tried like the dickens to get a read on the boy. "You the one told on him?"

His head took to wagging again. "Mista Frank woulda give me his blessin', if I had," he said, dragging a Lucifer across that low table. "Tan caught up *himself* when he told the thing to Rosie Thibbedeaux."

Couldn't trust anybody this side of the river.

Not even kin.

My last hope came to mind. "Think you could take me home?"

Silver smoke swirled from that colored boy's nostrils like an uncommon lust, a thing meant to be seen. "Suppose I could," he said softly. Those fingers of his, so delicate with touch, slipped easily beneath my chin, raised my gaze to meet his. Something familiar showed itself in his eyes. "That time to Granddad's, when you let me kiss you—was you bein' for real?"

The boy still had a way of putting me warm and slippery where it counts most with a girl.

"If Tanyon hadn't barged in…" I said, losing the rest of my words in his kiss.

'Cept it couldn't come to this. Not now—not with everything coming apart the way it did.

I pulled back from him, showed off that ring says I belonged to another boy.

DeShay eyed the shiny band like maybe it escaped from one of Pig's jars—as if the thing hitched a ride on my hand with wicked intent. "Was you his when you let me kiss you?" he asked.

"Ain't even his *now*," I confessed, "—at least not in *that* boy's way of thinking."

"He the one shoot the fat man?"

My head tipped a nod. "He didn't mean to, though."

DeShay gained his feet. "Yeah, well," he said, drifting toward the front window. "If he'd got it right, wouldn't none of this matter no how."

He heard it before I did, that low rumble common to Henry Ford's machines.

Panic put my bones to shaking like they meant to come a-loose beneath the skin.

Fear stretched my voice high and tight. "You having company?"

DeShay tossed a gawk past his raggedy drapes, let it fall in the street. "Musta been one of them boys showed you to here gave 'em a call."

"Gave *who* a call?" I demanded, still frozen to that loveseat.

"Mista Frank," he said, like maybe that name meant nothing at all to the moment.

I broke free of the sofa, met him face to face near to the window. "You gotta hide me," I pleaded. "I don't know anything about his sister. I wasn't even born when Papa and Tanyon knew the girl."

DeShay's countenance took up with a thing looked an awful lot like shame. He managed a weak, "I'm sorry, Emily Ann," before releasing the door's lock.

Frank Rydekker strolled in like a notion from hell. That angry gaze of his fixed tight to me with some kind of hatred. "Had to go and foul everything up, didn't ya?" he said. Then he flung a handful of words at the colored boy. "Anybody else know she's been here?"

Stupid DeShay wouldn't even look at me anymore. "Jus' them three sent her to me," he answered, eyeballing some stain laid against the floor at his feet.

Rydekker closed the door, cut off my escape. "You got a way to the alley without going round front?"

I wedged myself between those two, got face to face with that colored boy. "You can't just turn me over," I cried, hopeful my tears might stir in him a need to protect me.

'Cept DeShay couldn't be moved. "Back door," he said, "through the kitchen."

I'm the one stole *that* plan, though. I bolted headlong for the alley, stumbled recklessly toward my only hope.

If DeShay wouldn't save me, I'd have to do it myself.

Big Fella's the one caught me—as if he just *knew* I'd be out there, tumbling through the night. The man fell on me like the devil himself come to claim my soul.

I never did see the knife.

Felt its rage, though. The sting of its blade pierced my belly, tore a jagged hole in my life that could never get properly fixed. Sharpened steel scraped the bones of my spine, brought me low against that dusty patch of earth.

I meant to scream; tried like the dickens to draw a saving crowd into this moment. 'Cept nothing came out—nothing but a pitiful wet wheeze.

A crimson stain spread across the front of my dress like an ignorant girl's flowers suddenly come to bloom.

Big Fella tugged that knife a-loose of my belly without any discernable malice. His voice came low, hushed, almost paternal. "I never did hate you, doll face," he said, wiping his blade with my ruined dress. "Never hated you at all."

I can't say for sure where he'd gone off to. Didn't really matter much, neither, I reckon. Bleeding out is a thing demands a certain intimacy. An act like that could never find proper satisfaction in the company of gawkers.

Can't nobody hold your hand when crossing *this* river.

CHAPTER SEVENTEEN

Sharp white light stung my eyes wide with fear.

Eager voices buzzed through my head like fat mosquitoes gone drunk with blood.

My blood.

Hands got hold on me, held my arms, my legs, my body; pinned me tight against that cold metal table.

Shiny scissors cut a straight line right up the front of my soiled dress.

Panic jabbed hard at my belly.

"*Stop it!*" I cried, tasting copper on my tongue.

My legs went to kicking, my feet searching for traction, for a foothold on something, anything.

Some fella over my shoulder hollered, "Hold her still, dammit!"

My own voice came wet with blood. "*Papa!*"

"Give her the ether," said that same fella.

*   *   *

Darkness thick as cold sorghum painted my sight black. Shadows conjured shapes against corners inside my head.

That old familiar creaking sound came at me first. I knew it to be him, alone, in that chair of his.

"Use that voice," he'd said. "Get you someplace ain't Rayford." Said it back when it meant something.

The motions of his oak rocker drew him closer, though he'd never come close enough to see, to touch, to climb on his lap just one last time.

Soft words fell into my hearing, a delicate sound, an easy saying wrapped in a whisper. "Come up for air, Baby."

My head broke the smooth surface; cool water caressed my soul like the hands of a brand new mother.

"Papa?" I called, though the word died in the air.

Songbirds jazzed in that green canopy above, thought to lure me from the pond for a dance—or maybe for a tune of my *own* conjuring.

'Cept I couldn't find my voice.

Couldn't find my legs, neither.

Movement shook at those low trees back of that rickety dock; something wild meant to come on through, put me to the test, to see was I worthy or not.

"Who's there?" I demanded, still unable to raise much sound.

A colored girl traipsed into the moment like an image not quite real. Her feet slapped an eager rhythm against those loose wooden slats. Her determination promised a quick end to Mister Kuiper's ancient dock.

Still, it held beneath her meager weight, presented the girl like a sacrificial offering above the water, bare as she'd been that morning in my bed, beneath those peach-colored sheets.

A lovely sight, really.

'Cept for that hole in her belly.

I tried for an explanation, said, "I didn't mean for…"

The effort wore me to a frazzle, though.

And Neesie, she wouldn't so much as look at me; she acted like I no longer existed in her world. And maybe I didn't, in *her* way of seeing. The girl just muttered a notion sounded an awful lot like, "Gots to make me clean," and tumbled headlong into that cool, clear drink.

She never did come up again.

It's as if she clean dissolved away, let all her parts get mingled with the things that make up life, death, and everything after.

My body floated on the water like maybe this is where I meant to spend all eternity.

Hands came up all around me. Hands connected to arms, arms connected to—nothing. Fingers entered that new black hole at the center of me, tugging and pulling on things inside, searching no doubt for my soul, for proof I'd once been among the living.

Tommy Letts spoke his piece next.

The boy spilled into view from back of the same tree spat up the colored girl. That hole in his head had gone dark and void, though it didn't bleed anymore. Wasn't anything in his eyes, neither. Nothing, 'cept emptiness.

His voice came with effort, as if spoken from a place beneath the water.

"Why July?" he said, gawking at some far-off place. "Why July?"

"July?" I slapped at those groping hands, tried like the dickens to sit up. 'Cept you can't sit on water. "What about July?" I demanded.

"Why July?" Tommy repeated. "Why'd you lie? Why July? Why'd you lie?"

"I *didn't* lie!"

'Cept Tommy knew better. "All liars go to the lake of fire."

Those hands got at me again; their fingers took up with needle and thread, and commenced to closing up that hole in my middle.

Words spilled a-loose of me soft and sad. "I'm sorry, Tommy. I swear I am."

'Cept Tommy Letts held no answers, nothing to put a girl's mind to ease. The boy just dove on into whatever space laid claim to Neesie, and the two of them left me to myself.

*   *   *

Words swirled around me like a lazy dust devil, turning up dirt and grit and things meant to draw my ire. Lord knows Aunt Frannie has that way of churning up all my bad points.

"Nothing but trouble," she proclaimed to whoever lent an ear. "Since day one, that child. And she has no qualms toward taking others down with her. We all just sort of get sucked right in."

Jobie Pritchett's voice cut at the darkness like a fresh-struck Lucifer, splashed its pale glow against the back of my mind. "You ain't been through what she's been through," he argued, "so don't talk about her that way."

"She's to blame," is all my aunt said.

The colored girl's name went unspoken but I heard it just the same.

Jobie's lips brushed my ear, raised goose bumps across my skin. "Can you hear me, girl?"

I could hear that boy just fine; could feel him, too, the warmth of his breath on my neck. The scent of his shaving cream filled my head with a thing both familiar and yet new.

His whispered plea found its mark. "If you'll just open your eyes, Emily Ann, I swear I won't so much as *look* at another girl as long as I live."

My own voice came strained and ragged. "Liar."

Aunt Frannie's words fell out a frantic mess, like frenzied bees shook a-loose of their hive. "Lord have mercy! The girl's *alive!*"

My eyelids gave a flutter like brand new butterfly wings hoping for flight. I fixed on her through a lazy squint.

My only living kin, this woman.

"You're right," I said. "I'm to blame."

She tipped a subtle nod, wiped away a lone tear, and promised we'd have all the time in the world to talk about it once I got to healing.

That's when that sterile tang stung my nose, put me in a mind to recollect the pain in my belly.

"This one needs her bandages changed," said a nurse come to take charge of our moment. She wedged herself between me and that boy called himself my husband. "We'll be needing some privacy."

'Cept Jobie held firm. "Ring on my finger says I'm entitled to stay right here."

"It's not a pretty sight," that nurse promised.

"I *ain't* leaving her side."

Even through all its vagueness I could still decipher a smile behind the woman's intent.

"Fine then," she huffed, "—but you're gonna help."

Aunt Frannie's the one retreated; she had no intentions of gawking over the work Big Fella had accomplished on me.

Truth be told, I can't say *I* wanted a looky-loo, neither.

Old Florence Nightingale swooped down on my body as if she had a mind to pick the bones clean. Withered and spotted hands went to tugging at the linen sheet, yanked up the front of my flimsy gown, took to peeling away that stained bandage from my belly.

My new gash ran a heap longer than my memory recollected. Five inches, I'd suppose—if I ever got a notion to lay a measuring stick against the thing. The wound began—or ended—just above my navel, and pushed its way toward my sternum.

Angry black stitching kept my insides where the Almighty intended them to be.

"Toss this in the bucket by the door," Nurse Nightingale ordered, handing Jobie my soiled gauze.

'Cept the boy's gaze remained fixed to that rip down the middle of me. Couldn't hide the horror in his stare.

Old Florence, she caught on quickly, gave him a nudge meant to draw him down. Softly, she said, "She's gonna heal up just fine, son."

I hated all that gawking, spoke a piece just to lure attention away from my belly. "How'd I get here?"

"A colored fella," claimed the nurse. "He didn't stick around long enough to give up a name." She laid out a clean gauze, set about taping it over my wound. "He the one did this to you?—the colored fella, I mean."

Jobie's blue-eyed gaze took up with that naked place where my legs come together.

Indifference, I reckon you'd call it, that haze clouding his sight. Maybe even disappointment.

My hands yanked that stupid gown back down, covered all that I lacked. "Wasn't no colored that cut me," I argued, angry over the way Jobie Pritchett still saw me.

At least Tommy Letts appreciated all I managed to offer.

Jobie's voice came low and soft, a thing I ain't too awful sure I really even heard. "That fat man did it, didn't he?"

I could have lied, made claims of mad Earl Mouton taking revenge for that bullet in his shoulder. At least that way a certain preacher's boy might stumble into feelings of guilt, might could come to consider me in way a husband ought to consider his wife.

'Cept a lie like that would never quit Frank Rydekker from his intentions to put me under.

Instead, I said, "And neither did Pig do this."

Jobie gathered up his full height, all the means needed to keep a girl safe. "Then who's the one did it?" he demanded.

Maybe it *was* guilt nibbling on that boy, sprinkling its dark pall over his countenance, had him yearning to put things right.

But Old Florence, she's the one held final say on affairs concerning me. Once again she wedged herself between me and Jobie, announced an end of visiting hours, and searched out a ripe spot on my arm.

"Morphine," she promised, sticking me good with a silver sliver.

My breath fell out soft from my lips. Blood in my veins tumbled warm and slow; my chin took rest against my chest.

Called to mind that night with Moss, it did, on that houseboat on the Atchafalaya. Wasn't no dirty-spoon ritual this time, though.

The nurse snatched Jobie by his arm, angled him toward the door. "Leave her be now," she ordered.

'Cept that narcotic put me in a mind to make a thing known.

"Either we're a married couple, Jobie Pritchett, or we ain't," I proclaimed softly. "The choice is yours, boy."

*   *   *

They got together in my room, there at the hospital, those two lawmen, each issuing promises of a quick resolve to things done to me.

Such was the talk.

Officer Luc Doucet sought to determine Big Fella's true identity—if only could I recollect a fair description of the man—and his reasons for running a knife through the middle of me.

Sheriff Dantley, he only took issue with whoever put a bullet in Tommy's head over to Rayford. Whatever befell me in the Big Easy was of no concern to him.

Truth be told, I didn't trust neither one of the two. No doubt Rydekker's sawbucks found place in that Cajun copper's pockets. Anything I thought to mention would surely come to *that* wicked man's ears.

And the sheriff—I still recall the hunger in his gaze at finding me bare in Mister Kuiper's pond. Even that foolish old pointy Klan hat couldn't conceal such a bold gawk.

"Nola Patterson," Dantley claimed, "she's the one filled in the missing pieces once we found the Letts boy. Says a car with Louisiana plates came calling after you."

Doucet took offense at the intended implication. "That don't mean one of ours did this mess."

Dantley's grin tipped sideways. "And still we find the girl on *your* side of the river. With a *knife* in her belly. Ain't no gangsters calling the shots over in *my* town."

I flung my own words into the sterile air, hoped like the dickens to run the both of them off. "I didn't see *who* did it. I don't even know *why* he did it."

'Cept that crafty Cajun, he parked his scrawny existence on the end of my bed. A mottled hand found my feet beneath the sheet. "Was a Negro brung you in," he said, tracing a doodle against my left sole. "Boy carried you right through the front doors and put you on the floor before turnin' tail toward the night." He dared a move along my calf. "Did you come to my city to miscegenate?"

Any sort of answer I had notion to speak got lost in that foggy swirl back of my eyes.

Doucet nudged it a little further. "Ain't no big thing this side the river. We like to think of ourselves as *progressive*, more open to such predilections than, say, folks over to that other side of the river."

Lies and denials failed me; not a word of protest came a-loose of my lips.

The creaking leather of Sheriff Dantley's gun belt tore a much needed hole through the tension. His words attempted a fatherly tone. "Who's the one snatched you and Neesie from over to home, Emily Ann?"

It stole all my air just to hear that colored girl's name spoken aloud. Wouldn't a lawman-one give a single moment to hunting *her* killer.

Doucet's eyes narrowed like someone pissed in his cup and made claim it's whiskey. "I ain't convinced anybody got *snatched.*"

Dantley's thumbs rested snugly in his belt; confidence bent a smirk around his lips. "Got a witness says they were."

Witness?

What witness?

My heart beat inside me like it meant to come straight through that gash along my belly.

I swallowed hard at my words. "Who saw?"

'Cept old Florence Nightingale barged on in, laid a squelch to those two lawmen and their jurisdictional bickering.

"Just quit badgering the poor girl, will ya?" she hollered, shooing my interrogators toward the door.

Sheriff Dantley wouldn't let it go, though.

He fixed his gaze on mine, offered up that sideways grin of his. "We'll talk all about this once you come home, Baby Teegarten," he promised, tipping his hat. "We'll have all the time we ever gonna need."

CHAPTER EIGHTEEN

I slipped away to that tiny water closet as soon as I got home. Jobie's the one made claim my wound would practically vanish outside of a year. Just don't look at it, he said. Give it time to heal. Still, I had to see the thing for myself. I needed to see it the same way that long looking-glass saw it.

I took my time with the matter, though; didn't rush in for any sudden gawk. The look had to come natural, like a passing glance.

That? Oh. I once had stitches, is all. I almost forgot it was even there.

'Cept Jobie interrupted the moment; his knuckles laid an easy rhythm against the bathroom door. "It's only been a month, Emily Ann," he said, a hint of pleading in his voice. "Just leave it be for a while."

I offered the mirror my back—the only part of me liable to ever look normal again. My fingertips took after those lower buttons along the front of my blouse. 'Cept fear put me still.

"I can't do it, Jobie," I confessed, taking perch on the edge of the tub. "I can't bring myself to look."

That preacher's boy pushed past the door, closed us up inside like the water closet was our own cocoon. Couldn't anything bad get at us inside that scrap of space.

He offered nothing by way of explanation; the boy just set about working a-loose the buttons of his shirt, gave his trousers an easy tug off those narrow hips.

A warm giddy thing swam freely through my belly.

Married in the eyes of the Almighty, we were, and I'd yet to see him completely bare.

I came up off the tub, got pulled into his orbit. "Need help with those?" I asked, dropping a subtle nod toward his britches.

Jobie's head went to wagging back and forth like I just might be the dumbest girl in all the world. "Look at it, Emily Ann," he ordered, showing off that familiar pink scar spoiling the lower end of his stomach. "Gonna look exactly like this, it will. Only give time to heal."

"Getting your appendix out ain't the same—"

"A scar's a scar, girl, no matter *how* you come to it."

My hands came alive, moved eagerly over all that smooth skin kept hidden beneath his clothes.

"Think you might consummate me?" I asked, breathing in his scent.

His voice came soft as goose feathers—and just as light. "Doctor says we can't. At least not for a few more weeks."

"Won't hurt I should get a look, will it?"

He got hold on my wrists in a gentle sort of way. "Doctor says you probably can't get with child, neither."

Blood and all its heat left my face and settled in my feet. A lump got caught in my throat, promised to choke off my air.

I coughed up a handful of words. "Gonna hate me now?"

"Ain't gonna ever hate you, Emily Ann," he said, his fingers working at all those buttons down the front of my blouse. He pulled the garment open, pushed it off my shoulders.

It glared at me from the mirror behind him, that angry red line running along my middle.

"It's ugly," I lamented.

'Cept that boy, he didn't care nothing about no scar. "They're getting bigger," he said, laying a gentle caress to my breasts.

My voice fell soft, needful. "Think so?"

"Gonna draw only you," he whispered, his fingers twisting a-loose the hitch on my skirt. "Make you my muse."

'Cept real life wedged its foot between us, shoved us apart.

I rehitched my skirt, closed the front of my blouse. "Suppose you want children?" I blurted. "And that's all your mother ever talks about, always yammering on about grandbabies."

His brows furrowed as if ideas bumped headlong into his mind. "Plenty of orphans to go around."

"Ain't the same," I argued, trying awful hard to tamp down on that swelling panic.

Jobie's lanky frame found rest against the edge of the tub. "You're the one talked all big about me being an artist and you singing in clubs." Muscles roped around his long arms. "Thought you wanted the big time."

"Ain't no big time in Mississippi." My body moved on its own, got closer to him. "Besides, suppose I can't sing anymore? A thing like jazz, it comes from the belly."

"Then I'll be a preacher and you'll still be my wife."

Jobie's kiss came delicate, a thing sweetened with Co-cola.

I pulled a-loose of those arms. "They'll come for me again. Ain't no way they'll just leave me be."

The blue in that boy's eyes burned hot. "They the ones killed Tommy?"

My body moved again, carried me over to that long mirror. I opened my blouse and studied Big Fella's mark on me. "They killed Tommy, Neesie and Tanyon," I told him. "And they'll kill me, too."

"What'd you do?"

"Ain't what *I* did, it's what *we* did. Tanyon stole from him and so did we."

Jobie fled his perch, backed me into a corner. "Thought you said it wasn't the fat man."

"Pig's dead, I think."

Those words lingered in the space between us like the smell of something gone rancid in the heat. It's a confession, he expected, a statement setting him free from his own part in this mess.

'Cept I'd never speak on such a thing to another living soul. If Pig died, it didn't mean the blame belonged only to me.

Jobie backed off, allowed me some room. "They coming for me, too?"

My shoulders flinched a shrug.

The blue in his eyes dipped cool, focused. "Who is it?"

The name came sour against my tongue, sharp and jagged. I spoke it aloud and cringed at the taste.

Jobie stumbled a-loose of the moment. A thing akin to fear wrapped itself around his countenance. "*Rydekker?*" he hollered. "The *gangster?*"

"He ain't the one stabbed me," I explained, trying awful hard not to tumble over my own words. "Ain't the one killed Neesie, neither. He's the one gives all the orders, though."

I was in the middle of connecting Pig to Frank Rydekker when that sudden knock laid us quiet, dripped a sticky darkness into the moment.

Jobie fetched up his full height.

The boy seemed smaller this time.

His straight razor fit snugly against his trembling hand. "Stay put," he whispered. "If a commotion commences, open that window and get to screaming."

If Frank and Big Fella lurked outside, wouldn't no straight razor save anybody.

I shut myself inside the water closet, leaned my weight against the door, sifted the silence that promised to bury me. They'd lay me between Papa and Mama up to the graveyard. The whole family together again.

Course, that didn't make me eager to join them.

Hushed voices conspired like conniving schoolboys back of that thin door.

I crawled to the window, shoved it open. Only Nola Patterson would likely hear my cry—if they hadn't got at her first.

A curious jiggle found the doorknob.

My throat squeezed down on a scream; watery pain filled my belly.

Jobie's tone lacked panic. "It's all right, Emily Ann. Open the door."

I slid back the lock, met the cautious gaze belonging to Billy Blood.

"I watched them snatch you," he said, standing back of Jobie. "Saw them kill Tommy, too."

My body got a mind of its own, breached the threshold. "*You're* the witness?"

The Injun's head sagged low, a thing sure to come a-loose of his shoulders. "I shoulda stopped them," he said, drawing down on a deep hurt. "Coulda saved Neesie."

'Cept he couldn't have. And I told him so. "They'd have done you like they did Tommy," I assured the boy.

"I just wanted to watch, is all—what you and her were fixin' to do," he blurted.

I peeked at Jobie, returned to Billy. "Who told you?"

"She did." That Choctaw narrowed the space between me and him. "I want their names, Emily Ann." A shiny pistol glowered at me from the boy's waistband. "And you're gonna tell me where to find them."

To give up names and locations would be to send Billy to his grave.

I couldn't be part of any more killings.

"Gonna have to find them on your own," I told him.

'Cept Billy reckoned otherwise. "You *owe* her, Emily Ann."

His point jabbed me like the sharp end of a stick.

I owed Neesie more than a measure of justice. "Frank Rydekker," I said. "He runs the Crescent Club."

"Across the river?"

My nod fell heavy, final.

The boy spun toward the door.

"You mess this up," I hollered, "they'll kill you, Billy Blood." I waited until he'd gone before tossing up my last fear. "Gonna come and kill *me*, too."

*   *   *

Those old ladies dabbed at their eyes with handkerchiefs pilfered from the pockets of nearby husbands and sons. "Amazing Grace" put them up to it again. That's probably the last certainty left standing in my life. I mean, suppose I had taken up with that Eunice Spatch and her fancy Mister Stanley Duncan. Imagine where my station might lie nowadays.

Wouldn't be no gash down my middle.

Wouldn't be responsible for Neesie, neither.

'Cept I'd never find happiness at a school teaching folks how to sing—especially since I already know how to do it better than most.

Pastor Pritchett tossed his nod, dismissed me from up front.

I took perch beside Jobie in a pew near the back.

Pastor flung a jagged tirade at the evils of big city living, jazz music, and everything else a decent man of God ought to rail against. Truth be told, I understood his rage. Maybe even agreed with him—to a point.

But still…

My body fell into Jobie's. "Let's go to Biloxi this weekend," I whispered.

The subtle rise of his eyebrow put a giggle in my belly.

"Ain't got a thing to do with Della, boy," I said, "so you can go on back to forgetting you ever knew the girl."

Jobie shifted in his seat, played like he meant to hear all the hellfire his daddy dished up. From the side of his mouth, he asked, "Then why go to Biloxi?"

My own voice dropped low like a marble rolling unseen along the floor. "To see can I still sing."

"You can sing *here* all you want."

"*Jazz*, boy."

There went that brow of his again. "Thought they wouldn't let you in."

"There's a speak," I said. "Tanyon took me once."

His head got a wag to it. "Ain't a good idea, Emily Ann."

"I ain't asking permission." I pulled away from him, tugged my spine nice and straight. "Besides," I informed him, "if you won't take me, I'll find someone who will."

*   *   *

The state road lured us along like the flow of that ancient dirty river I so meant to avoid. One last time, is all I hoped to squeeze from this ripe moment. I mean, to sing jazz with a colored band in a genuine speak? Ain't a feeling like it to be had anywhere else on God's green.

'Cept maybe...

Jobie found third gear, slung us headlong toward Biloxi. I'd catch him in the green glow of the dash from time to time, snatching gawks at me, trying to decide if he really ought to mention whatever curiosities he'd cooked up behind those blue eyes of his.

"A hundred dollars," he said, drawing a pack of Luckys from his shirt pocket, "—that's what Tommy offered if I'd let him run off with you."

I snatched his proffered cigarette, dipped the tip into a hot Lucifer, sucked smoke from its back end. I wondered aloud, "Why'd he make an offer like that?"

"Had to do with that day you two got together."

I tossed a smoke ring into the space between us. "Bet the only reason you didn't take his money is on account of you'd be stuck explaining to folks where your wife had got off to."

He swiped the Lucky from my fingers, pulled hard on its smoke. "Would you have gone?" he asked. "I mean if I'd took his money."

Not in a million years.

And that ain't a knock against Tommy, neither. He just ain't the sort of fella a girl ought to throw her lot in with.

I didn't tell that to Jobie, though.

All I said to him is, "Don't know."

Old Satan's grin took up with the corners of his mouth. "Tommy claims he dished you a lickin'," he said, bouncing his gaze between me and the road. "Says you liked it."

I paid the boy no mind, set my face toward the window, let the wind toss about my hair. It wasn't short anymore; it got long again, reached past my shoulders, made me feel normal, the way I felt before life came all undone.

Jobie's hand found mine like maybe *he'd* been the serious one concerning the vows tying us together. "I wouldn't turn you loose to nobody," he swore. "Not even for a *thousand* dollars."

"Liar." The word just sort of slipped through my lips before I had a chance to examine it to see if I meant it.

'Cept Jobie, he didn't cotton to my way of thinking just then. The boy mashed the brake pedal level with the floor, put that old flivver of his sideways in the middle of the road, and jerked my body up close to his.

"Don't you call me no liar, girl," he hollered; said it like I'd gone hard of hearing. "You don't know the first thing about how I feel."

I meant to speak, to spit out some smart-alecky thing for myself. 'Cept words of any sort refused my tongue.

Jobie's kiss came along and sucked all the air from my insides, let me know his true feelings for me.

His voice spread a warm fog inside my mind. "I would die protecting you, Baby."

My own words came soft, low. "Might come to that—and still you couldn't…"

"Suppose we pay him back?"

My head twisted left and right. "He'd kill us both anyway."

His fingers found my chin, raised my gaze to meet his. "Then we have to do what we have to do."

I took his hand, kissed those fingers. "And what's that?"

"Find out can you still sing."

"Then what?"

Jobie tipped the pattern back to first gear, tossed his rattletrap in the direction of Biloxi. "North," he said. "Way up where nobody knows us."

New York, he meant—though he'd never utter its name until Mississippi was at our backs.

The old general store lurked in shadows gathered thick along the edge of the road. Notes from a saxophone fluttered through the air like familiar butterflies come to guide us home.

Jobie wrestled that gray-primered contraption of his into the dirt lot, angled for cover around back, shushed his engine with a subtle turn of his wrist.

Music wafted through the back door.

I knew the song being played, could sing it in my sleep. 'Cept there'd be nobody to hear it like that.

Jobie flung his door wide, worked over the remains of a Lucky. A thing like fear sneaked into his eyes.

"You say Tanyon brought you here, huh?" he asked, tossing the spent cigarette to the ground.

"It's safe," I assured him.

He scratched his chin like he expected to find fresh whiskers there. "Ain't worried about some pitiful speak, Emily Ann."

I scooted closer to him, took his hand again. "What's got you spooked, then?"

Those broad shoulders of his flinched a shrug. "Did you and him fool around?"

"*Tanyon?*" My head went to twisting again; declarations of my innocence fell from my lips like the plucked petals of a thorny rose. "He didn't even like me that way."

Jobie grabbed hold on my closet door, yanked it open, let all those bones tumble out into the light. "Tell me about you and that colored girl. What'd Billy wanna watch?"

Stupid Injun; had to go and open his yap.

"She ain't here anymore," is what I told him. "Anything I say is only gonna be gossip."

It's that low, steady chuckle of his I always hated. A thing like that makes a girl feel dumb, soft in her head.

My fist collected his shoulder, promised his chin what-for, should the boy not mind himself.

"Just saying, is all," he said, rubbing where I socked him.

"Saying what?" I demanded.

"You let Tommy Letts lay a tan to your backside and you're worried about *gossip*?"

"Let me out," I ordered, climbing over his lap.

'Cept those long arms of his got hold on me, held me tight. "I could learn to love you, Baby Teegarten."

I pushed clear of him, let my feet settle in the soft dirt outside his door. "Love ain't a learned thing, boy," I told him. "Either you do or you don't."

His nod called to mind a fella negotiating a deal of some sort. The kind of deal puts everybody involved in high spirits.

"You're entitled to your own secrets, Mrs. Pritchett," he announced.

"And so are you, Mr. Pritchett."

Jobie tipped that nod again and met me in the dirt. "Let's go hear this jazz singer you're always going on about."

Beem Weeks

Beem Weeks is the author of short stories, poems, essays, and novels. Among his literary influences he counts Daniel Woodrell, Barbara Kingsolver, and Stephen Geez. A pop-culture trivia buff, Beem's passions include indie films, loud music, and a well-told story. He has also penned a collection of short stories entitled *Slivers of Life*.

❧

Find Beem Weeks on Social Media

www.FreshInkGroup.com
Blog: BeemWeeks.WordPress.com/
Twitter: @BeemWeeks
Google+BWeeks
About.me/BeemWeeks
GoodReads: Beem_Weeks
Amazon Author Page: Beem Weeks
LinkedIn: Beem Weeks

The Fresh Ink Group

Publishing
Free Memberships
Share & Read Free Stories, Essays, Articles
Free-Story Newsletter
Writing Contests

Books
E-books
Amazon Bookstore

Authors
Editors
Artists
Professionals
Publishing Services
Publisher Resources

Members' Websites
Members' Blogs
Social Media

www.FreshInkGroup.com

Email: info@FreshInkGroup.com

Twitter: @FreshInkGroup

Google+: Fresh Ink Group

Facebook.com/FreshInkGroup

LinkedIn: Fresh Ink Group

About.me/FreshInkGroup

SLIVERS OF LIFE

By Beem Weeks

These twenty short stories are a peek into individual lives caught up in spectacular moments in time. Children, teens, mothers, and the elderly each have stories to share.

Readers witness tragedy and fulfillment, love and hate, loss and renewal. Historical events become backdrops in the lives of ordinary people, those souls forgotten with the passage of time.

Beem Weeks tackles diverse issues running the gamut from Alzheimer's disease to civil rights, abandonment to abuse, from young love to the death of a child. Long-hidden secrets and notions of revenge unfold at the promptings of rich and realistic characters; plot lines often lead readers into strange and dark corners.

Within *Slivers of Life*, Weeks proves that everybody has a story to tell—and no two are ever exactly alike.

www.FreshInkGroup.com
ISBN: 978-1-936442-10-2

PAPALA SKIES

By Stephen Geez

Chicago native Rochelle DuFortier likes to imagine the future, her world a series of picture postcards so vivid they sometimes seem real. When a foolish mistake at thirteen causes her mother's death, she's sent to a secluded Hawaiian valley, an outsider "haole-girl" among pidgin-speaking boys who hurl flaming papala spears under the full moon to summon her mother's spirit. After boarding school and a prestigious university back east, the ambitious young woman is torn between chasing new career opportunities, discovering her mother's heritage in a remote French village, and meeting obligations pulling her back to Hawaii.

On this island steeped in ancient mythology and modern superstition, Rochelle tests the possibility of sharing pieces of her life with those whose beliefs she barely understands and never intends to embrace. She dives the depths of a pristine coral lagoon, conceals bodies in a subterranean lava tube, and challenges the eruptions of a living volcano, even as she deciphers the truth about her mother's death and struggles to satisfy new debts born of old betrayals.

Papala Skies is the story of a young woman who makes all the right choices, only to find herself living an unexpected life. It is about the need to belong, and seeking one's own version of truth amid such differing cultures' responses to wrenching loss and abiding grief. It is about yearning for a sense of place, yet having to confront new ways to honor the love of family and friends.

Will Rochelle lose what matters most, or might she learn what the smart octopus already knows?

www.FreshInkGroup.com

ISBN: 978-1-936442-07-2

COURAGEOUS LADY:

A Woman's Alaskan Quest for Native American Spirituality

By Mark Allen North

In the first novel of The Lady Trilogy, auburn-haired beauty Leigh West travels to Alaska's majestic and mysterious Tongass National Forest in search of self-discovery and harmony with nature. In her journal, she chronicles all she learns from native Tlingit tribesmen, the cunning wolves and belligerent brown bears, and the transforming seasons of the region's glorious landscape. It is through Native American spirituality that she sparks new passion within herself, a new appreciation for the physical world, and a life filled with love.

www.FreshInkGroup.com
ISBN: 978-1-936442-12-6

TWO FRIENDS, TOO OLD

By Robert Scott

What would you do if you saw your best friend for 60 years slipping over the edge into mental oblivion? You would do anything to help him, right? Frank and Clay have been friends since the first day of first grade. Now both in their mid-sixties and retired, Frank is looking forward to spending a lot of quality time hanging out with his lifelong friend. But all that is threatened when Frank sees Clay going around the bend.

Clay denies he has a problem and rejects Frank's initial suggestions for help. But when Frank stumbles upon a drug that might help, he renews his efforts to help his buddy and he talks Clay into taking the drug. That works great, for a while. But Frank couldn't quite bring himself to tell Clay the entire truth about the drug, and that deception has tragic consequences, not only for Clay but also for Frank.

www.FreshInkGroup.com

ISBN: 978-1-936442-11-9